LOVE AND OTHER WILD THINGS

MOLLY HARPER

COPYRIGHT

ACKNOWLEDGMENTS

Thank you to the good people of Slidell, Louisiana for hosting me as I wrote a good portion of this book. Your eerily beautiful, Spanish-moss laden environment was the perfect inspiration.

As ever, thank you to Amanda Ronconi and Jonathan Davis for giving my characters a voice and for taking my extensive notes (read: bossiness) with such good grace. Thanks to Jaye Wells, who helped me come up with a better name for the series than, "That Audio Series I Can't Seem to Come Up With a Good Name For."

Thanks to www.spirit-animals.com for all of the information about llama spirit animals and their personality traits, and to a number of comic book fandom sites that helped me understand what the heck I was trying to express in terms of Dani's talent.

PROLOGUE

I f she got any closer to the rift, there was a good chance her head would explode.

She'd fought through the waist-high ferns and gone far beyond the rock circle that marked the safe distance for humans to approach the rift that purportedly separated this world from the next. For that matter, she'd gone beyond the rock line that marked the safe distance for the *magique*, the population of shapeshifter, fairy folk, and assorted monsters that populated Mystic Bayou. She'd ventured farther than anyone had ever dared, forcing her feet to carry her into the vast sacred site surrounding what the locals called *la faille*, and she was feeling the effects of it. The air felt too thick and heavy to breathe and it had nothing to do with the stifling heat of Louisiana in August. Her skin prickled, like fire ants were crawling up and down her bare arms. Her ears popped with the fluctuations in air pressure as it pulsed with pure energy just a hundred feet away.

But still, she'd come this far, too far, to stop now.

She set her backpack of supplies at her feet and admired what looked like the aurora borealis, hovering too close to the surface of water rippling beneath it, a living vortex of shifting color. Others described it in banal terms, as "a haze" in the air that could barely be detected without binoculars. But she could see what they couldn't, the mesmerizing dance of prismatic flashes in the air. Her eyes ached with the intensity of the light, but she forced herself to stare into it.

There was no known explanation for this mystical vortex. There were no ley lines, no atmospheric anomalies, no massacres on the site. The rift in the fabric of what kept their world separate from whatever lay beyond just *was* and nothing could be done about it.

Being this close, she was witnessing something that perhaps no one had ever seen before, but she didn't have time to stop and appreciate the moment. She had a job to do, and she had three, maybe five minutes before the pressure overwhelmed her and she passed out. And there was no one else around to drag her to a safe distance.

She forced her body into a relaxed standing position, shoulders loose and feet spread. She faced the light of the rift and drew the energy into herself, like a lover breathing in a kiss. She felt the burn of it sizzling through her cells and held it, focused on it with every bit of her concentration before taking a deep inhalation. She pictured the rift like a tear in fabric, holding on by the thinnest of strands. She pressed her palms to her chest as if in prayer and slid them away from her body, picturing that fabric splitting. She felt hesitation, push-back from seams that had no interest in separating and releasing more of the destabilizing force that was radiating out into Mystic Bayou. She inhaled and pushed her mind out even further, as if her own hands could grab either side of that visualized fabric and rip it apart.

The tension in her head eased the tiniest bit, and she took advantage, focusing as hard as she could on her target. The fabric ruptured and she watched the colors writhe even more frantically as the rift opened just a tiny bit more.

She smiled to her herself, reluctantly turning away from the change she'd made and jogged toward the rock circles on legs that still shook.

It wouldn't be long now.

1

ZED

The old washtub was plotting against him, intentionally trying to mess up his day. That was the only explanation.

Zed Berend yanked at the old galvanized tub, perched precariously on top of Miss Lottie's sun shower, but it would not budge. He was not a weak man. He was a brown bear, for shit's sake. He'd managed to pull it off the mounts connecting it to the wooden slats that made up the shower walls, but the water kept sloshing around, the momentum working against his efforts. And he was afraid if he pulled any harder he would break the wooden slats and destroy the shower.

He'd promised Jillian he would have an actual shower installed —with plumbing, she'd been sure to clarify that—before anyone else moved into the *maison de fous*. Dr. Jillian Ramsay, Ph-damn-D, was an International League for Interspecies Cooperation anthropologist who'd been expecting to sleep in a tent in the rainforest before she'd been redirected to Mystic Bayou to study how the humans and *magique* managed to live there in relative harmony for so many generations. The League wanted to use Mystic Bayou as an example of how other communities might create safe, productive environments where *magique* and humans could live together. The League believed that someday soon, modern technology would shove the *magique* out of the shadows and into the light of the twenty-four-hour news cycle. The plan was to prevent pitch forks and panicked mobs by breaking out Jillian's studies, which were now in full force. The League was sending dozens of researchers, scientists, and other paper-shufflers to make sure she got results sooner rather than later.

Jillian insisted that the League personnel being sent to Mystic Bayou over the next month would not be as accepting of the "Bohemian" showering conditions as she had been. And because Jillian was perhaps one of his favorite humans and definitely his favorite ILIC employee, he'd agreed to the minor renovation. Also, a mama nutria had birthed a litter of little baby swamp rats in the beaten copper tub by the sun shower, which had sort of proven Jillian's point about the need for modernization. And walls around the bathing facilities.

So, he was converting Lottie's old sun shower with brand new pipes from Burton Boone's hardware store and one of those *Time Life* home improvement books from the 1980s. The faded hardback was the only one Miss Bardie would allow Zed to leave the parish library with, despite him being the mayor of Mystic Bayou and technically, her boss. But Bardie Boone was a dragon shifter who guarded her horde of library books the way most dragons protected their gold. And she'd never forgiven Zed for teething on a copy of *Tom Sawyer* when his adult canines were coming in.

Enclosing the shower in its own little cubby with walls and a critter-proof roof would take a few weeks. But still, he enjoyed working outdoors for once, soaking up some sun and fresh air. Since his election, Zed had often felt caged in his mayoral office. He'd jumped at the opportunity to be out in the sunshine, by the water, working with his hands. He enjoyed the veneer of quiet over the swamp, the illusion that everything was peaceful and serene and then the sudden bursts of noise—generally caused when some predator snapped up an unsuspecting snack—that reminded you that you were not in some safe little meadow.

This was Louisiana. Mother Nature—whichever incarnation of Mother Nature you happened to believe in—had a way of reminding you that she was still in charge.

Just like this stupid tub was showing Zed that it was still in charge. Growling, he yanked at the tub one last time. It suddenly popped loose of its moorings, only to have the water surge toward him and the container tip over, soaking him in lukewarm rainwater. He fumbled with the tub, feeling the perforated bottom give as he tried to catch it, before it landed with a *clank* on the wooden boards.

"*Merde!*" he grumbled, grateful that the screen that protected the water hadn't smacked him in the face on its way down. And that Bael hadn't been present to see Zed embarrass himself so thoroughly.

Zed shook his long dark hair out of his face like a dog. In the heat, it only took a few seconds for his clothes to feel like they'd been vacuum sealed to his body. He stripped out of his soaked shirt and threw it aside with a wet *slap* against the boards. Just then he heard his favorite lady anthropologist calling from the front of the house. He froze.

What was the etiquette for being shirtless in front of your best friend's mate? Jillian was a doll, and he'd even considered making a play for her before he'd realized Bael was hung up on her.

Zed certainly didn't have anything to hide. He was just as tall and muscular as every Berend male had ever dreamed of being. But he'd chew off his own paw before he made Jillian uncomfortable. And he didn't want to have to deal with an angry, possessive dragon sheriff, either.

Could he wrestle his way back into his wet shirt, he wondered, eying the pile of wet cotton at his feet. No, that would just mean

Jillian would walk back here to find him with his head and arms trapped in sopping, uncooperative material, which wasn't exactly a step up from his current situation. Shifting into his other form and running into the depths of the swamp as a bear seemed like a good option, but it also involved dropping his pants. And Jillian could end up seeing him naked, which would compound the dragon jealousy issue. Could he dive into the water? Sure . . . if it wasn't tail end of mating season for the local gators, who were not particularly choosy. He did not want to tangle with an amorous bull gator on top of everything else.

"Hey, Zed!" Jillian yelled as she came around the corner with a tall brunette. Her voice trailed off and she said, "Are you here? Oh . . . Zed."

Right, no escape. He lifted one of his large hands and waved it at her. "Hey there, *catin*."

Zed stood a little bit straighter and refrained from hitching up his jeans, even if they'd drooped just a little bit. He would not be embarrassed about this. He'd smile and brazen his way through it, which was most of politics, anyway. Jillian sighed, and rolled her eyes, a gesture he now expected from someone who'd come to think of him as her idiot older brother. Zed grinned and turned his attention to the lady at her side.

Man, she was pretty. Jillian was, of course, very attractive with her tall, slender frame and fair hair but this girl . . . Zed cleared his throat to cover the faint, interested chuffing noises he was making. She was tall and curvy, with riotous curls the color of chicory that fell far past her shoulders. His eye was caught by the generous cleavage displayed by her gauzy red sleeveless top, but only because it seemed to be embroidered with tiny llamas leaping between blue flowers. He'd never seen a girl wearing leaping llamas, but definitely wouldn't mind seeing it again.

Her wide green eyes were the color of the tiny algae that bloomed on the swamp. He loved those little plants, for their purpose and the brilliant color they lent to the water, but he would never tell her that her eyes were the color of what most people considered pond scum. Most girls would find that sort of thing to be insulting.

She was gorgeous and he was staring.

Zed's cheeks flushed red under his dark beard. His *maman* would be appalled to find him shirtless and ogling some perfectly nice girl's . . . llamas. Oh, well, she was smiling, which was a good start.

"Mayor Zed Berend, this is Danica Teel," she said. "She's the consultant the League hired to investigate the issues surrounding the *faille*. Danica, this is Mayor Zed Berend, who believe it or not, is the person the good people of Mystic Bayou elected to be in charge of them."

Danica, she of the bee-stung lips and delightfully rounded thighs, attempted to suppress her grin as she extended her hand to him, but failed utterly. "Nice to meet you, Mayor Berend."

"You can just call me 'Zed.'" He grabbed her hand with just a little too much enthusiasm and pumped it up and down. Her hand was warm and now that she'd stepped a little closer, he could smell a hint of ginger on her skin, and the faint green sweetness of clover. He tried to inhale deeply without being obvious that he was scenting her.

Despite the fact that he'd been shaking her hand far beyond what was socially appropriate, Miss Teel just smiled and gripped his hand right back, which he found . . . intriguing. Zed hadn't met a lady with such a firm grip since Maddie Angrboda moved to town, but she was descended from a line of Norse stone giants and had an unfair advantage.

"Well, then you can call me, 'Dani,'" she told him. "I look forward to working with you."

"Not nearly as much as I look forward to working with you," he said, finally releasing her hand.

Jillian cleared her throat as she glanced at the bent copper tub and the slats Zed had pulled loose while trying to free it. "Um, Zed, do I even want to ask what happened to your shirt?"

Zed shook his head. "Not really."

"Dani here was hoping to move in today, but I can see that there's still an issue with the shower," she said, chewing her bottom lip.

"I tried, Jillian, but I wasn't expecting you for another two days. And there was the small matter of my town to run, while you and your League buddies plan your invasion," Zed noted.

Jillian very subtly scratched her nose with her middle finger. Zed was teasing her, of course. The citizens of Mystic Bayou needed the League's resources as much as the League needed information from Mystic Bayou's citizens. They'd been too long without a proper healer. Hell, they'd never had a dentist who could treat all of the different teeth amongst the Bayou's population. Half of parish school's teachers were well past retirement age and leaning towards 'older than dirt,' but stayed on because there were no trained educators to replace them. There wasn't enough in the parish accounts to cover the badly needed repaving, because thanks to the otherworldly mojo bouncing around the bayou, the roads kept moving around like the freaking staircases in *Harry Potter* and it was damn near impossible to estimate how much asphalt would be needed. And then there was the small matter of the rift de-stabilizing and spreading its chaotic energy amongst the Bayou residents and changing their very genetic make-up.

But Dani didn't know he was teasing and she frowned slightly at Zed's mention of an invasion.

"Not that I mind. Sometimes a little invasion can be good. Like the Beatles or how all of the sudden all actors seem to be Australian," he said.

Jillian lifted a brow. "Um, sweetie, did the tub hit you in the head?

"Not that I can remember."

"Dani, it's not a problem for you to stay with me and Bael for a few days until the shower's fixed and the house is livable," Jillian protested.

Dani shook her head. "Oh, I couldn't possibly. I wouldn't want to impose. Besides, I've stayed in much rougher places than this. A couple of days of sponge baths won't do me any harm."

Zed found his mouth suddenly going dry at the thought of the beautiful Miss Teel and sponge baths.

"Besides the house is amazing. I love it already. And compared to my last accommodations in Mongolia? It's a luxury suite," Dani said.

Zed felt a sudden rush of affection for the newcomer. Anyone who could appreciate the otherworldly charms of the *maison de fous*, without even going inside yet, was a person worth knowing.

Jillian sighed. "You could always stay with us for a night or two."

"I make it a policy not to draw the attention of law enforcement whenever possible," said Dani. "That includes sharing a breakfast nook with your sheriff. Besides, this way, I can settle in, be able to concentrate. And that means getting to work that much faster."

"All right, but if you need anything, call and I will come running. Even if it's just clean towels."

Dani held up her fingers in what looked like a Girl Scout salute. "I promise I will."

"In the meantime, I can take you back to town to get the rest of your things," Zed offered.

Jillian jabbed a finger towards his chest. "Dani does not need the full Near-Death-Experience-on-the-Back-of-Zed's-Harley just yet. Besides, don't you think maybe you should concentrate on fixing the shower?"

"That's your Springer Soft Tail Classic out front?" Dani asked, delighted.

Jillian muttered, "The one with the extremely unsubtle claw marks painted down the body?"

Zed's grin ratcheted up even further. "Sure is. You know bikes?"

"Only because a boyfriend in college rode one. He taught me how to drive because I threatened not to give him..."

Zed's eyebrows rose.

Dani didn't look remotely embarrassed. She just grinned cheekily and added, "Handshakes anymore. Very firm, loving handshakes."

Zed smirked at her. "Mmmhmm."

"Nice save," Jillian added.

Unabashed, Dani gestured to her shoulder bag. "Besides, there's no need to run back into town."

"That's all you brought?" Zed asked, side-eying her bag.

She jiggled the bag lightly. "Everything I have in the world."

Zed shuddered. He wasn't a dragon when it came to hording stuff, but he enjoyed his cave and its creature comforts. He had no desire to live anywhere else. He couldn't imagine a nomadic life where he could carry everything he owned around in a backpack.

Dani laughed, a rich, bright sound, like thrumming a harp. "I'm just kidding. I have equipment and clothes coming in a few days. It's being shipped. I like to travel light, but I'm not pathological about it."

Zed snorted. "Yeah, I had that coming."

Dani grinned at him, and he went all warm and gooey inside, like he'd just drunk a mug of hot apple cider. He shook his head, as if wiggling his brain back into place. Maybe he did get a concussion from the tub.

Jillian patted his arm, as if she could sense his distraction. "Okay, it's so hot out I can feel the sweat between my toes, which is not a good look. Zed, how about you focus on fixing the shower and I'll show Dani around."

Zed found that he didn't want to agree. He wanted to follow them through the strange fairy tale house and see Dani's face as she saw all of the charming little quirks, the trees lit by spirit bottles, the haint-blue porch crowded with hanging baskets of geraniums, the odd little tower where Miss Lottie had held her rituals. And the bed that swung from the ceiling on ropes made from spider-shifter silk, that was always a point of interest.

But instead, he chose not to behave like a lovesick preteen girl, looked at the mess he'd made of the shower and realized he was going to have to visit the hardware store. In his effort to try to catch the tub, he'd stepped on several of his pipes and bent them beyond repair. Sure, he had the strength to force them back into shape, but they'd never thread together properly and run water without serious leaks.

"Hey, *bebelle*! I'm gonna have to run into town!" he yelled through the kitchen door, into the house.

"Put on a shirt!" Jillian shouted back from upstairs. "Otherwise, Bael will arrest you for public indecency!"

Zed called back. "Not likely! He's been in a much better mood since you moved in! He's only a grumpy bastard every other day!"

Zed pulled his wet shirt over his head, Jillian's bell-like giggle ringing through the open door. The shirt clung to him like an overprotective mother, but thanks to the summer heat and the breeze from riding his motorcycle, the material had almost dried by the time he reached the town square. His bike rolled smoothly down Main Street and its collection of shops. The town square centered on a wooden gazebo and a large fountain, carved by dwarvish craftsmen, featuring nearly every creature included in the town's population, all sheltered by a dragon's unfurled wings. The Boones weren't exactly subtle about their "patronage" of the town.

The Boones owned almost everything: the bank, the boat dealership, the grocery, the apothecary shop, the beauty salon, the hardware store, the book shop and, of course, the pie shop marked with "Bathtilda's Pie Shop, Home of the World's Best Chocolate Rhubarb Pie." Each building was freshly painted and decorated with baskets overflowing with bright red geraniums. It was practically the town's official flower, what with its mosquito repellent scent.

Resisting the muscle memory that demanded he pull the bike into its usual parking spot in front of the parish hall, he parked in front of Boone's Hardware and Dry Goods. He picked at his damp shirt and sauntered into the store, with its strange collection of tools, hardware, pixie traps, and bottles of toadstool remover. Waving to Burton Boone, a stooped, ancient dragon-shifter with mutton-chop sideburns meant to hide his abundance of ear hair, Zed searched the plumbing section to replace the supplies he'd damaged. He crouched in front of a display of couplers, trying to remember the size he needed.

"I thought you'd already bought the supplies to fix Miss Lottie's shower," Bael said.

Zed jumped slightly and glared up at his closest friend in the world, who happened to be leaning against a rack of wrenches, his arms crossed over his tan uniform shirt. Zed prided himself on his senses, his ability to keep track of any predators that might try to sneak up on him. But dragons had almost no natural scent, and they moved as quietly as death. "*Couillon*! You know I hate it when you do that."

"Watch your language in my shop, Mayor Berend!" Burton yelled from the front of the shop.

Bael scoffed at him. "You hate that I'm *able* to do that."

"That, too," Zed admitted, standing from his crouch. "I thought you were writing tickets out by the school this morning."

"Eh, I caught Emily McAinsley speeding on her way to the yarn

14

store again and we were both so traumatized by our last experience that I decided to call it a day."

Zed gave a sage nod. "Probably for the best."

"So what happened to the pipes you bought already? You step on 'em and turn them into U's?" Bael grinned.

Zed winced, scratching the back of his neck.

"I was just kidding!" Bael cried. "What did you do?"

"I don't want to talk about it."

"Did you break anything that was meant to hold up the house, that's all I want to know. If it collapses, I'll have to fill out a shit-ton of paperwork . . . Wait." Bael stepped closer, sniffing lightly. "You smell like Jillian. Did she drop by the house?"

"Bael, you're my best friend, but please don't smell me. We've talked about this."

Bael shrugged. "When you have a mate, you'll understand."

"I doubt it. A lot," Zed told him. "But yeah, she drove that new League consultant by the house to show her around."

"The dark-haired one? Dani? With the, uh...?" Bael paused to find the right word.

"Really nice llamas?" Zed suggested.

Bael nodded emphatically. "That's the one."

Zed's dark brows rose and Bael jerked his shoulders. "I'm happily mated, not blind."

"She is a looker, that's for sure," Zed responded. "And she and Jillian seemed to be getting on pretty well, which means she could be around a lot, so you should try to be a bit more blind to her llamas."

"Thanks, but I am also not stupid."

Zed carried his supplies to the counter, where he paid cash for them. Burton had not extended credit in the two hundred years he'd been in business. Zed noted that Burton did not so much as nod at his distant cousin in acknowledgement. Bael had been on the outs with most of his family since his relationship with Jillian had gone public. Bael was already considered *drole* among his family anyway, to the point that Bael was in danger of being disinherited by his grandfather, and being cut off from his portion of the family's treasure horde. Once it got around that Bael was mated to a woman who was human? It didn't even matter that Jillian had been transformed into a phoenix, after living so close to the rift's energy. As far as the Boones were concerned, once human, always human, and Jillian was not worthy of carrying their precious dragon babies or the family gold. Bael was cast out and officially disowned.

Of course, for Bael that just meant he was left his own football-field-sized horde, as opposed to being Bill Gates-rich. But still, it was a big deal to dragons.

Zed watched Bael slide his aviator sunglasses on, as if being cold-shouldered by his own family didn't gnaw at him. Burton was known to be a grade-A asshole when a beer hit him wrong, and had been personally driven home by Bael on multiple occasions instead of being charged with drunk driving. And yet, here he was, ignoring his cousin like Bael was somehow less of a dragon for falling in love with someone who was smarter *and* nicer than the awful scaled harridan that had been making Burton's home life miserable for more than a century.

"Here's your change, Mr. Mayor. Now please take that person out of my store," Burton drawled, without looking at Bael.

Zed shoved his change in his pocket. "You're an asshole, Burton. I've always thought so."

Burton's mouth fell open as Zed snatched his bag off the counter. Bael followed at a sedate pace as Zed stomped out of the shop.

"That wasn't necessary," Bael told him. "I appreciate it, but being called an asshole isn't gonna change Burton. Also, you probably just lost his vote."

"Well, it chaps my furry ass to see your family treating you that way when you're the best of the lot. If they want to know real family shame, they should come meet some of my cousins."

The corner of Bael's mouth lifted, which was practically gushing since he wasn't one for bro hugs.

Zed asked, "What were we talking about again?"

"Your fascination with the girl with nice llamas."

"I wouldn't say 'fascinated.' I just want to know who's going to be living in one of fair town's beloved landmarks."

"Mmmhmm," Bael murmured.

"What is it exactly that she does for the League?" Zed asked.

"I know it has to do with the rift, but not much else. Jillian said it was really complicated and I tried not to be offended that she didn't think I was smart enough to understand it."

"It's probably not so much a question of smarts, as that time she was trying to explain 'ethnomusicology' to you at dinner and you fell asleep with your face in your pasta."

Bael cried, "That happened once!"

"You snored. Loudly."

"Once!"

Zed patted his friend's shoulder. "That's the sort of thing a girl remembers."

2

DANI

D ani liked the look of the *maison de fous* very much. Most of the waterfront houses she'd passed had look like cracker boxes on stilts, all faded paint and slowly disintegrating wood. The layers of faded blue-gray stories were accented with eaves dripping with rust runoff. Each story had its own wraparound porch, protected by the scent of hanging geraniums. The top floor offered a cupola, which she imagined gave the inhabitant an amazing treetop view of the bayou. A dock extended from under the "ground floor" to the water, and some thoughtful soul and had set out a ring of comfortable looking, mismatched chairs, so one might enjoy the sunsets.

Dr. Jillian Ramsay, her liaison with the League, was leading her on a room-by-room tour of the house. As its last inhabitant, Jillian was clearly fond of each little nook and cranny. She pointed out the small animals carved from peach wood standing guard on the window sills, meant to protect the house from negative energy. She mentioned how meticulously Miss Lottie had cared for her furniture. And when they reached the bedroom that was to be Dani's, Jillian just blushed and gestured for Dani to walk in.

It was a beautiful room, with high cathedral ceilings, white-washed walls and a huge bay window looking out on the trees. And the bed was . . . hanging from the ceiling?

Dani tilted her head as she examined the thick white silk ropes keeping the bed suspended from the high ceiling. "Hmm."

Jillian's cheeks were still tinged quite pink, but she found voice enough to say, "Actually, it's a few years old. Theresa Anastas helped spin the silk for the ropes herself."

"On a spinning wheel?"

Jillian shook her head. "Theresa is an *arachnaed*, a spider-shifter from Greece. She made the silk herself. She was very fond of Miss Lottie."

Dani grinned broadly. She'd only met a handful of locals, but she liked this strange town full of nightmares and monsters. It wasn't the smallest town she'd had ever stayed in, but it was close. Still, she felt safe here, despite the heat and humidity and the abundant wildlife that could do her serious harm. She'd spent so much time being different from everybody else. It hadn't exactly filled her with angst. She was proud of her talent and the life she'd built with it. But it was nice to be in a place where she didn't stand out. In Mystic Bayou, everybody was different, so no one was.

It had been particularly nice to meet the Mayor, Zed Berend, he of the god-like build and aversion to shirts. At first, Dani thought she was being set-up in some sort of awkward "welcome to the swamp" stripper prank, walking around the house to find a shirtless, wet man, shaking out his long dark locks in the breeze. But the show stopped at the shirt removal, not that it wasn't enough to enjoy on its own. Because Zed had *all* of the muscles. She tried to be a better, more evolved person than someone who was attracted to a man because of his body, but seriously, all of the muscles.

And beyond the body, the man had a face forged by a divine hand—long, straight nose, ambitiously high cheekbones, and . . .

probably a full mouth? It was kind of hard to tell under the thick dark beard. Dani normally preferred a clean-shaven face, after a boyfriend with a bizarre commitment to scruff had left her with rampaging beard rash on her thighs. But Zed clearly took care of his beard, probably with those artisan beard oils that always seemed to be on sale on Etsy. It looked really soft. She'd been tempted to reach out and touch it, but she figured that was a violation of personal space . . . and probably seven different kinds of etiquette here in Mystic Bayou.

His fog-over-ice gray eyes might have come across as hostile, if they weren't so damn warm. They crinkled when he laughed, when he talked. If hints hadn't been so broad about his bear shifter status, Dani might have guessed that he was one of those sexy woodsmen from a fairy tale. Or a sexy genie. Or a sexy huntsman. Basically any fairy tale stock character that required advanced upper body strength.

But she wasn't here to ogle supernaturally attractive men. She was here to do a job. And she was being super-rude to Jillian by ignoring her tour.

"So why do they call it '*maison de fous*?'"

Jillian smiled at her. "It's a long story. Do you want to hear it over a cup of tea? I think I left some chamomile in the kitchen cabinet."

"I'd love a cup, even with this heat. I haven't gotten used to the iced tea thing, yet," Dani said.

Jillian gave her a sympathetic look. "Did you get confused when they offered you 'sweet or unsweet?'"

"Yes. What in the hell is 'unsweet?' I've traveled around the world twice and I've never heard of it. And when I said so, the waitress at the truck stop in Houma gave me water."

"You've mostly traveled outside of the American South, huh?" Jillian asked as Dani followed her down the rickety wooden steps to the tiny dollhouse kitchen, with its ancient refrigerator.

"I was born in Wisconsin, spent some of my toddler years in Arizona, and then I lost count of the places my dad decided we needed to visit. My passport couldn't hold any more stamps by the time I was eight."

"That sounds nomadic," Jillian said as she pulled a kettle down from a hook over the sink. Dani shrugged, sitting at the tiny breakfast table. "Well, for the record, they're just asking if you want a plain glass of iced—unsweet. Some people prefer to sweeten it at their tables with the tiny colored packet of their choice. Others want the real deal—basically, rock candy added into boiling hot tea so the sugar dissolves evenly through the drink. I do not recommend trying it without a half-and-half mix of sweet and unsweet on the first try. Otherwise your dental enamel could spontaneously dissolve."

"That sounds really complicated. I think I'll just stick with Diet Coke."

Jillian filled the kettle. "Probably for the best. Anyway, the house has been called *maison de fous*, the Fool's House, since it was constructed more than a century ago. A sea captain named Worthen built it for a water sprite he'd fallen madly in love with. He retired from his navy commission and followed her into the bayou. He built the house to show her how much he wanted a life with her, to show her the sort of future he could give her. But she was just not that into him, rejected him pretty much at every turn, and he was so distracted by the constant refrains of 'let's just be friends' that he didn't really pay attention to what he was doing when he was building, or that his house in no way resembled anything that his neighbors lived in."

"Are all sea sprites so freaking mean?" Dani asked.

Jillian set the kettle on the stove and pulled two mugs from the cupboard. One that said, "Loveland, Ohio—Home of the Loveland Frog," and another that said, "Knitters grab life by the balls" in hot pink script over two round skeins of pink yarn.

Jillian spotted Dani staring at them and said, "They were a gift, which I should probably take home with me, before Mel's feelings get hurt. I forgot them in the move. Bael already thinks I'm a mug hoarder, but he's one to talk. But yeah, in my experience, they're kind of the bitches of the sea. River nymphs, mermaids, *rusalki*, all much nicer."

Dani threw her head back and laughed. "You know how weird it is, to cite that experience and be able to prove it's not bullshit, right?"

Jillian pursed her lips. "I'm aware."

"I'm assuming that the sea sprite never saw the error of her ways and came swimming back to the good captain?"

"Nope, she continued back-stroking through the swamp, breaking hearts left and right. Worthen met a local lady, a healer, who thought he was everything that was amazing. She married him, kept him fat and happy and gave him six children. Lottie was the last of their descendants, and the local healer, a very popular woman among her neighbors. Despite the house being so old, they couldn't bear to just let it fall down, so the residents of Mystic Bayou do little repairs whenever they can. And they rent it out to *drole* like ourselves, whenever the need strikes."

"*Drole?*" Dani repeated the strange word, letting it roll over her tongue.

"A term you better get used to. It's sort of a blanket word that applies to anything funny, strange or 'other.' Anyone who didn't grow up here, basically. It's not an insult. I've been accepted, thanks to Bael, and I'm still *drole*."

"Eh, I've been traveling around long enough that I'm sort of used to being the outsider," Dani said. "Doesn't bother me. So, I'm assuming your assignment here in Mystic Bayou is going to be long-term?"

"Most likely permanent, considering the resources the League is investing here," Jillian said.

"Isn't that sort of unusual for the League?"

The kettle whistled and Jillian rose to grab it from the burner. "Incredibly. But, I'm fortunate in that I impressed the right people at the right time. It wasn't that difficult, really, considering I'd been brought in at the last minute to replace a unicorn fondler."

"I'm sorry, what?"

Jillian waved a free hand dismissively. "It's a long story, better told over tequila. Out of Zed's earshot. How long have you worked for the League?"

"Off and on, freelance, for three years. Mostly traveling around, recording energy anomalies and making 'adjustments' where it's appropriate."

"I will admit, I envy you that, just a little bit," sighed Jillian. "I was on my way to my very first international assignment in Chile when I got re-assigned here at the last minute. I mean, I love my life here, but I was looking forward to seeing a bit of the world, you know?" Jillian poured hot water over the tea bags in her colorful mugs. "So, if you've been traveling, I'm assuming you're not familiar with the political nightmare-scape that is the League's office in DC?"

Dani snickered. She had intentionally written her contracts so she never had to visit the DC offices. Oh, sure, on paper, the International League for Interspecies Cooperation was a benevolent collective that was founded centuries before by a particularly open-minded group of shifters and humans, striving to promote understanding and peace between all creatures. It was a lovely party line.

The League wanted to show humans that there was nothing to fear from the otherworldly. That shifters and fae and other creatures had lived among them for centuries and for the most part, humans had been unscathed. But somehow, the hippie genes from Dani's father just wouldn't allow her to trust a shadow government organization with seemingly unlimited resources and influence.

Dani didn't mind working for them, when she thought the project was an appropriate use of her skills and unlikely to do any harm. That didn't mean she wanted to be under their permanent control. She was approaching this job with the cautious optimism she applied to all of her League jobs, while carefully keeping her eye on the exits.

Dani had done her research on Jillian, just like she'd done her research on Mystic Bayou and its history. Jillian Ramsay was a new voice in the field of paranormal anthropology, but that voice was bright and strong. She trusted Jillian. She could practically feel the good intentions rolling off the good doctor in waves, along with some "other-ness" that she couldn't quite name. From her background reading, Dani knew Jillian was born human, to humans. But somewhere along the way, her very being had been changed into something more . . . and never thought to mention it in her work. Dani respected that. She was a fan of boundaries and personal integrity.

"No, I have been very careful to avoid the DC office," Dani said.

"That just proves how smart you are. All I can say is that as long as you can do your job without pissing off the higher-ups, you'll be better off. I'll help you there, wherever I can. I don't like the in-fighting and position-jockeying, particularly when it distracts from the point, which is the work we're supposed to be doing. Keep your head down and your job done, and you'll be fine. Do you have questions for me?" Jillian asked.

"Oh, just a few dozen."

Jillian sipped her tea, despite the boiling temperature. "I have time."

AFTER TEA, CONSIDERABLE ANSWERS FROM JILLIAN, A SPONGE

bath, and change of clothes, Dani took out her phone and dialed her aunt's number. Trudy Timmons was only twelve years older than Dani, a *surprise!* baby for her grandparents. She'd been more of a sister to Dani than she'd ever been to Dani's father, and was one of the few people Dani trusted absolutely.

Still, her hands shook slightly as Tru's "ring-back" song played. She loved Tru, but her predilection for the BareNaked Ladies after all these years was deeply concerning.

As soon as *All Star* stopped playing, she sighed, "Hey, Tru, what's the damage?"

"Oh, hon, you don't want to open the conversation that way."

The corner of Dani's mouth lifted. While she'd never been in Wisconsin long enough to pick up the regional accent, she always found it comforting in Tru. That "doncha know?" tone meant home to Dani. It meant Gramma's apple crumble and riding the orchards with Grandad. It meant staying up all night giggling over magazines with Tru. It meant she was loved.

"Hi, how are you? How's Grandad? Is his hip still acting up? How's the weather? What's the damage?"

Trudy sighed on the other end of the line. "It's bad, hon."

Dani's heart sank.

Her father had been born John Mason Nilsson III in Elkhorn, Wisconsin. But by the time he'd met her mother on a cold desert night in 1987, he'd changed it to "Journey Windsong." He'd missed the hippie era by about twenty years, but Journey was a big proponent of free love and free spirits and well, anything that was free. He'd never quite figured out that what was "free" for him usually ended up costing someone else—usually his parents.

While Trudy had been a much-cherished baby, Gramma Nilsson had spent several decades spoiling her golden boy. As much as Dani loved her grandmother, it was not a mystery as to where Journey got the impression that there would always be people just waiting to hand him whatever he wanted, all while he proclaimed that he didn't need to work for a living because "the universe would provide." When Dani was twelve, she asked Gramma how she felt about being called "the universe." Dani got grounded for the weekend.

Dani felt fortunate that her parents knew themselves well enough to leave Dani with the Nilssons for most of her childhood. Her mother, Susan, was certainly more financially responsible than Journey, but her academic research meant a lot more to her than parenting. Oh, sure, they took Dani on summer jaunts across Asia or northern California or Bolivia, but as soon it was inconvenient to have a minor around, Dani was sent right back to Wisconsin. It could have been worse, she realized. Her grandparents made sure she went to school, got braces, went to the prom, and did all of the things that normal teenagers with involved parents got to do.

It was when she was in college that everything started to fall apart. Trudy had married the nicest cranberry farmer you could ever meet and moved to his bog. Grandad and Gramma seemed fine at first, tending to their empty nest. When Dani called from school, Grandad told her everything was "peachy keen, jelly bean." Sure, Gramma was getting a little more confused as she got older, and lost her keys more often, but little old ladies earned a bit of dottiness in their later years. Other than that, Grandad insisted they were the picture of health.

Grandad didn't mention that her father was visiting the farm more frequently; or that, on more than one occasion, Grandad had walked into the kitchen to find Journey sweeping paperwork into his backpack. Oh, sure, Grandad knew that Gramma was slipping some cash into Journey's pockets. Living a nomadic life was surprisingly expensive. Love and peace didn't pay for food or laundry or hostel stays. Or the child support from the handful of Dani's half-siblings whose mothers were smart enough not to let them near Journey.

Grandad had known that Gramma had been wiring him money

for years. Grandad didn't know that now that Dani was "grown," (at thirteen), Journey decided he was no longer content to drift around. He wanted to feel a "part" of something bigger than himself so over the years, he decided to invest in an artist commune in Oregon, an alpaca farm in Texas, an organic carrot cooperative in Georgia. The problem being that he had no funds to contribute, so of course, every time he came across an opportunity, he went to Gramma for a "loan."

Journey's investments never prospered. Well, except for maybe the alpaca farm, which had looked promising until an infestation of llama mange had taken out the herd's wool yield.

As Gramma got more "confused" over the years, it became easier for Journey to get her to agree to home equity lines, credit cards, loans to fund Journey's grand visions. The family had no idea what was happening until Gramma had passed the previous fall and Tru started finding financial papers stashed all over the house. Tru and Grandad had met with a forensic accountant earlier that week just to figure out how much debt was totaled in their name. Journey had, predictably, disappeared to a remote ashram in India for a "silent yoga" retreat of indefinite length.

"How bad?" Dani asked.

Trudy sighed. "The farm's been mortgaged twice."

"But the farm's never been mortgaged!" Dani exclaimed. "It's been in the family for six generations without so much as a promissory note."

"Well, when the deed to the farm is in the name of John Mason Nilsson and Abbigail Nilsson, the bank doesn't spend too much time checking to see whether it's the correct John Mason Nilsson signing the paperwork."

Dani gasped, sinking into the nearby kitchen chair. "He never did a legal name change. He said the fire ceremony was legal enough for him. I'm assuming he drove her to the bank to get the mortgages, when Grandad was out working?"

"Twice, according to the security footage," said Trudy. "Which the bank was somewhat reluctant to give, considering their screw-up. He also very helpfully drove her to two other banks in town to secure home equity loans."

Dani wouldn't cry. She couldn't. But somewhere, deep in her chest, something broke. She'd always told herself that her father might be lazy and self-centered, but he didn't seem to have bad intentions. He seemed to truly believe in the principles of love and truth and openness. He just wasn't good with the whole "responsibility" and "work ethic" thing. He lived in the now, to the point that he never really grasped how his actions affected other people. But this? There was no way to explain away what he did. This was fraud. This was theft. Her father had taken advantage of his own mother's illness for his own financial gain.

And for him to go after the family farm? How typical of her father to assume just because he didn't care about it, that no one else had any attachment to it. He probably told himself he was doing the family a favor, taking something he considered a "burden" off of their hands.

If she ever got to India, there would be no silence in his yoga. Only missing teeth and Journey unintentionally putting his legs behind his head.

"Just give it to me straight, Tru. How much?" Dani sighed, slumping to the table as Trudy named a number that—while not astronomical—was certainly well beyond the limit of all of Dani's credit cards combined.

Dani closed her eyes, breathing very carefully through her nose. Rage boiled up from her belly, settling around her heart like acid. She blew out a long breath through her mouth and inhaled deeply. She had to calm down. Getting this upset was terrible for her talent. She wouldn't be able to work for days if she kept this up. And she had to work. She had to impress the hell out of Jillian and the other League muckity-mucks with her amazing work on the rift. She had to earn her full fee, plus the built-in contract bonuses for working effectively and quickly. She had to kick ass, while staying very calm and collected and not rushing through and hurting herself.

Right, no problem.

"I'll get it, Tru. This job I just started, the contract is pretty big. With that and my savings, I'll be able to pay it in a few months."

Trudy clucked her tongue. "Oh, hon, I think I can talk the bank into a payment plan if we can pay off a little bit now. But it won't be just your money. Grandad has agreed to sell off some of the older farm equipment, the stuff he doesn't use as much anymore. Jim and I have some savings.

"No, Tru, that money is for taking care of your kids, the kids I can hear yelling in the background for fruit snacks. They'll need college tuition and braces and a never-ending stream of expensive shoes they'll outgrow after two wears because you chose to have five children with a half-Viking with enormous feet."

Trudy snorted on the other end of the line. "The girls' feet are growing faster than the boys. It's terrifying."

Dani snickered. "I'll wire you the money for the down payment as soon as I can get a dependable internet signal. This is my father's debt. He made this mess. And I'm going to take care of it. It's the least I can do for Grandad, for limiting how much damage that jackass was able to do to my life."

"That's not how Grandad would want you to think of it."

Dani pointedly ignored that and asked, "How's Grandad handling it?"

Trudy sighed loudly on the other line. "He's quiet. Real quiet. He misses you, but . . . honey, I think he's just a little too upset to talk to you right now."

Dani covered her face with her hand and willed the hot tears welling up in her eyes to go away. She sniffed, standing and crossing to the ancient stove to heat another potful of water for tea.

"I'll FaceTime him this weekend," Dani said.

"I'll let him know to watch for your call, hon. So, where are you again? Is it still Hungary? Taking pictures of those old churches?"

Dani cleared her throat, a habit she'd never been able to break right before she lied. Trudy didn't know about her talent. No one in her family did. For years, she'd excused her extensive travel by telling them that she was a photographer for a stock photo company that specialized in travel photos for brochures and advertising. And she definitely didn't tell them when she was sent to the outer reaches of the known world, instead substituting pretty stories about picturesque tourist spots. She hated misleading them, but it was a lot safer than them having any knowledge of the League. The only problem came when they asked for shots of her enjoying these exotic tourist destinations. Dani had gone to some pretty extreme lengths to fake pictures of her on the beach in St. Martin or visiting the moors of Scotland.

"Nope, I wrapped that up last week," Dani said. "I'm back in the States as of yesterday morning."

"What?! Where?"

"My editor asked me to move on to Louisiana. The agency would like me to take some French Quarter photographs."

"Topless 'wooo' girls are a little outside of your usual subject matter, aren't they?" Trudy asked dryly.

"There will be no 'wooo' girls. I'm talking tasteful French Quarter photographs. Fancy restaurants and courtyard bars with fountains and flowers. Wrought iron beds, *café au lait* and beignets. There will not be a plastic bead in sight."

"Well, that's a relief," Trudy said. "Are you staying in the decent part of town? You're staying safe?"

Dani glanced around the house. This was probably the safest place she'd stayed during the last five years.

"Always. And the place they have me staying in is really nice. More of an Airbnb situation than a hotel. Very quaint. Quiet.

"Quiet? In New Orleans?"

Dani cleared her throat. "It's pretty far off Bourbon Street."

"Well, remember to have some fun, sweetheart. Maybe meet somebody. Settle down somewhere in this hemisphere so we can see you every once in a while."

"I'll come home after this assignment. I promise," Dani swore.

"I'm holding you to it."

"Love you, Tru."

"Love you, too, hon. And that conversation about you carrying all of the debt. It's not over."

"Sorry! Can't hear you! Signal's breaking up!" Dani called while she made static-y "shhuurh" sounds.

"I know that's bullcrap, what with your fancy space phone! You can hear me! Danica Hubble Teel!"

Dani snorted as she hung up the phone. "That never gets old."

3

ZED

Zed intended to enjoy every minute of his ride into town. He didn't get to ride his bike nearly enough to suit his passion for it. And he never seemed to make it out of town long enough to do a distance ride.

He had plenty to do that day—meeting with Jillian and his *maman* to finalize plans for a "welcome boil" for the League employees, meeting with Theresa to plan further expansion of the "trailer village" of temporary League offices, plus holding a meeting with all of the locals renting property to the League employees about which amenities were guaranteed to those employees through their contracts. And to remind those locals that they were not allowed to shift into their *magie* form to intimidate the *drole* into not complaining about the lack of amenities. Those *drole* who could not rent their own places would be stacked like cord wood in the temporary housing trailers, so complaints would be given.

Zed had to walk a delicate line with the League. He had to give the League enough information and access to ensure that Mystic Bayou was provided the resources they were promised. Yet at the same time, he had to protect his citizens from being intruded upon and his town from getting overrun. And subtlety wasn't exactly his strong suit. His campaign platform had been, "Let's get shit done." He'd put it on his campaign signs and everything. His *maman* had even threatened to endorse his cousin, just for the obscenity.

He figured that Jillian and her colleagues would not appreciate him canceling all the planning meetings to go back out to the *maison de fous* to keep working on the defunct shower, which was what he preferred to do, far above anything he had scheduled for that day.

Walking that line every damned weekday was stressing him out. As much as he loved taking care of the residents of Mystic Bayou, he'd felt buried in work lately. He wasn't sure if it was the increase in town business or because he suddenly had more free time to fill with town business now that Bael was spending all his evenings with Jillian.

He tried not to be jealous or to begrudge the time Bael spent with his lady love. But watching the games alone in his man cave was getting kind of old. He actually had an excess of beer for the first time in his life.

There were times lately when he was lonely, though he thought that might have been sparked by seeing his long-time best friend matched so blissfully to a girl who was not only beautiful but funny as hell and scary-smart. Zed figured it wouldn't be so bad to be paired up with somebody if she would just let Zed be, not try to polish him up to take home to her mama. Bears usually turned on those who tried to tame them.

So here he was, putting off his arrival at work by taking a few extra meandering roads, just to get some quiet time to himself. He figured it counted as that "self-care" thing Jillian was always talking about . . . and it was less destructive than day-drinking.

Zed sped through a curve just beyond Stolen Pearl Crick,

prepared to gun his engine for the last mile to town. And then he damn near fell off his bike.

The sight of a person out in the grass, propped under a dead live oak tree, not moving, startled him so badly that he barely missed slamming on his brakes. All he could think was, "Please God, not again!"

His hackles had never quite relaxed since the town had been subjected to a series of murders, right after Jillian arrived in town. They'd lost several good people to a madman, and Zed still felt their loss, the guilt of knowing he had failed to protect his own.

It took him skidding to a stop and leaping off of the bike onto the grass, before Zed registered that the person sitting in the grass was Dani. He felt a peculiar rush of panic, seeing her sitting there unprotected. What in the hell was she doing this far away from the *maison*? Had she gotten lost trying to get into town? He didn't see a car parked nearby, though as far as he knew Dani didn't have a vehicle. Had she walked two miles from her rental house in the sweltering heat just to take a nap under an enormous dead tree? She was wearing sensible nylon pants and hiking boots, so she seemed to know what she was doing there. Was she not aware that she was a sitting duck in one of the most dangerous ecosystems in the world?

Also, she didn't seem to be stirring, despite the fact that a pretty loud motorcycle had rolled up within twenty feet of her. He could hear her heartbeat. And he could see her chest moving just a bit every few seconds. So she was alive at least, just . . . odd.

And she still wasn't moving or acknowledging him.

"Miss Teel? Are you okay?" he asked quietly.

No response. But she was still breathing. Zed frowned, and studied the tree she was sitting under. There didn't seem to be any fire ant hills or snake holes nearby, so that was something. The tree itself was covered in Spanish moss that had grown so thick in its branches that the tree hadn't been able to get the light and nutrients it needed. It was a grand old tree that had died a slow death.

And Dani still wasn't moving. He couldn't just leave her here alone. Abandoning sweet-faced ladies in the middle of the swamp was not something a Berend did. Or really any self-respecting shifter in Mystic Bayou.

But should he just sit here and watch her? That seemed sort of creepy. He knew he wouldn't be happy to wake up with a relative stranger standing over him. It would be better to do something besides stare at her while he waited for her to wake up—the problem being that he didn't carry a knapsack full of books and puzzles on his back when he was riding around town. And his phone had no signal, which meant Words With Friends was out.

His stomach rumbled, reminding him that he'd only had ham steak, fried eggs, hash browns, grits, and coffee for breakfast that morning. He knew a pretty good hive, just over the bend, near a huge patch of honeysuckle. The bees wouldn't begrudge him a little honeycomb at this time of year. He could faint away without a mid-morning snack.

But his debate of the merits of honeysuckle infused-honey over Dani waking up to find his bike near her and possibly scaring her was cut short by Dani's eyes snapping open. She seemed a bit out of it, as if waking up from a wrestling match with Jim Beam. And Zed was glad that he'd stuck around after all. Jillian wouldn't have wanted Dani left all alone *and* feeling like she couldn't remember whether the day ended in Y.

Zed was filled with a rush of relief so profound he actually felt his heart give a little. He sprang forward, throwing his arms around Dani's body, damn near knocking his head into the tree. Tucking his face into her neck, he squeezed her tight until he felt her wheezing for breath. A guilty expression pulling at his mouth, he leaned away from her ever so slightly to let her catch her air. This put his mouth just level at hers, breathing in her exhalations, lips nearly touching. She tipped forward, meeting him in the middle for the softest, most tender brush of a kiss Zed had ever experienced. He cupped one massive hand around her jaw, gently pushing her back against the rough bark of the tree.

Her tongue darted out, easing along his lower lip, until he parted his mouth and allowed her to taste him. Her long fingers slipped down his shoulders, caressing the warm skin of his arms, leaving agreeable little trails of sensation wherever she went. The urge to possess, to claim and mate and make her belly full of cubs, was almost over-whelming. He felt a little spark of embarrassment under all the delightful charms of discovery, to leap so far from the affectionate warmth she was offering him. He liked this girl. There was a lot to like about her. He wasn't about to treat her like a plaything here in the dirt, when she deserved the comfort of his cave and proof of his devotion.

Also, he was still kissing her, which might be a problem.

He pulled even further away from her, breaking the kiss. And because she was still so damned pretty, even a little addled, he couldn't think of anything to say. Zed blurted out, "You know that some people think that Spanish Moss started as hair from the meanest man who ever lived? People say that one day, that mean old man was running through the swamp and his long white hair got all gnarled up in some tree branches. He yanked it out and walked away, but he was so awful mean that the hair took on a life of its own and took over the whole damn tree in revenge?"

Dani blinked sleepily at him, her lips spreading in a slow smile. "No, I've never heard that before."

Zed dropped to the ground in a cross-legged position a few feet away from her. "Well, that's not surprising. I've lived in the swamp my whole life and I'd never heard that story until Jillian moved into town. She lives for that sort of thing."

"That sounds about right. What are you doing out here, Mr. Mayor?" Dani asked.

Zed scoffed. "What am *I* doing out here? What are *you* doing out here? Did you walk here? In this heat? Do you have any idea how dangerous that is? Not just because of the snakes and the gators and the bugs, but the heat!"

"Just give me a second." She took a long pull from a bottle of water, took some deep breaths, and then more water.

Zed felt sweat gathering between his shoulder blades and soaking into his t-shirt.

She shook her head and inhaled deeply. "Sorry. It always takes me a minute or two to perk back up after that much focus. It's like waking up from surgery."

"So you weren't asleep?"

"Oh, no, I was fully aware of what was happening around me. I heard your motorcycle pull up, just like I heard a car pass about forty minutes ago, and the herd of deer that trotted by a few minutes after that."

"So you heard me talking to you and you didn't respond? Woman, do you realize I thought you might be dead when I saw you sitting motionless out here?" he exclaimed.

"I'm sorry, but it's really important that I don't break out of that level of concentration. Not because I'm self-centered, but for my safety. This is my first day of work here in Mystic Bayou and I don't want to mess anything up."

Zed frowned. "What is it exactly that you do for the League?"

"It's kind of complicated. There's not really a name for it, even."

"I'll do my best to keep up," he said dryly.

"So the simplest term for what I do is 'energy witch.' It has fancier names, 'dynakinesis' and 'atmospheric consultant,' that kind of thing, but it boils down to this." She held out her hand and spoke in a soft, but focused tone. "No matter where you are, on planet Earth, you're surrounded by multiple forms of energy. Light, wind, waves in water—hell, the momentum of a speeding car moving down the road. It's all energy."

Dani held her open palm up. "Most people move through their everyday lives and don't even think about it. They might feel a little zing of static electricity when they touch a lightswitch, but eh, they just walk on and ignore it."

She closed her eyes. "Well, if I picture that energy in my head, the wavelengths, the bright light of it, coming together at a point and collecting, morphing into a mass that I can control, that I can manipulate to do what I want..."

Zed watched as a pinpoint of blue light sparked to life, just over Dani's palm. It bloomed, growing to the size of a tennis ball. It rotated constantly, the light shimmering over its surface and glimmering with tiny stars.

He'd seen weather witches work before, playing around with water vapor and barometric pressure until they created mini-storms in their hands. He'd seen healers set bones in seconds. But he'd never seen someone pull light itself from the air and turn it into a tiny spinning universe in their palms.

"I thought I was psychic, when I was younger. But I looked into it, read a lot of titles that got me funny looks at the library, went to some meditation masters, studied. And now I can do this." She opened her eyes, smiling down at her creation.

"What is it?" Zed whispered as if he was afraid to jar the ball out of its stasis.

"What keeps the world spinning and the universe expanding. Energy. Life. Electricity. All of those things and none of them at the same time."

Zed barely restrained the urge to poke at the ball with his finger. "And what can you do with it?"

She grinned, holding her free hand over the ball and making it expand ever so slightly. "A lot of things. I can help crops grow. If you're sick, I can push this into your skin and it won't cure you, but it will make your cells get moving, and you'll heal a little faster. Or I can just light a room with it, which doesn't sound like a super-power until you're stuck in a hotel in Moscow and there's a black-out. Some can launch these at other people, weaponize them."

Zed leaned back ever so slightly. "So what are you going to do with that one?"

"I'm not going to throw it at you. I said *some* people weaponize them. I don't because I'm not interested in hurting people."

She raised her hand to her pursed lips and blew on the ball. It floated in a straight line, never wavering, until it reached the tree. It melted into the dry, dead bark like warm wax. Zed watched as the branches overhead sprouted tiny green buds that would even-tually become leaves. He stood, his eyes following the healthy flush of life that seemed to be traveling through the surface of the tree like a blush. His head whipped toward her, an expression of wonder lighting his face.

"It was dead."

She shrugged. "It was sleeping. It just needed a little boost to fight off the moss."

Zed reverently ran his fingers over the healing bark. "I've never seen anything like this."

"Well, there's really no real-world name for my discipline. I just sort of pieced together techniques from bits here and there, including stuff I read on comic book forums. I'm really more of a half-assed superhero than a witch. And I'm not the only one, but I'm one of the best."

"It's just so hard to believe."

"The guy who can turn into a bear has a hard time believing I can manipulate air and light?"

"Point taken. So how do you use this for the League?"

"Well, Dr. Ramsay informs me that the rift is de-stabilizing. That it's leaking energy and causing some issues? She said there was some super-secret rift-related appendix to her book that I would have to sign about ten non-disclosure agreements to read," she said.

"It's one of the universe's little jokes. The very thing that drew shapeshifters and fae to the Bayou in the first place, the thing that made us feel that this place was a safe haven. We feel anxious if we get too far away from it . . . which is kind of screwing us over. The very thing we need is causing us all kind of headaches," Zed said.

"In my experience, the universe can be a real asshole like that."

Zed chuckled. "The League has some sort of 'advanced math' guy tracking the patterns to make sense of it, but yeah, we started noticing little differences about thirty years ago. Babies with *magie* gifts being born into families where every single family member was human. And trust me, we're sure nobody was bouncing on the wrong side of the sheets. We're getting shifters and fae breeds we'd never seen before. You ever heard of an *aswang?*"

"I'm not really as familiar with shapeshifters as I probably should be, considering that I work for them . . . "

"Well, it's just as scary as it sounds. Imagine a toddler running around town, turning into a tiny bat-monster-ghoul thing in the cereal aisle, when his mom won't get him Fudge Marshmallow Sugar Pops."

Dani shuddered. "That does sound terrifying."

"Well, the real eye-opener was when human adults started shifting. It started off slowly, so spaced out that we thought it was a freak occurrence, but now it's happening every year. We figure it had to be the rift, because we've never heard about humans randomly developing super-powers."

"The League confirmed that, right?"

Zed nodded. "Yeah, we double-checked before we let their consultants rampage through the town like pissed-off grizzlies in spring."

"Smart. Jillian said you're not really telling people that there are problems with the rift, like not even the locals know what's going on?"

"We didn't want to cause a panic. If our residents happen to ask, we explain it away with recessive genes. When you live in a town where everything is a little weird, you can get complacent about it, ignore what's right in your face. Especially if part of you doesn't really want to know. And we definitely didn't want word to get outside of the community. We'd have every crazy person who had internet access camping out in town, trying to force a change."

Dani chewed her lip. "There are a lot of people on those furry internet forums."

"What?"

She held up her hands in surrender. "Nope. I will not be the one to explain that to you. Google it on a non-work computer."

"Even if I make a pouty bear face at you?" He gave her his best impression of "puppy eyes."

"I think Pouty Bear is one of the lead moderators on the furry internet forums."

"Dammit, now I have to Google it."

Dani laughed. "So the rift is changing people at a genetic level?"

"That's the theory. Jillian has the League's genetics department coming up with some sort of test, to see if there's a 'marker' to make you more likely to be changed or have a child that's changed. That's the big trailer in the back of the village with the sign on it that says '*No, Zed, you can't come inside and play with the test tubes, Love Jillian.*'"

"I haven't seen that one." Dani cocked her head to the side, squinting at him. "So what's the deal with you and Jillian?"

Zed frowned. "What do you mean, *cher?*"

"Well, you two seem close. You were pretty comfortable without your shirt around her yesterday. And you tend to bring her up a lot. Just curious. I like to know if I'm going to step on any toes."

Zed felt his cheeks flush and his mouth drop open. She really just came out and said that? She didn't seem to be brazen for the sake of being provocative. She came across as . . . sincere. She just wanted the information. Maybe she was one of those rare *drole* that actually said what she thought? The more time he spent with her, the more interesting she became.

"What you're seeing is two people who look at each other like a brother and sister," he said. "My *maman* has all but adopted her. She's my best friend's mate. And I would never do anything to hurt him or her. She's dear to me, but because she's also dear to people I love, I will do anything to keep her happy and healthy. That's all."

"That's a lot."

"So why would the rift de-stabilize in the first place? It's been a contained system for centuries. That doesn't just change in a decade or two."

"If I knew that, the League wouldn't have had to send a consultant in."

"Good point. So, what is the payoff for the town, in terms of cooperating with the League?"

Zed grinned at her. "Money, medical support, access to a lot of resources we haven't had for years."

"Well, just be careful about accepting help from the League. They're considered a shadow government agency for a reason."

Zed nodded. He doubted that Dani knew the half of it. The League took control of the *magie* population worldwide without that population having much of a say in it. Sometime in the Renaissance, they simply informed the shifters and fairy folk of the world that their organization was in charge and that any disagreement with their policies would be met with silver bullets. Not that the superstitions about silver bullets were true, but a bullet to the head would kill just about anybody. This explained why so many *magique* complied with the Pact of Secrecy in 1800, cornering them into an extensive list of behaviors meant to keep humans from finding out about the supernatural world. And when the League got all compulsive about keeping track of the *magie* populations in 1908, the *magie* agreed that filling out a census questionnaire was a reasonable alternative to silver bullets.

"So was the town built around the rift?" Dani asked.

"No, the original settlers were human and had no idea what they'd built their homes next to. The first shifters started straggling into this little swamp village called *le Lieu Mystique* early in the 1800s. All of the *magique* were called here like homing pigeons to the roost—shifters, fae folk, witches, any and all of them. We just feel *better* here, welcomed, wanted. Our shifts are easier. They take less out of us and we can change back to human faster. The fairy folks' gifts are turned up to eleven. Witches whose powers have been out of balance for years? Perfectly at peace and in control. It's the best place for us."

"At first, our forefathers tried to tell their new neighbors that they were plain old humans. But the locals were already pretty suspicious of all the new people suddenly dying to live in the middle of a backwater swamp, and they noticed that there seemed to be a lot of weird creatures running around. It got real clear that the humans weren't buying our excuses, so our great-great-great-great-great-great-great-granddaddy, the guy who felt he would be able to best fight the humans off if they got pissy, met with the local town fathers to try to explain what was really happening. They didn't believe him, of course, because despite all the odd happenings, who would actually believe that the supernatural circus had come to town? So my great-great-great-great-great-great-great-granddaddy dropped his drawers, changed his skin. The town fathers collectively lost their shit, one of them literally, because there's this big brown bear standing on his hind legs, offering to shake hands. *Maman* says this particular ancestor was known for being a smart ass. The humans are shouting prayers against hoodoo and witchcraft, calling down God and whoever else was listening to save them from the demon bear."

Dani giggled, tilting her head against her palm like a child being told a story. "I actually feel sort of sorry for the guy who lost his shit."

"Finally, the one elder who still had some sense in his head told everybody to shut the hell up, handed around glasses of homemade brew and they all sat down and chilled the hell out. Then my great-great-great-great-great-great-great-granddaddy promised them that their new neighbors had no intentions of starting any problems." Zed chuckled, charmed by her response. "They just wanted to live a quiet life in a quiet, safe place. And if the humans were willing to live in peace with them and keep their secrets, then the *magique* would share all of their knowledge and magic. I'm sure the town fathers probably didn't feel like they had much of a choice, given that we had major apex predators on our side, but they agreed. Those that didn't agree moved out of town or got into ill-advised arguments with the *magique*, taking care of themselves on their own."

"My great-great-great-great-great-great-great-grandaddy became the unofficial leader of the *magique*, and eventually the Berends took over leadership of the town. The humans and *magique* have trusted us for generations to do what's right for them. And we take the responsibility pretty seriously, even if it seems like we don't take anything seriously. I think we've done a fair job of it so far. Over the next hundred plus years, the humans adjusted to having us around, especially when the fairy folk helped the crops grow and the healers kept the yellow fever at bay. Soon enough, we all started to intermarry, except for the Boones, but that's a whole different story, narrated by assholes. The separation between the locals' culture and *magique* culture blurred and Mystic Bayou just became 'our culture.' Everybody tries to cooperate, but we're people just like anyone else. We try to get past our differences faster than other towns, because it's more important here."

"I noticed your accent is a little different than I expected. Less *Swamp People* and more Davy Crockett."

Zed jerked his broad shoulders. "Well, we're not a true Cajun community. There's so many languages and accents floating around that they kind of fought each other until we have a sort of 'general Southern' sound. We kept some of the French sayings, and most of us have accents, to varyin' degrees. We have some of the same food customs, but we've also mixed in our own traditions, our own flavors and our own languages from the places where we come from. It's a big mess sometimes, but it works for us."

"Do people ever leave?"

"Well, we're not forbidden from leaving. We're not like *Children of the Corn* or anything," he said. "We just don't leave very often. I mean, I've been to New Orleans and Shreveport when it was called for, but I never wanted to wander much farther. I don't know if you know this, but bears are pretty territorial."

"But what about going away to school or getting a job somewhere else?"

"Sure. We had Will Carmody, who left a few years ago to go to medical school. Nice guy, a selkie, but I doubt we'll see him again, once he starts making big city doctor money. So why are you out here, giving this random tree CPR?"

She crossed her arms. "Well, I need to work up to dealing with the rift. I'm not ready for it yet. I have to get used to the local atmosphere. It can be dangerous to mess around with energy at those levels, especially if you're not properly prepared."

"What do you mean?"

"You can deplete yourself really quickly. Or, if you take too much in and don't offload it somehow, that can be dangerous," she said. "Any sort of energy work puts stress on your body—your cardiovascular system, your nervous system, your organs. Generally speaking, with the jobs I'm usually working? It's pretty minor. A slight increase in heart rate and blood pressure that you can cancel out with the right teas and meditation. Or if that fails, chocolate usually does the trick for me."

"That makes sense," he agreed. "Everybody who tries to get too close to it ends up in a six-month coma while they heal from the internal trauma caused by . . . whatever the hell the rift is made of. The closest we *magique* can get to it is about three hundred yards. Humans? You can get five hundred or so."

"You might be surprised how close I can get. But I will be careful, I promise. With a case like your rift, the physical side effects could be, well, fatal. Someone could stroke out pretty easily if they didn't prepare themselves. Someone who doesn't know what they're doing could end up dead. I don't mess around with that."

Something in Dani's pocket beeped. She pulled out a chunk of glass and plastic considerably thicker than the average smart phone, and seemed to be checking her text messages. "Sorry, it's my aunt. Just some family business."

"You're getting texts? How do you get a phone signal all the way out here?"

Dani held the phone up for his inspection. It was an ugly, utilitarian thing, without any of the cute little touches women tended to pretty up their phones with, no decorative case, no apps, no photo background, nothing. "Satellite phone. You travel around the world long enough, you learn the tricks. I can make a call from the Amazon River basin and you'd think I was calling you from the next room."

Zed cringed. "I'm suddenly afraid of what will happen if you and Jillian become friends. You know too much about too many things. If you organized, you'd be dangerous."

"Reasonable response."

"Well, good, now, how about I take you into town? Get some pie, recharge your witch-y cells?" Zed stood, offering her his hand to help her up. Even with assistance, her legs were pretty wobbly and she stumbled forward like a baby deer, face first into Zed's T-shirt. Zed caught her arms but not before her full weight fell against his body. She was so *soft*. The last couple of girls he'd dated had been all sharp angles and bone. It was nice to pull a warm, soft shape against him. He wanted to burrow against her and press his face against the curve of her hip. But that would probably be considered forward, definitely not something you did before the first date.

He was definitely going to have to ask her out. Some other day, when she hadn't woken up to him staring at her and ended up in a surprise liplock. Because that seemed like too much for one day.

"Thanks, Zed. Jillian asked me to come to her office today to get some League employment materials, plus sign about five more releases saying my estate won't sue the League if I die."

Zed slung his leg over the bike and offered her the spare helmet he kept for just such a purpose. "About that, I don't think I want you going out to the rift by yourself."

"That's also probably reasonable, considering I don't know where it is. And Jillian said something about alligator shifter creepers roaming the swamp?"

"Yeah, you're gonna want to close your curtains when you change," he said.

"Says the man who's left me with an incomplete outdoor shower."

"Hurtful," he said before starting the engine and pointing the bike toward town.

4

DANI

Dani had expected Zed to offer her a ride into town. She had expected him to feel solid and warm between her thighs as she tucked herself against his back on the bike. She had not expected him to drive like her dear, deceased Gramma.

Seriously, the man drove like he was balancing a raw egg on his seat.

He took so much time driving into town that she had time to compose an extensive grocery list in her head. She saw quite a bit of Mystic Bayou, though. While there were plenty of houses, the woods were so thick that it was sometimes difficult to see them, or to even know how to get to them. They drove past creeks and marshes covered in thick floating carpets of algae. Most were occupied by alligators, so intent on sun-bathing that they didn't move as Zed's loud engine approached. But Dani spotted several large rat-like creatures scampering away from the roadside, chattering angrily.

"What in the hell was that?" Dani yelled over the wind. She leaned closer to Zed, the smell of leather and woods and good clean sweat drifting up from his t-shirt. She may or may not have rubbed her cheek against his shirt to get a little closer to that pleasant smell. And then immediately leaned back because sniffing someone without their permission had to be an etiquette violation of some sort.

"Nutria!" Zed yelled back. "It's kind of a cross between a possum and a prairie dog. Louisiana's damn near overrun with them!"

These sights, while different from what Dani was used to, were to be expected in the swamp. And now that Dani thought about it, she remembered seeing a nutria on the "Welcome to Mystic Bayou" sign. It had read, "Home of the Fighting Marsh Dogs" and showed a rat standing on its hind legs in a boxer's stance, like the Fighting Irish Leprechaun.

But she nearly fell off the bike when they drove past an open expanse of brown water and she spotted an enormous blue-green horse's head curved over the surface. The horse tossed its head, slinging a spray of water from its iridescent blue mane. Its long serpentine tail flicked over the water, propelling it forward, toward the road.

"Was that a sea horse monster?" Dani yelled.

"Yep! A hippocampus. They're an old Phoenician creature, liked to swim alongside the boats to give the sailors protection. That one swam all the way to the Gulf of Mexico and then forged his way upriver. Determined little bastard."

"He's hardly little," Dani shot back. "That thing is bigger than my car."

Zed laughed and picked up his speed. She wondered whether she'd passed some sort of test to provoke him out of his granny-driving, proving that she wouldn't flop off the bike when surprised. The increase in miles per hour was delightful, zooming down the surprisingly smooth blacktop past trees overgrown with Spanish moss and waterways haunted by the otherworldly. The air in Mystic Bayou was considerably more pleasant than the "Devil's Armpit" area Dani had to drive through to get to Mystic Parish. The air she now inhaled was a mix of honeysuckle, pine and *growth*—the green, earthy scent of living. If Dani could burn a candle that smelled like that, she might never feel tired.

She was feeling more than a little tired at the moment. She often felt drained by calls from her mother, which was why she sought out a meditation spot *al fresco*. Susan's number popped up on Dani's satellite phone while she was making breakfast that morning, and for a moment, Dani considered ignoring the call. But considering that she hadn't spoken to her mother in eight months, morbid curiosity had her hitting "accept."

"Hello, mother," Dani said, spreading strawberry jam on her toast while balancing her phone on her shoulder.

"Danica, hello. How are you?"

"Just fine, thank you. And you?"

"I'm well, thank you. My research is progressing at a satisfactory rate."

It felt like the sort of conversation prisoners had when they knew the warden was listening in, stilted, cold, and uncomfortable. How had this careful, controlled woman managed to catch her wayward father's attention, much less make the irresponsible choices that led to an unplanned pregnancy? Dani had long suspected there were pot brownies involved, but she was afraid to ask. There were some mental images that could never be unseen.

"I'm calling to wish you a happy birthday."

Dani pressed her lips together to keep the annoyed grunt behind her teeth. "Thanks, mother. Only three months late this year."

"There's no need for that tone, Danica. You know how busy I am. You know how important my work is to me. You know how important my work is to the scientific *community*. Considering the hours I keep at the lab, it's not surprising that I become distracted.

Our relationship has never depended on emotional displays of sentimentality."

"You're right," Dani muttered, though she wasn't sure what their relationship did depend on. She hadn't lived with her mother for any amount of time since she was ten years old. Her mother hadn't given her the birds and the bees talk, Trudy had. Her mother hadn't helped her pick out a prom dress, Gram had. Her mother hadn't attended any of her piano recitals or graduations or birthday parties. They simply didn't have that sort of relationship, and the sad thing was that Susan seemed to think they were somehow more evolved for it. Dani couldn't come up with a reason to stop talking to her mother, who was distant, but never as problematic as her father.

"So where are you this week?" Susan asked.

"I'm in Louisiana. I should be here for some time."

"Good. It's not healthy for you, drifting about as you do. You need structure in your life, Danica. Routines. A real job. I've always said so. If you would only take a job with a publication or a studio, it would be much more convenient for all involved."

Dani made a non-committal noise and took a bite of her toast. And she made four more pieces of toast while her mother droned on about the various things Dani was doing wrong with her life. Dani's only consolation, beyond the excellent strawberry jam, was that her mother wouldn't call again until she thought it might be Dani's birthday. So Dani had at least six months before she had to have another achingly awkward prison conversation.

Dani had accepted that each of her parents was pathologically selfish in completely unique ways. And while she was a big believer in self-care and self-esteem and all the good things associated with the word "self" she was terrified of behaving like either of them— being so self-centered that she failed to realize other people actually had the nerve to exist. That was part of why she enjoyed her work so much. Sure, she was getting paid, but she was helping people, protecting them from dangers they didn't even realize were there. She was the anti-Journey.

Dani pressed her cheek against Zed's back, enjoying the warmth seeping through his shirt. Eventually the houses became better kept and more organized, and suddenly they were approaching the improvised village of trailers that housed the League offices. The trailers, located right across the street from Parish Hall, were prefabricated to look like charming little Cape Cod style cottages, but it was very clear they didn't match the town's down-home aesthetic. Dani noted the location of the grocery store, the post office, and the library. She would definitely have to make a stop at Bathtilda Boone's Pie Shop.

Zed slowed his bike to a (gentle, of course) stop in front of the Parish Hall and offered his hand to help Dani off the bike. Her legs had regained some of their steadiness, but she appreciated the gesture.

"Thank you for the ride, Zed."

"You're welcome. If you need help getting back to the house, ask me or Jillian—hell, come to the Parish Hall and ask Bael—for a ride. No going wandering around, got it?"

"Wouldn't dream of trying," she promised.

"Jillian's office is in the biggest trailer, right there. Building One. So everybody knows she's the one in charge."

"Thanks. I think I'll stop by the post office first. I need to set up a PO Box. It will be kind of nice to have a real address for a change. My grandpa will finally have a place to send letters. He hates email with a passion."

Zed grinned down at her. She had no issues with her size, but being around Zed made her feel like a delicate little flower. And she was going to enjoy that feeling.

"You should know that our postmaster, Bonita De Los Santos, is a touch-know psychic, meaning she can tell what's happened to an object, or around an object when she touches it. It makes her sorting the mail really easy, but you have to be careful what you hand her."

"So stop delivery on my Sex Toy of the Month Club membership while I'm here. Got it."

Zed's eyes bugged out and he choked out a laugh, so hard he bent over at the waist and propped his hands against his knees.

"Okay, so I'm gonna go. Sorry about the choking."

Zed was wiping at his face. "No, no, *cher*. It takes a lot to make me choke on my own air. Good job. Go, but keep your sex-toy-purchase-thoughts to yourself."

"No promises!" Dani was grinning all the way to the post office. There was a tremendous feeling of power in bringing a man of Zed's proportions down with a slightly crude joke. And she appreciated that he didn't get all grumpy about her using "blue humor." There was a certain comfort in spending time with a man who could laugh at a sexy joke without making it weird.

And Dani found that she was much more uncomfortable around a known psychic than she thought. While Bonita, a short Hispanic woman with soft, rounded features and a crown of braided salt-and-pepper hair, had been perfectly sweet, Dani hummed show tunes in her head to avoid thinking of anything incriminating or sexual. And she was careful to use a pen from the post office cup to fill out her form. It was probably hyper-optimistic to rent a box for six months, but it would be nice to have a place where she could order internet deliveries. She hadn't used her Amazon account in three years. She thought maybe that was grounds to have someone declared legally dead.

Dani emerged onto sunny Main Street and debated seriously between a visit to the pie shop and visiting her boss. She figured that a responsible adult whose family was depending on her should probably go visit her boss.

She glanced across the street at the pie shop. "Soon, you will be mine."

She scanned the street as she walked toward the League village, a habit developed while traveling in less than hospitable countries. She took in the white-washed Parish Hall building topped with a spire and a golden dragon. It was very similar to the dragon that hovered over the fountain in the center of the town square. She got the feeling that dragons played an important part in local history. She really needed to read Jillian's study.

"Hey, Miss Dani!"

She turned to see Sheriff Bael Boone, Jillian's boyfriend, jogging across the square. He had a foil wrapped square and a to-go cup of coffee in his hands.

"Hi, Sheriff, are you all right?"

"Hi, there." Bael grinned at her. "Thanks for asking. I'm fine. I just stopped in over at the sweet shop to get some mid-morning pie for Jillian. Can you run it to her office for me? I've got a call on the other side of the parish. The twice damned Beasley boys got stuck in Charlie Deeds' shrimping nets again and Charlie's threatening to fill both their asses with buck shot."

Dani tried to contain her laughter. She really did. But she failed. "The Beasley boys are the pervert gator shifters Jillian warned me about?"

"Yes, they are." Bael nodded, a grim expression on his face.

"But you're not a gator shifter, right?"

Bael frowned. "Beg pardon?"

"I'm picking up a reptilian sort of vibe from you, but not alligator. Something bigger? Does that make sense? Am I wrong?"

Bael cleared his throat. "I'm sorry. I'm in a bit of a hurry. If you could just run this in to Jillian's office, I'd appreciate it."

"Sure thing." Dani frowned, watching Bael running across the parking lot toward his squad car. Had she said something to offend him? She figured that asking about someone's shifting ability was a fairly standard question in Mystic Bayou.

Shaking her head, she walked into Building One, which was far more impressive than the tiny faux New England structures. She noted that there was no signage indicating that these buildings housed League offices. She supposed this was because tourists could make a wrong turn, end up in Mystic Bayou and drive past the village. Considering that the League was a secret organization, that was probably a bad idea.

The air-conditioning practically slapped Dani in the face as she walked in. She shivered, shutting the door behind her quickly. Despite the manufactured chill, the auburn-haired receptionist at the front desk was still fanning her face with a copy of *Popular Photography*. A painfully thin girl with dark hair was staring at the receptionist, in a manner that would have made Dani distinctly nervous, like she was imagining a towel rack made from the receptionist's ulna.

"I don't understand why I can't just see Dr. Ramsay. I only need five minutes of her time," the brunette seethed.

"Because you don't have an appointment, Dr. Portenoy," the receptionist replied coolly. "No appointment, no access to Dr. Ramsay. She's a very busy woman and she can't have people just showing up and interrupting her day."

"Which is why I will only take a few minutes of her time to discuss this acquisition form, Lara. Somehow, half of the supplies I ordered for my lab were left off of the order form, leaving me without vital equipment I need. If I can't run the required tests, I might as well be back in the morgue in Baltimore."

The word "morgue" had Dani taking a step back.

"Lara" stopped waving her magazine and cast Dr. Portenoy an exasperated look. "Is that the corrected form?"

"Yes. I need to make sure each and every item is in my lab, by Monday."

"Fine, I will place the order myself, if it means that you leave my office and stop trying to interrupt Dr. Ramsay's schedule." Lara said primly.

"Thank you," Dr. Portenoy sighed. She turned and the laser focus of her blue eyes landed on Dani. She didn't flinch, but it was a near thing.

"You're Danica Teel," Dr. Portenoy said, squinting as if she could see through to Dani's thoughts.

Stop thinking about how off-putting she is, Dani told herself. *She'll hear you!*

Dani cleared her throat. "Yes?"

"Ivy Portenoy. I work for the forensics department. It's so nice to have another girl here working for the League. Besides Dr. Ramsay and Lara, and a handful of others, most of the other League employees are male."

"I had noticed that. And it's Dani, please."

Dr. Portenoy sent an annoyed look Lara's way. "Some people are more agreeable to those ratios than others."

Lara frowed at her. "And some people should remember that their supply order hasn't been placed *yet*."

Dr. Portenoy rolled her eyes. "It was nice to meet *you*, Dani. I look forward to learning as much as I can about you.

Dani's chin felt like it wanted to retreat back into her throat as Dr. Portenoy passed and walked toward the trailer door. When the door closed, Dani said, "She's intense."

"Yes, she is." In a sweet, professional tone that was obviously contrived, Lara asked, "Can I help you?"

"I'd like to speak to Dr. Ramsay please."

Lara's pleasant expression melted away, leaving only cold rejection. "Do *you* have an appointment?"

Dani smiled her best smile. "Not exactly."

"No appointment, no access to Dr. Ramsay," Lara said in the exact same tone she'd used with Dr. Portenoy. "She's a very busy woman and she can't have people just showing up and interrupting her day."

"Well, she did ask me to stop by," Dani said.

"For a Monday morning social chat?" The receptionist eyed the foil wrapped package in her hands. "To bring her coffee? That ruse won't work with me. I've heard every sob story—"

Jillian's head poked through her office door, shooting a slightly embarrassed look toward Dani. "Lara, really, it's okay. This is Danice Teel, one of our newer employees. I asked her to stop by and see me today."

Lara nodded sharply. "Yes, Danica Teel, no PhD, independent contractor, non-specific tasks. Your office is in Building Eleven. There was no picture attached to your profile."

"I didn't realize headshots were something that people did . . . with professional positions . . . with a secret organization," said Dani.

"This is the International League for Interspecies Cooperation. We hold ourselves to a higher standard."

Dani's eyes widened. "I don't know how to respond to that."

Jillian snorted. "Come on back to my office, Dani. Lara, hold my calls."

Lara nodded sharply. "Yes, ma'am."

Dani followed Jillian into a spacious office. "What in the actual hell? Where did she go to secretarial school? The CIA? Mossad?"

"Sorry about that, Lara is a little intense when it comes to protecting my schedule," Jillian told her.

The office was lined with different maps of Mystic Bayou, the largest showed the entire parish with several clear plastic overlays marked "new *magique*," "family territories," and "rift influence." One map showed the *faille* clearly marked in a place called the Afarpiece Swamp. The only personal item in the office was a large framed photo of Jillian and Bael grinning at the camera like a couple of smitten kittens, and another frame Dani couldn't angle around to see.

"Glasses, glasses, where did I put the glasses?" Jillian sighed, searching her desk.

Dani "ahemed" and pointed to the top of Jillian's head, where her glasses were stuck through a golden bun secured with a pair of bronze sticks carved with sea serpents.

Jillian groaned. "That's embarrassing. I don't really need the darn things anymore. They're more of a comfort item, like an academic security blanket."

Jillian gestured toward the plush blue wingback chair across from her desk. "So, Lara wasn't wrong. We do have office space set aside in Building Eleven. I can take you over in a bit."

Dani shuddered. "Ugh, no, that sounds like hell. I wouldn't be able to concentrate at all, with this many people and the phones going off and—I would be a complete mess in a few days. I'm much better off working at the house."

"Fair enough. I'm all for knowing your limits. So, how are you settling in?"

"Better than I expected. I love the house. I don't think I've slept this well in years."

Jillian smirked. "The swinging bed is pretty comfy, once you get used to the idea. Scenery's not bad either."

"Yeah, either Zed's going to have to finish up my shower quick, or I'm going to jump him and ruin our working relationship."

"Oh, I meant the view from the bedroom window, but I see your point." Jillian nodded toward the cup and plate in Dani's hands. "So did you let Siobhan choose for you, or did you brave potential pie disappointment?"

"I'm sorry what?"

"The to-go order from the pie shop."

Dani laughed. "Oh, no, the sheriff asked me to drop this off for you. He said it was your 'mid-morning' pie? Which would imply there are several pie points throughout the day?"

Jillian chuckled as she took the pie and coffee from Dani's hands. She unwrapped what looked to be a coconut cream pie and sniffed appreciatively. "Yeah, pie is pretty much an all-day food around here. To balance it out as a complete breakfast, Bathtilda usually serves it with bacon."

"I think I'm gonna like it here."

"Was there a reason Bael asked you to deliver this instead of bringing it himself?" Jillian asked.

"Something about the Beasley boys being up to no good again," said Dani.

Jillian shuddered as she sipped her coffee. "If the bayou had the *Dukes of Hazzard*, the Beasley boys would be it, only with less folksy charm and way more of a voyeuristic creep factor."

"I think I might have offended the sheriff in some way during this conversation."

"Bael? That's pretty difficult to do. I mean, he has tourists call him an 'inbred asshole with a badge' on a regular basis, and it doesn't even phase him."

Dani frowned. "I don't know. We were having a perfectly nice conversation, and then I asked him what sort of shifter he is and he just sort of shut me down."

The corners of Jillian's mouth pulled back into a grimace. "Yeah, you're really not supposed to do that, it's considered rude in shifter culture."

"I don't understand."

"Are you a fan of *The Office*?" Jillian asked.

"Sure."

Jillian leaned forward, squinting at Dani's face. "Wow! You are very exotic-looking. Was your dad a GI?"

"Wha—" Dani's jaw dropped at the implication of one of the cringier quotes from the show. "Aw, man, am I the Michael Scott in this scenario?"

"I know you didn't mean anything by it, but it's considered intrusive." Jillian nodded. "You could literally ask some of these people about their favorite sexual positions and they wouldn't bat an eyelash. But direct questions about their species? The height of rudeness. They can throw out hints. And if you guess correctly, they'll confirm it. But you don't ask."

"But direct questions are my primary means of communication!"

"Trust me, I get it. Haven't you read my handbook?" Jillian asked. "The League was supposed to send copies to all its employees. It's required reading if you plan on working for the Mystic Bayou Initiative."

"Well, I was working in Outer Mongolia when the League contracted me to move here, so no, I didn't read your handbook. They didn't have wifi in my yurt, so it wasn't like I could order it on Amazon. And despite the fact that I am a League employee, I haven't had a lot of experience with shifter culture before. My mother using her lab's de-contamination airlock as a babysitter? Sure. Naked people dancing in the mud to the music of the wind? Yes, on my twelfth birthday. But not shapeshifters."

Snorting, Jillian reached into her desk drawer and pulled out a blue-bound soft-covered book entitled, *Mystic Bayou: A Whole-Hearted Approach to a Blended Community*. "Here. I keep these handy for moments like this."

Jillian unlocked another desk drawer and handed her a much thinner volume marked TOP SECRET. "And here is the appendix regarding the rift. Please don't let that get into the wrong hands."

Dani nodded. "I will do my best."

"And for future reference, Bael is a dragon shifter."

"Really? Good for you," Dani said, raising her brows. She couldn't imagine calm, collected Bael as an enormous, fire-breathing creature. Then again, she'd only mildly annoyed him. She hadn't pissed it him off royally.

"And since you're working with the rift, I feel the need to tell you…" Jillian snapped her finger, and a tall blue flame flickered to life on the end of her thumb.

Dani sat back in her chair, a confused expression on her face.

"Jillian, I mean this in the nicest way possible, but what the fuck is going on with your thumb?"

"Exposure to the rift earlier this year turned me into a phoenix. I'm one of those 'remade *magie*' the League is so concerned about. After spending just a few months in this town, I can now do this."

Jillian's body exploded in a plume of blue and gold flame, forming into a blindingly beautiful bird whose wingspan stretched all the way across the office. Dani didn't topple her chair backwards in a panic, but she came awfully close.

"Okay, okay, go back to human before you set off the smoke alarms!" Dani shouted over the roar of Jillian's fire.

Jillian was laughing when she became human again, ducking behind a privacy screen painted with a writhing golden dragon. Over the top of the screen, she called, "The first time I changed, it was in the League offices. In front of Akako Hayashi herself. I didn't know I could do it. But she could sense that something had changed in me. I'd spent a little too much time around the rift and it changed me."

"Well, it's a good thing you're living in a fireproof house."

"If it makes you feel any better, the office is fireproofed, too."

"Do you think the rift is going to change me?" Dani asked.

"Well, there's no way of knowing, really," Jillian said. "But your genetic make-up is already pretty different, so I wouldn't worry about it too much."

"Zed said you have the genetics department working on some sort of test. But you visited the *faille* site, at least once, right?"

Jillian nodded. "I got close for a few minutes before I started getting dizzy. Bael basically had to carry me out. And then I lived here for a few months, absorbing who knows how much residual supernatural radiation. It may be that I carry some sort of gene that meant I would change no matter how close I got to the rift. Honestly, this whole conversation is probably me being a worry-wart. I just want you to have a realistic understanding of the risks involved with your work. And frankly, I didn't trust the League to fully inform you."

Jillian Ramsay was someone whom she could trust, maybe not with all of her life's secrets, but at least Dani knew that Jillian didn't consider her employees cannon fodder on Jillian's climb up the League career ladder.

"So, how do you feel about the whole, 'working with the League changed my entire life as I know it' thing?" Dani asked.

Jillian snapped her fingers again, snuffing out the pretty little flame. "Believe it or not, it's made things a bit easier on the relationship front. Dragon boyfriends suffer way less anxiety when you're fireproof."

"That makes sense."

"And everything else . . . I'll figure out. I didn't have much of a home before I came here. I mean, I had Mel and Sonja, who are the closest things I've ever had to family." Jillian paused to tap a picture frame showing herself with her arms around a short, balding Japanese man and a lovely dark-haired woman in a slick red power suit and matching lipstick. "But no place where I felt like I absolutely knew I belonged, where I wasn't the weird girl obsessed with monsters. I've found that here. And even after the League is no longer interested in Mystic Bayou, I'll still be here."

"You'd give up your job for a man and good pie?"

Jillian smiled. "I don't like to think of it as 'giving up' so much as changing what I think of as a fulfilled life. Plus, you've never tried Siobhan's pies. They're life-changing."

"You could let me try that pie that I happened to carry in here for you."

Jillian took the plate and scooted it across her desk, cradling it like a newborn against her chest. "Oh, no. This is my pie. You should go get your own."

"That's not nice."

"I wasn't trying to be nice," Jillian said, taking a big bite of pie.

Dani's eyes narrowed. "You're diabolical."

Jillian grinned broadly. "Just do yourself a favor, when Siobhan says it's better to let her choose, believe her."

"Why wouldn't I be able to choose my own pie?"

"Just let Siobhan choose. Trust me, it saves time. If you choose your own pie, you'll only be disappointed."

"That's cryptic."

Jillian smacked her lips. "Yep."

Dani accepted her pie-denial with a modicum of grace, she thought, and carried her new books down the street to the Boone Mercantile and Grocery. She'd expected some little bodega-style market, but to her surprise, the store offered a pretty impressive range of ethnic foods, from lutefisk to guava soda. She imagined that was due to the wide spectrum of cultures and tastes represented in the Bayou. Cultures that she was apparently going to have to figure out on her own, without asking a lot of direct questions.

Dani had to be careful about how she ate. She wasn't so much worried about weight management, but the fewer processed foods and chemicals in her system, the better she was able to perform. So as much as it pained her, she'd given up her beloved diet soda and Sno-balls. She rarely drank coffee anymore. But she was going to eat as much pie as she damn well pleased, because as far as she was concerned, sugar was a natural substance that kept people around her from getting injured.

Fortunately, the health food section of the store was equally impressive, so she was able to find almost all of the ingredients she needed to stay reasonably fed. She stopped in the baking section and stocked up on spices and staples. She had a feeling she was going to need some chocolate and coconut sugar cookies, even if they weren't a good substitute for real Girl Scout cookies. The produce section, tagged with a sign that said, "Proudly grown on local farms!" was stocked with over-sized, beautiful fruits and vegetables. She stocked up on strawberries the size of her fist, but noticed that all of the apple baskets were empty.

She frowned, staring down at the empty bushels. She had really been looking forward to some fresh apples. There were no Granny Smiths in Outer Mongolia.

"Apparently, they sell out of the apples really fast."

Dani turned to find a tall, gorgeous blond man with a jawline like a ruler standing behind her. He was giving her a sympathetic look while holding up a bag of Bartlett pears the size of softballs.

"I'm not a pear person," said Dani. "They're too soft. As a fruit, that seems so non-committal."

He snickered, his blue eyes crinkling behind black square-framed glasses. "Well, we're fighting the entire town for supply. Apparently, this shifter lady grows them near a whole complex of bee hives and between the cross-pollination and the weird mojo in the air, they're enormous and taste like the original apple of Hesperides."

"That's probably a reference I should understand, but I've been living in a yurt for the last six months," Dani said.

"Well, that's considerably cooler than my nerdy Greek mythology reference. I'm Rob Aspern, head of the League's remote advanced math department. I've been spending too much time with the guys over in cultural anthropology."

Dani extended her hand for a shake. "Danica Teel, independent consultant for the League, head of nothing. Advanced math has its own department?"

"Well, it's me and one other guy," Rob conceded. "But he has to use blue Post-It notes if I tell him to. So . . . yeah, I'm a pretty big deal."

"You're right, that does deserve its own department."

"Nice to meet you." Rob shook her hand and gave her a smile that had to be the product of expensive orthodontia and possibly a demonic bargain. "But in all seriousness, it has to be sort of nice, not to have to share your office space with anyone, right? Tell me of a room unoccupied by someone else's crappy Spotify play lists or stinky yerba mate tea? Is it beautiful there?"

"I actually haven't seen it yet."

"What?"

"I just got into town and I've been more focused on settling in."

"You clearly don't understand the inner workings of the League. Your office space is a physical representation of your status," he said. "How will other people know that you are very important unless you have a window? Or ten square feet more than they do?"

Dani nodded. "I have much to learn."

"Well, my door is always open."

"Is it near a window?"

Rob wriggled his eyebrows. "Yes, it is."

Dani moved toward the check-out station. "Well, it was nice to meet you, Rob."

"You, too. Um, some of the employees have a regular Saturday night get together over at the 'residency court.' If you like card games and mediocre food, stop on by."

"Thanks, that's really nice of you." Dani pushed her cart to the checkout, where a bored teenager with a remarkable lip ring and blue-green hair scanned her groceries.

"Just so you know, when that guy says 'card games,' he doesn't mean, like, poker," the girl said.

"Does he mean strip poker?" Dani asked.

The girl shuddered. "Worse. *Magic: The Gathering.*"

"You have done me a great service." Dani handed the girl a hundred dollar bill for eighty-two dollars' worth of groceries. "Keep the change."

5

ZED

She was on her computer again. Zed had no idea what Dani was doing that required so much computer time. He always thought witches spent their time in the open-air communing with sunlight or some such thing. But he'd worked at the *maison* every morning for a week, and she hadn't so much as asked for the location of the *faille*. She mostly read and worked on her computer, occasionally taking breaks to offer him something to drink or sit on her front porch swing for what she called "meditation naps."

Zed wasn't making much progress with Dani's shower because it turned out that he was not nearly as handy as he usually was when he was distracted by the sight of Dani through her back window. Damn near everything she did was adorable, from the way she got a little line between her dark brows when she was reading to the way she cursed under her breath when she messed up her hunt-and-peck typing.

He was going to have to ask this girl out on a real date or he was going to wind up with a restraining order. And considering that he was the highest authority in town, it was going to be really awkward to sign a restraining order against himself.

Dani emerged from the house in a pair of shorts and a tank top with a llama dancing across the chest. Her long, shapely legs were on full display in the heat, and he couldn't help but notice the little constellation of dark freckles right over her left knee, that bore a striking resemblance to Ursa Major.

She asked, "You all done for the day?"

"Yeah, I got a bit done."

Dani seemed to be eying the shower skeptically. "Okay."

"Are you heading over to the boil my *maman's* hosting tonight, *cher*? It'll be the best food you've ever had for the low, low price of small talk and being reviewed as possible dating material by all the matchmaking grannies in town."

Dani pulled a reluctant face. "I was thinking about just staying in for the night. I've got some work I need to catch up on."

"Is it anything that you absolutely couldn't put off until another night? Because most of your coworkers are going to be there. It's a big welcome for all the personnel working in the bayou, a good chance for you to get to know your coworkers, put your best foot forward, and all that."

She chewed on her soft lip. "Normally, I would be all about it, but I just got to a critical point I'm trying to make."

"There will be pie. Lots of pie. Magical pie."

She grinned. "Isn't all pie magical?"

"This pie has something extra. You'll have to see for yourself."

Dani sighed, then laughed. "This better be some amazing pie."

Zed changed into the fresh shirt he'd saved in his saddlebag while Dani freshened up. She emerged from the house, wearing form-fitting jeans and a purple t-shirt that said, "Como se llama?" next to a dancing alpaca. Her long dark hair wound around her head in a shining coil. She'd accentuated her full lips with gloss the color of ripe strawberries. He loved strawberries.

"Any chance you'll let me drive this baby sometime?" she asked as he handed her the spare helmet.

"Probably not, but if you hop on, I will fulfill all of my pie promises."

Dani's smile grew even wider as she whipped her leg over the seat. "Fair enough."

As impressive as it might have been to speed out of the driveway, he took the long winding gravel path at a reasonable rate that wouldn't risk tossing gravel. And it gave Zed a chance to savor the way Dani's arms wound around his waist, while he shouted over the grind of the engine, "What have you been typing away on in there? I thought your work was more physical."

"Just a bit of academic writing. The urge to publish is hereditary, you might say."

"Are you working on your PhD, too?" he asked.

"No, there's no such thing as a degree program in my field."

"Well, that's a shame."

"I'm writing what I'm hoping will be the end-all-be-all work on energy rifts. Or at least I hope I am. There aren't a lot of books written on the subject, and I thought, with the League's resources, they might get the book into the hands of people who need it. People like me, who are just trying to help."

Heaven save him from beautiful women who were several times smarter than him. They were apparently his heretofore unknown catnip. Or bear-nip.

ZED'S *MAMAN'S* YARD HAD NEVER LOOKED SO GOOD. THE GRASS, usually a riot of untamed nature, was neatly trimmed into a velvety green carpet. Outlining the property, torches and cheerful paper lanterns were strung between the heavily-laden fruit trees Clarissa planted to keep her bees entertained. The garden, boosted with energy from *la faille*, was bursting with spiky bee balm in stunning pinks and purples, broken up by patches of hardy pink coneflower, magenta foxglove, and bright lemon yellow snapdragons. The bees hummed sleepily in their sturdy box hives. If he knew his *maman*, she'd had a stern pre-party talking-to with each swarm's queen warning her of the consequences of attacking the guests. (*Maman* would plant nothing but stinkweed in the garden for the next three years.)

The *magique* seemed to have decided as a whole that their new neighbors were going to have to get to know them warts and all. The few merfolk the bayou could boast were doing the backstroke in the water beyond the grass, their rainbow fins flashing in the late afternoon sun. Fairy wings were unfurled, gossamer and glistening. Little kids scampered around the lawn in their shifter forms, wolf cubs and lion cubs and tiny bears. Bael was in full dragon form, huge and golden, keeping the cooking fires burning. While a handful of League employees were shifters, the new humans looked somewhat uncomfortable dealing with real live *magique*, as opposed to paperwork. But they were making an effort at polite conversation, and generally being sociable, so that was a good sign.

The whole town had turned out in force to welcome the League employees, shifters and fae folk and humans alike. There was so much food that Clarissa had divided it into stations. Gumbo bubbled over a fire in Bonita De Los Santos' iron pot. Another little rock-ringed campfire heated a giant pot of red beans and rice. Earl Webster was overseeing the roasting of several *cochon de lait*—suckling pigs, turning on spits over the flames—something they could only recently reintroduce to the menu after the Warburtons, a family of warthog shifters, moved out of town. Everything was served with cornbread and drowning in butter.

"You weren't lying, this is food paradise," Dani whispered to Zed. "Also, there's a dragon, which you don't see every day. Or in my case, ever. I mean, Jillian told me there were dragons here, but . . . wow."

Zed shrugged. "That's just Bael. Dragonfire is the steadiest cooking heat there is," he said, gesturing to the pair of police uniform pants secured around the dragon's leg with elastic. "He's very polite about keeping his pants on in public."

"I'm not sure whether to be more excited about the dragons, fairies and mermaids, or the fact that I smell sassafras in the gumbo."

"It's a toss-up," said Zed, noting that one of Bael's younger relatives had shown up, a rarity on the Mystic Bayou social scene. Ben, the son of one of Bael's more likeable cousins, was still debating whether to leave for college in the fall, a dilemma often faced by Mystic Bayou's youth—whether to stay in the protective bubble in a community that accepted their unique nature, or to explore the wider world. The main difference was that Ben's parents could afford tuition, so Ben's explorations could take him much further afield.

Bael's less likable relation, Balfour Boone, had skipped out entirely, instead of his usual habit of inserting his company where it wasn't wanted. But that probably had something to do with the fact that Jillian was in attendance, and the last time Balfour had gotten mouthy with her, she'd attempted to Tase him in the junk.

Zed spotted another unexpected face manning the rack of *boudin* smoking over burning applewood. Ash Webster, one of Earl Webster's boys, had been out of town for the last year, training as a federal Fish and Wildlife officer. Baldric Boone had pulled several strings to get Ash assigned to the district that included Mystic Bayou. It would come in handy when the town was trying to explain some of the odder creature sightings to the *drole* world.

Clarissa had been careful to arrange the picnic tables in one long continuous row. It was a pointed gesture to remind the League employees that they were all one big community. That they had to work together to accomplish the League's goals. His *maman* was the master of unsubtle social engineering.

Normally, *maman* would have made her famous honey-pecan cake for a fancy dinner, but this was Mystic Bayou, and when more than ten people gathered here, pie was required. Dani dragged Zed toward the pie table, three times Siobhan's normal pastry display, and he was happy to let her lead him. Her touch was warm against his skin, but not unpleasant, like a low electric hum that skimmed up and down his arm. He wondered if that was part of her gift, or just his response to her.

Siobhan, a squat, cranky brownie who as far as he knew, had no last name, stood guard over her pies like a watch-dog. She did not appreciate little cubs who tried to sneak sweets before dinner, particularly her sweets. She scowled a little as Dani and Zed approached. "No use, Mr. Mayor, your mama made me agree. No dessert until you ate at least one helping of real food. I will not be sweet-talked."

Zed raised his hands. "I accept defeat, Miss Siobhan. I've had your spatula smacked against my hand enough times to know when I'm beat. I just wanted to bring Miss Danica over here to survey the pie and let you get a feel for what sort of pastry she might need."

"I really don't get to choose my own pie?" Dani asked.

"Oh, sure, you could pick your own pie, and it would taste fine. But it wouldn't have that magical spark that Siobhan's choice will have. It's a fairy thing. Siobhan makes her pies to soothe a troubled soul, to heal a grieving heart, to ignite romance. She can tell just by looking at you what sort of pie you need. It's better to let Siobhan choose."

"What if my soul doesn't need soothing?" Dani asked.

Zed's smoky eyes twinkled. "Then she'll sense what your soul does need and give you that instead."

"Well, how do I turn down an offer like that?" Dani smiled at Siobhan. "I'll be back to visit you after dinner."

"See that you do. You need more than you think." Siobhan

sniffed, nodding toward the house. "That one didn't think she needed my guidance and she regretted it."

Zed turned to see Jillian walking into his *maman's* backyard. She was damn near glowing at the side of the Asian man who seemed familiar to Zed somehow. Jillian was chatting animatedly with him, pointing to the various food stations. Zed glanced toward Bael, who did not move between Jillian and the unknown male, despite being in his dragon form.

Zed was about to cross the grass to ask about the man when a whippet thin girl with dark hair and pale skin popped into view like a damn ghost in an internet meme. The girl dressed in unrelieved black and the way she stared at Dani made Zed a little nervous. He liked to think the shriek he let loose was a manly sound of warning, but it sounded like,

"Gah!"

"Hi, I'm Ivy Portenoy. I'm a lab assistant in the forensics department. Did Dani mention me?"

Zed frowned. The girl who looked like Wednesday Addams worked for the newly installed county coroner? Did his beloved Jillian have no sense of irony?

"No, I hadn't had the chance to bring you up in conversation, Dr. Portenoy. How are you?" Dani was keeping her social shit together in a much more impressive fashion, extending her hand and greeting Ivy with a handshake.

"Oh, you have to call me Ivy now, Dani. We're practically old friends. Have you had a chance to think about game night, Dani? Dr. Aspern mentioned he'd invited you."

Dani looked vaguely uncomfortable. "Oh yes, I'm not really much of a card game person."

"Well, we'd love to have you come by on Saturday, even if you don't play."

"Actually, Dani has plans on Saturday," Zed cut in.

Dani nodded, flashing a grateful look at Zed. "Yes, important parish-League cooperative business."

"Very important."

"Well, we'll just have to catch you some other time, then," said Ivy.

"Maybe," Dani replied.

Ivy nodded at them both and filtered back to the other League employees.

Dani cringed, the corners of her mouth pulling back. "She's . . . intense."

"Do me a favor, if she offers you anything to eat or drink . . . don't take it . . . And maybe don't let her have any of your hair . . . or blood or important personal possessions."

"That's pretty good advice. Now, if you'll excuse me, I think I hear the gumbo calling my name," Dani said. "And I suppose I have to talk to some of the other League people eventually."

Zed nodded. "I'll catch up with you at the tables, *cher*."

He crossed the grass to Jillian and the stranger. She beamed at him and waved him over. "Mayor Zed Berend, I would like you to meet Mel Yamagita of Loveland, Ohio."

Despite his confusion, Zed pasted on his best mayoral smile and shook Mel's hand. To his surprise, the old man had a serious grip on him.

"Nice to meet you, sir."

Mel gestured around the yard. "Hell of a place your mother has here."

Zed glanced toward Bael, who had shrunk into his human form and slipped into his spare pants. He jogged toward them, with a big smile on his face. He kissed Jillian soundly on the cheek and nodded to Mel. "We have more seafood than you could ever want to eat, Mel. Do you want a beer?"

Mel nodded his balding head. "That would be great, Bael, thanks."

Bael ran off to fetch Mel's food. Zed pursed his lips. Bael was behaving in an almost tame fashion. What was going on with his friend right now?

"Mel is going to be moving to Mystic Bayou soon," Jillian said. "He's been looking at buying Gladys Fider's old place. It's peaceful and it's right on the water—"

Mel curled his arm around Jillian's waist and squeezed her against his side, grinning broadly. "And it's near my best girl, so it's an ideal place for retirement."

Zed had so many questions about this strange little man who was giving Zed that familiar "hair standing on end" reaction that he had around most *magique*. Though their bond was clearly non-romantic—because Bael was allowing this man to live—Zed had no idea how Mel fit into Jillian's life. He'd assumed that the citizens of Mystic Bayou were the first *magique* she'd ever met.

And suddenly, Zed realized where he'd seen Mel before, the picture on Jillian's desk. This man was one of Jillian's closest friends, and while that explained Bael's polite tolerance of Mel's physical proximity, it didn't really explain the shifter energy crackling off of him or why Bael was almost . . . sucking up to Mel.

Relationships were weird.

Zed put his arm around Jillian's shoulder, pulling her loosely to his side. He nodded toward Ivy, who was now staring down Bonita de los Santos. "*Catin*, you know I don't like to pre-judge people, but that woman is . . . concerning."

"Ivy?" Jillian's mouth pulled back at the corners. "Ivy comes highly recommended, is even more qualified, but her bedside manner is appropriate for working with dead people."

"Why do we need a coroner again?"

Jillian tilted her head and patted his arm. "Um, remember that series of murders we had a few months back? And how we didn't have a medical examiner who could deal with it? This fixes that problem. Also, as long as the family members sign the right release forms, Ivy will do a sort of death census, recording the Bayou's life spans, causes of death, etc. It's going to provide a lot of helpful information."

"Dammit, I hate it when you make sense."

"And yet, it happens so often."

Across the yard, Ben Boone was lifting a wire basket filled with shrimp, crayfish, crabs, lemons, potatoes, and corn out of a cauldron of boiling water. He carried the basket—without protective gloves—and carefully spread the boiled seafood on a newspaper-covered table at the end of the line, for those who wanted to eat with their hands. The air was redolent with the scent of lemon, seafood and spice, and Zed naturally drifted toward his favorite scents. It had nothing to do with the fact that Dani had made a beeline for the crayfish table . . . or the fact that he'd been aware of where she was standing since they'd arrived, no matter where she moved amongst the crowd.

She was laughing with Theresa Anastas as she tied a cloth around her neck to protect her clothes. Zed watched as Rajesh Agarwal showed Dani how to pull the heads from the crayfish and claim the meat with her teeth. Rajesh was a tiger shifter from Kerala, India, a relative newcomer to the bayou who delighted in all things food-related. He was also very happily mated to a lion shifter named Analah. Otherwise, Zed would feel a little strange about Rajesh's hands being so close to Dani's mouth.

Dani licked her own fingers, grinning as she searched for the next delicious bite to eat amongst the jumble on the table. She peeled and bit into a shrimp, moaning at the explosion of flavor in her mouth. Her pleasured sounds were enough for Zed to need to move behind one of the high-top "drinking tables" for cover. The spicy juices from the garlic-rich seafood ran down Dani's arm as she ate. She laughed, and followed its trail down her skin with her tongue, licking it clean.

He could stand here for hours, enjoying the spectacle of her meal, without taking a bite himself. She ate like someone who loved life and enjoyed it to the fullest. And it was the sexiest thing he'd ever seen.

Zed noted that the intense girl who guarded the entrance to Jillian's office, Lara, was taking pictures of Dani's culinary delight with a fancy-looking camera. Jillian said something about using photos from the party in promotional materials. Zed made a mental note to bribe Lara with some form of pie to get a copy of Dani's photo.

Suddenly the seat next to Dani was occupied by some tool from the League's research department, one of the first League reps Zed had met after Jillian's return to town . . . Dr. John As . . . something . . . Assface? No, that couldn't be his legal name, but Zed was definitely comfortable calling him an assface at the moment. He slid onto the picnic table next to Dani, tied a cloth around his neck and began picking through the boil mix. He was blond with a perfect Ken doll jawline and Zed hated him on principle.

Dani was smiling as Dr. Assface made small talk. Though his ears couldn't quite pick up his voice over the noise of the crowd, Zed could imagine Dr. Ken Doll Assface saying, *"Oh, it's so nice being so much more worldly and sophisticated than every person in this town. I think you'll find I have much more in common with you than anyone else here, what with my fancy pants education. Would you like to leave this lame party to go enjoy a latte with me at my condo? We can watch a depressing documentary on climate change."*

Okay, that probably wasn't fair. Most people wouldn't open a conversation that way, particularly when Dani was obviously enjoying herself at the party. But he was sure a latte offer would be involved if Dr. Assface asked Dani out. These League people practically worshipped lattes.

He should walk over there and ask Dani if she wanted some gumbo. Or just pick up Dr. Assface and toss him to the mermaids

76

in the inlet. That would be a reasonable response to this situation, right?

"Hey, Zed, um, your claws are out," Bael said, appearing at his elbow.

Startling, Zed grimaced and stuck his hands behind his back.

Bael asked, "You okay, man?"

Zed swallowed the jealousy rising in his throat like acid. He was not okay. He didn't recognize these uncomfortable, dark feelings in himself. He didn't get jealous over women. He didn't get threatened by other males. And he for damned sure didn't suffer bouts of insecurity. Insecurity was for whiners. He was awesome, born of awesome, made of awesome. Fuck this shit.

"I'm fine, just got distracted," Zed said. "Let's get something to eat."

"Sure, Jillian's got seats over by your mom."

Zed glanced toward Dani's table with more than a little longing, then consigned himself to polite behavior and a good meal with people he loved. "So what's the deal with that Mel guy?"

"Well, you know, Jillian doesn't really keep up much with her family. But Mel, he was the one who introduced her to the whole world of the *magique* when she was a kid."

"Really?" Zed laughed.

"You ever heard of the Loveland Frog? That's Mel. Or at least, his family. Jillian grew up in Loveland and in high school, she set her mind to finding the mythical frogman. Took her about six months."

"Well, hell, of course she did." Zed guffawed, a loud, barking noise that had Dani scanning the crowd for him. She waved when she caught his eye. He waved back, a stupid happy grin on his face.

"Oh, we're talking about that later," said Bael.

"I plead the Fifth, man."

"Anyway, Mel has connections in the *magique* world even Jillian didn't know about. He's been easing her way through her whole career, not making opportunities mind you, just helping her along. He was the one who got her a job with the League. He's the closest thing to a true father that she's got. When he realized she was going to be settling in a *magique* community long-term, he decided to move closer to her. He's getting older, and he doesn't want to lose his time with her."

"And what do you think of that?" Zed asked.

"Whatever makes Jillian happy, makes me happy."

Zed made a noise that sounded like a whip cracking.

Bael scoffs. "Yeah, yeah, laugh it up. But if I'm going to ask her to marry me, I need to talk to him first."

"Married." Zed settled back on his heels and stared at his friend. As much as he knew that Jillian was Bael's mate, the idea of Bael getting married, it was so . . . adult and domestic. It made his neck itch in discomfort. Or that could be a mosquito, who knew. "Wow."

"I spent about a month going through my horde, trying to find the perfect ring for her."

"Did you swim through it like Scrooge McDuck?" Zed asked, smirking.

"I can't believe Jillian told you about that," Bael sighed.

"Hey, she refused to show me the video she took on her phone. You should take that as a true sign of allegiance in the woman you're going to marry.

Bael frowned. "I didn't know there was a video."

"So show me the ring," Zed insisted.

Bael turned his back toward his lady love—and Mel—to keep her from seeing him open a little jewelry box to show him a very respectable solitaire set in a gold band that looked like dragon scales. Zed clapped his hand on Bael's shoulders. "That's a beauty. She'll love it."

"I had Australian opals, Columbian emeralds, pearls from Atlantis. Nothing felt right. So I took a bunch of copies of her report, burned it with dragon fire. And then I took the ashes to this lab in New Orleans and had them compressed into a diamond."

The delighted grin abandoned Zed's face. "You burned her life's work?"

Bael pursed his lips. "Is that bad? I thought it would be romantic, because her work is what brought us together. And it was only copies."

"It's a calculated risk. I'll keep my couch free for you, just in case," Zed told him. "You realize when she hears you talked to Mel to ask permission to marry her, she's going to hit you with a stick. Because feminism."

"I didn't say I was asking for permission," Bael insisted. "I am asking for his blessing, big difference. I know my woman."

"Well, I'm happy for you. Even if it will leave you with even less time to see me."

"Right because that's what this is about. Your feelings," said Bael.

"I would make that whip-lash noise again, but we're getting close to her and Jillian might hear me."

Bael nodded. "Good call."

ZED SPENT THE NEXT FEW HOURS EATING HIS NEIGHBORS' culinary offerings and trying to hold conversations with people who did homework for a living. The usual after-dinner tradition of dancing had been done away with on Jillian's advice. She'd told Clarissa and Zed that bookish colleagues would be much more comfortable with just sitting and chatting.

In the spirit of good sportsmanship, Zed re-introduced himself to Rob Aspern, PhD, whose name was not, in fact, Dr. Assface. And Zed felt a little bad for his assumed dialogue painting Dr.

Aspern as a latte-loving douche. He seemed like a nice enough guy. Zed just wanted him separated from Dani by about three parishes. And an ocean. Full of sharks.

He lost track of her a few times as she milled about the crowd. But after most everybody was full and lulled into quiet, happy after-supper conversation, Dani approached their table with a beer in her hand and an empty pie plate. Zed was quick to hop up and make room for her, which immediately caught the attention of his *maman*.

"You must be Dani." Clarissa Berend was a broad-shouldered woman who gave Zed his gray eyes and dark hair. She eyed the newcomer up and down and extended her hand to Dani. "My Zed tells me you're living out at the *maison de fous*, and that he stomped all over your shower."

"He's right on both counts. I'm Danica Teel, it's nice to meet you."

Dani cleared her throat and reached out to Clarissa, who gripped her hand so hard that Zed could see the ripple of discomfort on Dani's face. Before he could tell his mother to back off, Dani squeezed right back and made a line appear between Clarissa's steely gray eyebrows.

"Well, Miss Teel, do you cook at all?"

"Not much beyond salads and soups," Dani admitted. "I'm more of baker."

Clarissa nodded. "You like children?"

"Depends on the child."

"Any genetic disorders in your family?"

"That strikes me as being none of your business," Dani replied.

Clarissa's lips quirked into a smile as Zed's brows shot up to his hairline. "All right, then."

"Zed, Lara mentioned she could give me a ride home," said Dani. "She's about to head out and I don't want to—"

"Nope, I'll be ready to go in a minute. I'm sober as a judge and ready to drive responsibly."

Under his breath, Bael made a "whipping" noise. Zed shot him a poisonous look.

"All right, then," said Dani. "I'm going to go say my goodbyes. Thank you, Miss Clarissa, for putting together an amazing welcome for us all. The food was delicious."

Clarissa gave her what could only be described as a mama bear hug. "Aw, you're welcome, sweetheart, you come back any time."

"Goodnight, everybody."

Dani walked away while everybody called their goodnights to her.

"I like that gal. Smart. Strong as hell." Clarissa shook out her hand as if Dani's grip was still stinging.

"So why were you giving her the third-degree?" asked Jillian. "I thought you wanted Zed to settle down with a nice girl and give you a passel of cubs to dote over? It would be smarter to give her the red carpet treatment."

"That girl would make me some beautiful grandbabies. But I gotta test the girl's mettle to make sure she's tough enough to breed with a bear."

Suddenly, Zed was struck with the image of Dani's already luscious curves padded further with his cubs. And he got a little dizzy.

"That makes sense," Mel told her. "We used to do something similar in my family. But it was more like a 'princess and the pea' test. We'd serve the prospective new family member a bowl of *matsutake suimono* soup, and if they didn't know we'd given them plain old *shimeji* mushrooms instead of rare *matsutake* mushrooms, they weren't sensitive enough to be a member of our family."

Jillian cringed. "Wow, that's . . . kind of mean, Mel."

"I never said I come from a particularly nice family, sweetheart."

Zed asked, "What if they were too polite to say, 'Hey, I noticed you served me plain mushrooms, you bunch of cheapskates?'"

Mel's wide mouth turned down. "That might be why my birth family died out."

"Mel's family traditions aside, shouldn't Zed maybe go on a few dates with Dani before you start talking about breeding?" Bael asked.

Clarissa shrugged. "Well, sure if you want to complicate things."

"Yeah, I'm just going to go before y'all truss me up and toss me on Dani's porch," said Zed.

Bael shook his head at his mate and his honorary mother. "I told you two to stop talking that way, it gives him too much warning."

ZED DROVE DANI HOME IN HIS *MAMAN'S* TRUCK. WHILE HE WAS a confident driver, it didn't feel right to drive her through the parish in the dark on his bike. Less than savory fae folk came out at night, the kind that didn't come into town and didn't interact with humans unless it was to hurt or trick them. And travelers on dark roads attracted unsavory fae like sharks to a bleeding baby seal. He wasn't about to expose Dani to that risk.

"Did you have a nice time?" he asked.

"I loved it," said Dani. "I haven't eaten that well in years. I'm so full, I can barely keep my eyes open."

"Nothing like a good meal on a warm night to send you off to hibernation."

Dani giggled sleepily, her head leaned against the glass of the passenger window. "You were right about Siobhan's pies. I've never had better. Well, except my Gramma's apple crumble, but since it's sort of a different dessert category, I'll let it stand. Ever since I ate it, I've just felt . . . peaceful? Does that make sense?"

"Absolutely. Siobhan must have sensed you needed to relax a little."

"Or she slipped me a supernaturally-boosted THC edible."

"Either one is possible, really. So how well do you know Dr. Ass . . . Aspern?" he asked.

"You mean Rob? Hardly at all. I met him at the grocery store a while ago. He seems like a nice guy who enjoys difficult math and fantasy card games."

Zed squinted at her. "What?"

"Long story."

Zed huffed. That didn't tell him much about whether Dani liked Dr. Assface. He was quiet for the rest of the short drive home. The spirit bottles were in full glow as Zed guided the truck up the driveway. Dani was too busy dozing against the window to notice their ethereal light. *Pauve ti bete* must have been tuckered out from working so hard. Zed parked the truck and jogged around to the passenger side.

"Curbside service," he told her, opening the door and catching her before she tumbled out.

"Thanks for driving me home."

"Wouldn't have it any other way."

While he hovered rather close, he didn't try to hold her elbow or support her as they walked to the door. She struck him as someone who wouldn't appreciate being condescended to, even when she was almost comatose on her feet.

Zed took the keys from Dani's hand on her fourth try to get them out of her purse. "I'm glad you came tonight. It would have been boring without you."

"I'm glad I didn't stay home in my pajamas." She admitted. She slipped her arms around his waist and hugged him. He hesitated for a beat, his hands poised over her shoulders, before pulling her close. He tucked his nose into her hair and smelled lavender and clover. He inhaled deeply and felt himself melt against her.

"Next time, maybe you'll let me drive the bike?" she mumbled into his shirt.

He burst out laughing, throwing his head back. "Nice try, *cher*."

"It was worth a shot." She snickered. "Good night."

He stared down at her mouth, so soft and full and bent his head toward it. He brushed his lips against hers, gently and when she answered by swallowing his next breath, kissed her properly. He approached her with tentative nibbles, followed by bolder licks and swipes. His hand slid down the curve of her back, settling over her hip. He squeezed, reveling in the soft, supple shape of her.

She bit lightly at his lip, parting his mouth with her tongue. He groaned and pulled her tight against him. She tasted like home and his favorite pie.

"You had the blueberry?" he murmured against her mouth. Dani nodded and Zed leaned in for another kiss. "I fucking love the blueberry."

Dani giggle-snorted into his mouth, but never stopped kissing him. She slid her hands into his mess of hair and he rolled the crown of his head against her touch. He pushed her gently against the door of the *maison*. She fumbled blindly for the handle and popped the door open. She pulled at Zed's shirt, guiding him through the door, but he put his hands on either side of the frame, stopping himself.

"I think this is where I leave," he said, not quite trusting himself not to throw her over his shoulder and run upstairs at a gallop. As much as he wanted to see what was going on under the llamas, he was half in love with this girl already, and if he had sex with her now, he'd give her the mating bite and they might not leave the house for the next week. And he had a small mountain of paperwork and half a dozen meetings to go to this week.

Though she looked vaguely disappointed, Dani nodded and gave him one last quick peck. "Thank you."

"*Dormez bien*," he whispered. Dani stepped back and let the door close in front of her. As the door locked, Zed hung his head. Sometimes being a grown-up really sucked.

6

DANI

Dani was pretty sure she was dying.

Wading through the waist-high ferns on the outskirts of the Afarpiece Swamp felt like fighting through quicksand that took her intrusion personally. She'd hiked mountains in Peru and jungles in Malaysia and she'd never felt the heat pull on her physical strength like this. Zed clearly wasn't struggling with the exertion, but he probably did considerably more cardio than she did. Her only consolation was the pretty picture he made, shoving the vegetation aside like unwelcome paparazzi to make way for her. Seriously, the man had a back side like a Greek marble sculpture. She would know because one of her favorite tacky souvenirs was a fridge magnet from the Bode Museum in Berlin, that was a framed close-up of a Greek marble sculpture's butt. And it looked exactly like Zed's.

Women would gladly give up their entire 401K's for a ticket to this show. She just had to keep the goal (and not Zed's formidable hip-to-shoulder ratio) in mind. She was here to work. As attractive and funny and cinnamon roll sweet as Zed was, she was here in Mystic Bayou to earn the money her Grandad needed. And yes, while she enjoyed Zed and his *ridiculous* body and the brain-melting kisses he'd bestowed on her under the almost-dead Spanish moss tree, she could not get distracted by them. Zed was a probably relationship guy, the most dangerous variety of potential hook-up partners. And a relationship would slow her progress down, and that would provoke Jillian's anger, which could get her fired, which would mean her Grandad would lose his farm. So there would be no boning of Zed. No matter how much she wanted to.

And she really, really wanted to.

Dani paused to adjust her backpack straps. She was wearing her sensible boots, nylon hiking pants, and a purple athletic shirt that wicked the sweat from her skin, and yet she still felt like she was swimming through a thick pudding of humidity. She'd carefully packed the backpack with water, snacks, sunscreen, bug spray, and camera equipment, but she was starting to wonder if she should have included a second set of clothes, because these were starting to feel particularly swampy.

She'd been pleasantly surprised when she'd mentioned going out to the rift over the morning coffee she'd taken to sharing with Zed on her back porch before either of them started their days. Rather than trying to convince Dani that she wasn't ready, Zed told her he'd brought a hiking pack for just such an occasion and he would gladly escort her to the site. She might have objected on principle, but Jillian had mentioned passing out, so she didn't want to take a stupid risk based on pride.

True to its name, Afarpiece Swamp was on the opposite side of the bayou from the *maison de fous*. The forest floor was carpeted with a thick layer of soft moss. Cypress and pine trees grew taller here than any spot Dani had seen anywhere in Louisiana. Honeysuckle blossoms the size of church bells hung from the trees, their scent so thick it almost felt unpleasant. Dani noted that the noises she normally associated with the swamp—the call of birds, chittering from small animals, splashing from underwater predators claiming a meal—were all pointedly absent. Nothing lived here but the plants. No animal could stand the constant pulse of energy from the rift.

Frankly, Dani was starting to feel a little unnerved by it. Like hauntings, each rift had its own personality. Some were angry, aggressive, like a drunk guy yelling, "FIGHTFIGHTFIGHT!" in a bar, encouraging others to violence. (Hello, Altamont.) Others were sad, the heavy, cloying weight of misery seeking to drag every living being around it into its haze of melancholy. This rift felt . . . lonely. It was calling Dani and Zed and every being in Mystic Bayou to it because it craved company. It was probably what drew the shifters and fairy folk in the first place. That made Dani wary. She'd never experienced a longing for attention from a rift before, and certainly not at this level. And yet, every time Zed said, "Just a little longer," she felt the prickle of anticipation along her arms. The weight of the heat and humidity lifted and she could feel the rift charging her cells with a welcome frisson of excitement.

Zed paused at a long line of moss-covered rocks that stretched as far into the woods as Dani could see. "Okay, *abeille*, this is as close as humans can get, without getting sick."

"*Abeille?* That's a new one."

The corner of his mouth lifted. "Means 'honeybee.'"

She laughed. "What about me reminds you of a honeybee?"

"'Cause I like honey, more than I like most things. And I like you more than I like most things."

She tried not to blush. She really did. But it was probably the sweetest thing that any man had ever said to her. "Thank you."

He snorted and held up the pair of hunting binoculars he'd taken out of his pack. He pushed back some tree limbs so she could see the water about five hundred yards away. "So you see through the woods and the clearing, over the water? That sort of haze floating a few feet in the air? It kind of looks like the wavy lines you see over asphalt during the summer."

Dani didn't need the binoculars. Her hands reached toward the spectacle, though there was no way for her touch it. "I don't see that at all."

What she saw was like the aurora borealis if it came down to Louisiana to play five feet over the swamp's surface. The blending and swirling of colors was so beautiful it almost made her eyes hurt. And yet, she was called to move forward, get closer. Her head whipped toward Zed and a smile broke out over her face. "Don't you see it?"

"Not really. It just looks a little foggy to me. I just feel, content? Settled, like this is where I'm supposed to be, even though there's enough pressure to make my ears pop a bit."

"Can you access it from the water?

"What, like canoe up from behind it? I have no idea. No one's ever been crazy enough to try it."

"How close can *magique* get?"

He pointed to an area far beyond the treeline, in a clearing between them and the water. "There's another rock line about two hundred yards in."

"I'd like to see how far in I can go."

Zed frowned. "I don't know, *cher*. I don't want you to wear yourself out on your first trip out here. What if you get sick? Or you hurt yourself and you can't do the work you're here to do in the first place?"

"And how am I supposed to know what my limits are if I don't test them out in a safe fashion with a partner who can get me medical treatment if I need it?"

"Damn you and your logic."

Dani raised her arms in triumph. "Scientific method, bitch!"

Zed chuckled. He crossed over the rock line and showed no signs of distress, except for staring back at her as if she was step-ping over a trip wire.

"It's going to be okay," she reassured him.

Zed grumbled under his breath and if she wasn't mistaken, those gray eyes of his were slowly changing to a tawny gold. She stepped over the rocks, expecting some sort jolt to her system, but like Zed, all she felt was contentedness. It felt like she was slipping into a bath with just enough heat to bite.

"If you start feeling off, I'm carrying you right back," he warned her.

"Agreed."

They kept a slow pace over the relatively even terrain, through thick moss and grass heavily perfumed with wildflowers the size of dinner plates. She walked right up to the *magique* line with no problem. When she stumbled over a patch of purple vetch that had formed a sort of rope across the ground, he caught her hand to keep her upright. And then he refused to let go, his fingers with their growing claws gripping her own gently as spun glass. Zed started shaking his head occasionally as they moved closer, twitching in mild discomfort, but Dani felt downright leisurely in her enjoyment of the rift's pulse.

"It's so beautiful," she sighed as the lights writhed in the distance. "Can't you see it?"

"No," he sighed, pulling her a bit closer to his side. "I wish I could see it the way you do."

"Imagine the most beautiful painting ever created, only it lives and breathes."

"Okay."

"And then another even more awesome painting busts through the wall Kool-Aid-Man style and kicks that painting's ass."

Zed threw his head back and laughed. "Finally, someone explains *la faille* in a way I can understand."

Dani stood, silently, letting the waves of the rift's energy wash over her like the tide. Blocking out Zed's discomfited chuffing, she closed her eyes and felt out the edges of the rift's space, and felt it leap to respond, throwing itself against the barriers of her gift like an overeager puppy against a pet shop window. It had so much to share with her, so much to show her, if she would only come closer.

The separation in the "fabric" surrounding the rift was immense, though it wasn't something Dani could measure in distance or even explain to someone who couldn't feel it inside their head. But something about the tear felt forced and manufactured, which didn't make any sense. Rifts were natural accidents and this felt like vandalism. Something was wrong here.

"I want to see if I can get closer."

"No." The smile slid right off Zed's face. "I won't be able to go in and get you if you pass out."

Dani reached into her backpack and pulled out a coil of climbing rope. "That's why I brought this."

"Your fancy scientific method is that I'm going to tie a rope around your waist and drag you back to safety when you push yourself too hard? Like in *Poltergeist*?"

"It *worked* in Poltergeist."

"Just when I think you may the smartest person I've ever met, you go and say something like that."

Shrugging, Dani secured one end of the rope around her waist in a double bowline knot and handed him the coil.

"I do not feel right about this," he told her.

"Duly noted."

Zed's eyes were fully golden now, as bears apparently started shifting when they were anxious. Dani would have to remember that. She didn't want to stress him out while riding on the back of his bike and end up riding shotgun with a bear, like something out of a circus.

Dani hopped over the *magique* line, turning to Zed and showing him that she was just fine. He was holding the rope like it was the only thing tethering him to the planet. And she wiped the cheeky smirk off of her face because he didn't seem to be amused at all.

She walked slowly toward the lights, her hands shaking from

the amount of push-back she was receiving. Every step seemed to require super-strength.

"I'm going to talk to you, so I can determine whether your brain is being scrambled."

Dani nodded as she crept toward the rift, her body overwhelmed by all of the signals it was receiving. "That seems sensible."

"Any idea of what it is? What caused it?" he asked. "I mean, I've lived near it my whole life, but no one really seems to know why rifts happen. And please try to explain it in Kool-Aid-Man terms again, because that seemed to work."

"Okay, imagine you're making the universe, but all the pieces don't line up, like mismatched print seams in a dress, creating a weakness in the piece."

"This is not up to your Kool-Aid-Man standard, but I get it." He nodded.

"Rifts are not that unusual, actually. You can find spots like this all over the world—Stonehedge, Machu Pichu, this really sketchy convenience store in Parsipanny, New Jersey. But they're not quite as dramatic. Those rifts are like when you don't quite seal a plastic baggie and a little fruit juice seeps out. Your rift is like the elevator scene in *The Shining*."

Zed shuddered so hard it jerked the rope around her waist. "Why? Why would you bring that up?"

Dani grunted against the strain of moving forward. The closer she walked, the lighter she felt, but in a less fun, "barely holding on to consciousness" way. She could feel the force of the rift pushing at her, like two massive hands were shoving at her shoulders.

"Look, energy is forever. You can't destroy it or create it. You can absorb it and move it somewhere else. You can remake it into another form, like that ball of light. The problem is your rift is one big interconnected system and I don't want to pull on the wrong bit and bring the whole thing down on our heads."

"I know we would all appreciate that. Do you think you're going to be able to bring the rift back under control, keep it from leaking?"

"I have no idea, but I hope so." She huffed out one last breath. "Toss me a rock!"

He selected one of the stones, yanked it out of the ground and rolled it toward her like a mossy bocci ball. She stopped it with her foot and marked her spot. "Okay! This is as far as I can go!"

"Great, now get that cute little ass back here before I stress myself into an early grave."

Dani laughed, and catching her breath, moved away from the rift and all its charms. The farther she walked, the better she felt, until she was running full tilt at him. Grinning, she leapt into his arms and Zed almost bobbled her, before he caught a double-handful of her ass to grip. Chuckling against her mouth, he dropped onto his back, and she landed on top of him, straddling his hips.

"So I take it you're feeling okay?" he asked, smirking up at her.

"I'm feeling great!"

Zed propped himself on his elbows to grin up at her. "Obviously."

"How would you feel about having sex right now?"

Zed made a sound that was between a laugh and a cough, clearly caught off-guard. "You're a direct little thing, aren't you?"

"No sense in tip-toeing around it. I want you. I think you want me. And the rift mojo just reminded me of how short and potentially awesome life is, and how stupid it would be to put off something we both seem to want, when the opportunity is right here."

She tore her shirt over her head, revealing a turquoise sports bra that was a wonder of modern brassiere engineering. She kicked off her hiking boots and shimmied out of the prison of her nylon pants. Fresh air on her skin never felt so good. Zed grinned even broader at the sight of her panties, a cute blue cotton print showing llamas prancing all over her generous ass cheeks.

"So what do you think?"

His face was very serious as he said, "I think you're one of the greatest philosophers I've ever met."

She beamed down at him and bit his bottom lip, making him moan and thrust his hips against her. How long had it been for her? Tribal customs had been too difficult to navigate in Mongolia for a casual partner, and she'd been there for two months. The Seychelles? No, she'd been so drained by that job that she didn't have the energy for blinking, much less sex. Alaska, that burly lumberjack guy who had turned out to be a werewolf. Sam something. Hell, that had been six months ago.

"If you don't catch up, I'll start without you," she told him, making him toss his head back and thwack it against the ground while he laughed. She lunged forward, licking at the hollow of his throat. He struggled to kick off his pants and his own boots.

She wasn't shocked to see that he was going commando. She couldn't imagine he liked being restrained, carrying something like that around in his pants. Maybe it was a bear shifter thing? But he put the werewolf to shame.

Ultimately, she didn't care, she just wanted him inside of her. She bit his lip again, since he seemed to enjoy that. He growled as she sank her teeth gently into his lip, his eyes flashing golden.

Rolling, Zed leaned toward his pack, hand scrambling like mad to unzip it. After a few seconds of fumbling, his hand emerged with a foil packet. She wrapped her fingers around the heavy length of him, pumping her hand up and down, as he arched his hips. He dragged a claw between the cups of her bra, splitting the fabric down the middle.

"There were clasps, you know," she mumbled into his mouth as his hands moved between them to sheath himself in latex. "Lots of them."

"Takes too long." He turned her so she was sitting in his lap, her back to his chest, and slid those claws carefully down her spine. He flexed them around her hips for a split-second before guiding himself upward as she sank down on him, keening with the sensation of her flesh being parted by his.

"Holy hell, woman." Zed panted against her spine as they both adjusted to the grip her body had on his.

He gently ground against her. She gasped, shrugging out of the remains of her bra. She ran her fingertips along his thighs touching each of the claw marks tattooed there. Her touch left little ripples of golden light on his skin, like she was leaving handprints of the rift's touch on Zed.

If she had her wits together, she would have asked what the tattoos meant, she would delight in this but all she could come up with was a string of babble that sounded like, "*Harder-pleaseyesthankyoutheremore*," while she reached over her shoulder and yanked on his long hair.

She deserved this. She deserved a good sweaty bout of reverse cowgirl in a sunny field with one of the most singular energy sources she'd ever experienced racing through her bloodstream. And she definitely deserved whatever strange rolling motion that was he was doing with his hips, because that felt amazing.

He mapped the curves of her body with his hands, caressing the soft skin with calloused hands, leaving trails of sweat and sensation behind. He caught her nipple between his callused thumbs, worrying it in patterns that left her breathless and dripping. A pleasurable coil of tension was building deep inside her, just beyond the reach of his thrusts.

She bucked her hips back, meeting his thrusts with abandon as her fingers tangled into the grass. It was almost embarrassing how close she was to coming so quickly, but against the double threat of his mouth nipping at her shoulder and his movements, she was spiraling toward the finish line in record time.

His teeth worked at her shoulders, giving her little nips and bites, but never breaking the skin. She wrapped her hand around the back of his head, pressing his face to her neck. His free hand snaked around her body and circled between her thighs.

The sudden spike of pleasure had her falling back against him, but he never stopped moving, never stopped touching. The thread of tension tugging through her snapped and she was screaming her release so loud that people in town probably heard it. She slammed her hands on the ground, the flowers growing larger and more vibrant in a large circle around them, the grass stretching and swelling like an ocean wave, and rippling outward.

Zed bit down lightly on her shoulder as his movements became more frantic. She was a limp weight, sagging against him. But he clutched her to him as he filled the condom, and they collapsed down on the fragrant green bed, sweaty and speechless.

For a second, Dani thought she'd fallen asleep. They were so quiet, laying in the grass, that she lost track of time. She felt Zed stroke his hand down the length of her thighs and then tried to subtly remove the condom without her noticing him tie it off and shove it and the wrapper in a plastic bag from his Mary Poppins backpack.

"Classy."

"I give a hoot. I don't pollute," he said solemnly.

Dani snickered into the grass.

"So, you are very comfortable in your own skin. That's sexy as hell."

"I come from a long line of very sturdy Northern European women. My bones are heavy and my shoulders are broad," she told him. "I'm never going to be tiny."

He held up his hands. "I like it. I like snuggling with someone that I don't feel like I'm going to break."

"Well, we can't snuggle here forever, you know. Your brain is going to scramble. And I probably just got pregnant with some weirdo bear-demon baby."

Zed cackled. "Nope, I have those League-made supernatural strength condoms. No weird bear-demon babies until you're ready for one."

Dani shook her head. "Thanks, I'm good."

A flash of hesitation showed across Zed's face, but he shrugged into his pants with a grin. "Did I hallucinate it, or did you just make all the flowers grow like a magic sexy green thumb?"

"Yeah, that's a new one. I'm not sure how I'm going to fit that into a progress report to Jillian."

"If you use the words 'reverse cowgirl' in a report to Jillian, I will give you all of the pie you will ever want."

Dani sighed over the remnants of a none-too-cheap undergarment. "You destroyed my sports bra. The girls are going to need support if I'm going to make the hike back to the truck. I refuse to free-boob it."

Zed reached into his pack and pulled out a small plastic box. "I brought a sewing kit in my backpack. I'll double stitch it back together."

"You brought a sewing kit?"

"I knew I was going out to the woods with you. The chances of one of our clothes getting ripped off was pretty high," he said.

"You know, I thought the condom was sort of presumptuous, but this is next level."

Zed stood, taking the bra shreds from her hands, and kissing her thoroughly. "I prefer to think of it as 'preparing in hope.' Also, I happen to adore your 'girls' and wouldn't want any harm to come to them."

He ducked his head and kissed the top of each of her breasts.

"I don't know whether to be charmed or annoyed," she confessed.

"I will accept a mix of both. How about we go back and clean up a little bit, I'll take you to the pie shop for dinner and make it up to you?"

She shrugged. "Nah, I'm good. I think I just want to go back home. Have a wash. Write up my notes and then drink about a gallon of water."

An expression of hurt bent his features into unhappy lines, but he busied himself, stitching her bra back together. True to his word, his hands worked quickly at whipping the needle through her damaged support garment.

Dani slipped into her pants and boots, feeling a little silly to be standing topless in the swamp like some victim in a scary movie. "I just have a lot of work that needs to get done. I don't really have time for a dinner out. Rain check?"

Zed smiled, and handed her the remade bra. "Sure, no problem. Ready to go home?"

She slid the bra over her head, impressed that it stayed together over the strain of her breasts. "Do you do alterations? I have a dress that needs to be re-hemmed."

"Smart ass." He slapped her on the butt and then held out her backpack like a ladies' coat, for her to slide into.

7

DANI

It became Dani's habit to visit the rift site every other morning, stopping at the *magique* line so she wasn't at risk for passing out. She needed to map the rift in her mind, to feel its vulnerabilities and figure out how to mend each one. It was arduous, painstaking work that took a lot out of her, so she alternated with days off, just to keep her strength up.

Zed's work on her shower continued, and somehow, things had gotten awkward after what she considered to be a pretty fantastic encounter in the swamp. He didn't seem to know how to talk to her anymore. His jokes fell flat and awkward and he didn't seem to know where to look. She found herself more disappointed by that than she thought possible. She had hoped to indulge in a healthy, enthusiastic affair while she was living in Mystic Bayou, but apparently sex had made things weird for Zed. She'd hoped maybe they could avoid that, but as she suspected, Zed was a relationship guy and that made things complicated. Dani couldn't help but feel that she'd lost a good potential friend. And then there was the possibility of Zed turning the populace of a very small town—and his good friend who happened to be her boss—against her, which was pretty damn distressing.

She'd started to leave her own house at the crack of dawn and make excuses to be somewhere else, just to pre-empt Zed's attempts at avoiding eye contact. She'd shopped at the Walmart in Slidell. She'd even camped out in her office a few times, but accomplished nothing because the ringing and rustling of all the other people drove her damn near crazy.

Her corner of Building Eleven was a tiny space that she was pretty sure would be a walk-in closet if the trailer was used as a house. Her doorway was marked by an enormous coffee splatter stain on the carpet just outside the waiting area, where someone had apparently dropped the world's largest latte. It had apparently geysered up to the ceiling and left creamy brown flecks up there, too. And now the entire building smelled like stale coffee.

Even with that and the portly ginger-haired socioeconomics consultant who insisted on microwaving tuna noodle casserole every day for lunch, it still wasn't the worst-smelling environment she'd ever worked in. That honor belonged to Rotorua, New Zealand, with its geothermal springs that smelled of dirty diapers and regrets. She hadn't been able to watch *The Hobbit* for years.

Still, having an office had its perks, especially at night, after everybody left for the day. The evening before, she had decided to take advantage of the office's wifi signal and make a FaceTime call to her grandfather.

She'd had a very difficult time holding back tears when her grandfather's face filled the screen. Because he was, as usual, leaning way too close to the laptop.

John Mason Nilsson, Jr. had been waking up at four-thirty in the morning to care for his apple trees long before Dani was born, and he looked it. His craggy, even-featured face was rough and weathered as an old boot. His lips, always on the thin side, were surrounded by a complex network of laugh lines and fine wrinkles.

Losing Gramma had been harder on Grandad than he ever wanted to admit. Abbigail had been the love of his life, his best friend, but in some ways, the dementia had taken her from him years before her death. He'd been sad but settled when Dani had left the country last.

Now? For the first time in Dani's memory, his dark green eyes were shadowed by heavy bags. Her grandfather wasn't sleeping, and not just in his usual the "early bird gets the worm" way. This was what Dani's father had really stolen, her grandfather's peace of mind.

And she was going to have to hide her fury behind a smile because she would not let Grandad see how upset she was. She would not waste their limited contact on Journey and his bullshit.

"Well, hey there, Dani-Girl!" Grandad's voice boomed through the speaker, making her cringe. Though his hearing was still sharp as an owl's, Grandad had never quite grasped the concept of "appropriate microphone volume." And he was using his to hum the tune to "Danny Boy," because that never got old.

"Hi, Grandad!" She waved her hands, because that's what he expected. It was like he didn't trust the video was live unless she was making jazz hands.

"Trudy says you're in Mississippi?"

She corrected him gently. "Louisiana. My boss wanted some shots of New Orleans."

"That sounds like an awful lot of crickets in the background for New Orleans."

Dani cleared her throat. Nope. Definitely didn't need to take Grandad for a hearing test. "Actually, I'm finished with my New Orleans assignments and the editors asked me to check out these weird little towns along the bayou for some nature shots, quirky tourist traps, that sort of thing. There's one town in particular that's really building their tourist appeal, so I might even stay there a few weeks. It's a little off the beaten path, but I'm having fun."

"I can't remember the last time you had a job in the good ol' US of A," he said, brightening.

Dani tried to control the shudder at the thought of her last assignment in Jersey. "It's been a while."

"Well, you be careful down there, even out in the countryside. Carry your pepper spray."

Grandad had given her a beautifully tooled pink leather belt holster for a very ladylike canister of pepper spray. Knowing FAA regulations as she did, Dani had never taken the canister out of Elkhorn, much less the country. Trudy was hiding it in her dresser on her own farm. But if believing that Dani had it made Grandad feel better, she would lie her ass off.

Dani cleared her throat. "I always do."

"Good girl. Now, what have you been up to?"

Dani kept her expression very neutral. "Um, just settling in, so far, meeting some really nice people. Visiting some beautiful places."

"Any nice *boys*?" her grandfather asked pointedly.

"I'm not looking for any nice *boys,* Grandad. If I was looking for anyone, which I'm not, I would be looking for a nice *man*."

"Dani-Girl, I know you didn't have the best role models in your . . . parents, but that's no reason to be scared off of relationships."

"I had the *best* role models," she countered. "I had you and Gram. I know exactly what love looks like. I'm just not looking for it right now. And I wouldn't say I'm alone. I enjoy the company of plenty of—"

Grandad's bushy gray eyebrows rose. Dani paused to search for the right words. "Gentleman callers."

"Well, *company* is one thing. Having someone to come home to at night is something else."

Dani narrowed her eyes at the screen. "Are you going to keep this up or am I going to have to tell Trudy where you've been hiding the Little Debbie cakes the doctor says you're not supposed to have?"

Grandad gasped in indignation. "You don't know where my stash is!"

"In the top cabinet, behind the matches and the emergency lamp oil. You haven't moved it since I was seven."

Grandad crossed his arms over his chest. "All right, all right. I'll drop it. Just so you know, this isn't me worrying about you being alone, honey. I just want you to have even a little bit of what me and your Gramma had."

"What you and Gramma had was irreplaceable. I wouldn't even want to try."

Grandad grinned from the screen, his eyes suspiciously shiny.

"I don't want you to worry anymore about the money, Grandad. With the contract fee for the work I'm doing now, combined with my savings, I'll have enough to pay it off."

"I don't feel right about that, Dani. I don't want to take your money. I don't need my granddaughter paying my way," he said.

"Well, it seems fitting, considering it was your son that put you in this situation in the first place."

"Your father." Grandad shook his head. "I never did understand that boy. He was born selfish, only ever thinking about whatever shiny thing he wanted next. I never would have thought he could trick his mama like that. And Abby, she would have . . . she would have been so disappointed."

Dani swallowed thickly. "I know."

"The only thing that boy ever did right was making you."

She preened for him, all false confidence. "Well, I am pretty amazing."

"I just don't feel right about taking from you. I'm supposed to leave behind something for you, not the other way around. You work hard, sweetheart. It's not right to take that to save a used-up old farm I'm probably going to have to give up in a few years anyway."

"Well, it's my money, to do what I want with, and I happen to love that used-up old farm as it's the only home I've ever known. So please don't sell it to some land developer for condos."

Grandad pinched his thin, trembling lips together and reached forward as if he was stroking the screen where Dani's face was displayed. "I love you, Dani."

"Love you, too, Grandad."

It was a good thing that the building was empty because the second she pressed the "end" button on the call, she put her face in her hands and wept like a baby. And then she sucked it up, wiped off her face, and wrote up a report containing her observations and thoughts on the rift. She submitted regular reports to Jillian, who didn't seem perturbed by her lack of immediate and concrete progress. Jillian was about results, but the right results. She seemed to grasp that rushing through the work could cause more problems, and Dani appreciated her patience.

Or at least, that's what she thought until she returned to the rift site one morning to discover she had company.

She moved beyond the *magique* line, toward "her rock," the marker she'd made to note how close she could get to the rift without suffering ill effects. The site felt off somehow, not from the vibrations of the rift, but some other presence, which didn't make sense because according to Zed, almost no one from town came out to the site, for the sake of their own ear drums.

Dani took her working stance, shoulders relaxed, feet apart, eyes closed. And she prepared to open herself to the rift, to begin the tiniest repairs to the edges of the rift to see what it would tolerate. But just as her lids shuttered close, she felt someone else's energy pressing at her back. And the warning klaxons in her brain shouted, "UNSAFE! UNSAFE!"

Dani turned around to find a thin redheaded woman with

pointed features standing nearly eye to eye with her. Dani shouted, raising her fist and swinging at the slight woman wearing head-to-toe khaki field clothes.

"Oh, my!" the woman sniffed as Dani stopped her fist just a few centimeters away from her nose. "That strikes me like an over-reaction."

"Well, sneaking up on someone in the woods strikes me as a great way to get punched in the face! What are you doing here! Get back to the human line before you get hurt!" Dani shouted.

The woman rolled her pale eyes slightly. "I don't 'sneak,' dear. I was merely walking quietly through the woods so as not to disturb the local wildlife, which from what I understand is quite 'varied.' Honestly, you probably shouldn't be out here if you're going to be so excitable."

"I don't know if you've noticed, but there is no wildlife in the area, because the rift chases them away," Dani said again, in her "talking to people who refuse to understand airport security proce-dures" voice. "Now, get back to the human line, before you get hurt."

The woman scoffed in a manner that was really beginning to piss Dani off. "There's no reason. I'm fine, you see. Just like you. It's always nice to meet another of my kind. I'm a dynakinetic, like you. Well, not like you. I'm sure I've been at it much longer."

Dani tilted her head and stared at her. "I'm sorry, who the hell are you?"

"Maureen Sherman, independent contractor with the ILIC. The League sent me to supplement your work on *la faille*. I've been doing my own research on rifts for a few years now. I'm currently writing *the* definitive book on the subject. And it takes many hands to accomplish great work."

Dani's brows knit together. "No one told me about this."

Maureen tilted her head in a gesture Dani had come to recog-nize as "oh, bless your heart" in the South. "Well, I'm sure they didn't want to undermine your confidence, dear. Besides the League hardly keeps us contractors updated on all of their maneuvering, do they?"

If this woman called Dani, "dear" one more time, Dani was going to punch her in the boob.

"That much is true, I guess. Does Jillian know about this?"

Maureen smiled blithely. "As of this morning, yes."

"So, I guess you got assigned office space in Building Eleven, too, huh?"

"Oh, who could work in Building Eleven with that awful stain on the carpet and the smell of stale coffee wafting about the hallways?" Maureen exclaimed. "I went back to Dr. Ramsay's office and demanded space in Building Three, which is much more commensurate with my position, nearest the key researchers. Lara, that rather high-strung girl behind the front desk? She was very accommodating, once she realized with whom she was dealing."

Dani frowned. Right, because she was a much more high-profile employee than Dani. Normally, Dani didn't worry about jockeying for position with the League. But something about Maureen's demeanor, like Dani'd had the job swiped out from under her, was sticking in Dani's craw. And the fact that Maureen was writing her own book on rifts? Well, that was just the cherry on the crap sundae of her morning.

"Well, you look like you're just getting started. I barely detected secondary pulses or reverberatory waves. Have you done any repairs at all?"

Dani had been working in this field for five years, and she'd never heard any of the words that were coming out of Maureen Sherman's mouth. Was Dani really so badly educated or was Sherman being a pretentious twit?

"No, I didn't want to rush and make any mistakes. A job done without preparation is dangerous and half-done," Dani said.

"And a job done with too much preparation is rarely done at all," Maureen told her.

Seriously, this woman was courting a double boob punch.

"I don't mean to get in your way, certainly. I've been out here most of the morning, so I'll just pop back to town and leave you to it."

"All right then," said Dani.

"It was nice to meet you, dear."

Dani hummed, but didn't returned the sentiment. Even with the politeness her Gramma had tried to drill into her bones, Dani didn't regret for one second that it was anything but nice to meet Maureen Sherman.

Dani turned her back on the woman, listening for signs she was sneaking up behind Dani again. But Sherman shuffled through the high grass, away from her. And no matter how hard Dani tried to concentrate over the next hour, she couldn't focus on the work in front of her. Dani wasn't prone to letting distraction derail her work, but with her grandfather's farm hanging in the balance, she couldn't help but feel anxiety creep up her throat like icy fingers. Maureen Sherman's presence nagged at her until she had to pack up her things, stomp back through the over-blown flowers and drive back to town in her newly rented car.

She knew that hiring Miss Sherman wasn't meant to be personal. It was the League's dime to spend however they wanted, as long as Maureen's work didn't interfere with hers. She thought that Jillian accepted her thoughtful approach to the rift problem. She thought Jillian appreciated her work. There was no reason for the League to send in backup. It felt like having a teacher she no longer needed double-checking her classwork.

She was going to have to be careful how she handled this. She didn't want to go to Jillian and complain because then she might come across as someone who couldn't manage conflict with her coworkers. But at the same time, she wanted to make sure her contract fee wasn't going to be split with someone whose hiring she had no control over. How was she supposed to pay off her father's debts with half of her fee? If that was the way Jillian was going to run things, Dani was going to have to set out on another assignment. Whether her next assignment was with the League or not depended on Jillian's response.

Dani blew out a long, labored breath at one of the few stop signs between the rift and Main Street. She really hoped that she didn't have to leave Mystic Bayou. She really liked it here. She liked her strange house on the water. She liked her friendship with Jillian and the connections she was making with residents of the Bayou. It had been a long time since she'd had a friend that wasn't Trudy. And she'd liked what she'd started with Zed . . . until it got weird.

She was going to have to think on how to bring that back into non-weird territory. But first things first, her job.

DANI CLIMBED THE STEPS TO JILLIAN'S OFFICE BUILDING, TAKING deep steadying breaths. She reminded herself that she was not approaching Jillian as her friend, but as her boss. She'd done nothing wrong, and she wasn't making any unreasonable requests. She had to remain calm, but firm. And she could not accept any bullshit from Lara, the cranky secretary, who was lurking at her desk like a watchful vulture.

Dani didn't even pause as she passed by. "Is Jillian free?"

"Almost never." Lara sprang up from her desk, following Dani to Jillian's door. "You can't just walk into her office, she's the head liaison! Do you have any idea what that means?"

"I really respect that you're about to throw yourself across me like I'm some sort of incendiary device, but I need to talk to my boss. And I happen to know she is taking a morning pie break at this time of day, so I don't feel like I'm interrupting any secret matters of the supernatural state."

Jillian opened the door, her glasses propped on top of her head. "What's all this noise? Dani, is everything okay?"

Lara jumped in. "I tried to tell her, Dr. Ramsay, but she—"

"I ignored her completely," said Dani. "She did her best to keep me out."

"Lara, it's okay, really," said Jillian. "You don't have to give me the full Buckingham guard detail. Why don't you go grab a cup of coffee or something? Decaf?"

"Well, who will watch your door if I do that?"

Jillian assured her, "I think I can survive a few minutes on my own."

"I don't like it," said Lara.

"I'll be sure to note that on your next employee evaluation."

"Thank you." Lara grabbed her purse and a camera bag from under her desk and walked out of the waiting room, locking the door behind her.

"She is going to have an ulcer before she's thirty," said Dani.

"Sorry. I know it's a hassle every time you need to talk to me," said Jillian. "Maybe we can set up some sort of cup and string system between our offices. Or, you know, email, like normal people."

"This felt like a conversation that needed to happen face-to-face."

"Is it about the thing with Zed the other day?" Jillian asked.

Dani gasped. "He *told* you about that?"

Jillian snickered. "No, but you've both been acting like a couple of scalded hens around each other. So I figure it had to be something sexual or Zed caught you in some sort of blood-letting ritual."

"Sometimes hanging around someone who is trained in the art of observing people is a real pain in the ass," Dani sighed.

Jillian blushed prettily. "Every once in a while, I need to practice my skills. So, as much as I appreciate the anthropological workout and you stirring up my already high-strung receptionist, what brings you by?"

Dani realized she'd already lost the plot in terms of approaching Jillian in a professional manner, considering she'd all but admitted to boning the mayor, potentially creating a tense situation between League and parish officials. So she did her best to recover some dignity by using her calmest voice to ask, "I just wanted to double check. The terms of my contract. They're not changing, correct?"

Jillian frowned, her shoulders straightening. "No, one thing the League takes very serious is contracts. Once we sign them, they're iron-clad as long as you fulfill the terms of your service. Why do you ask?"

Dani opened her mouth to lodge a detailed complaint about Maureen Sherman and her condescending invasion, but somehow just couldn't make words come out of her mouth. Suddenly, she felt like she'd overreacted, shoving her way into Jillian's office, upsetting Lara. Not to mention the slip-up revealing her . . . Zed issue. This had been an overreaction, based in panic. And now she felt like a colossal idiot.

Jillian groaned. "Is this about the other contractor horning in on your space? The redhead?"

Dani's mouth opened and closed, a bit like a giant fish. Maybe she wasn't a colossal idiot after all. "Yeah, it is."

Jillian sighed. "I know, it's annoying. I'm so sorry, Dani. I requested the exact people that I want working for me, carefully chosen from extensive lists, and then the League just makes these hiring decisions and don't even consult with me."

All of the tension that had been gathering in Dani's belly loosened, and she sagged against the chair. Jillian didn't think so little of her that she was about to be replaced. Her job was secure. She didn't have to worry about securing Grandad's debts. "Oh, well, that does make me feel better."

"It couldn't be helped. But I know that you're going to rise above it and get the job done."

Dani nodded. "I will. This job is really important to me, Jillian. I'm not going to do anything to mess it up."

"Of course you won't. Trust me, I know you're determined to do well, come hell or high-water. Like minds recognize each other," Jillian said.

"Thanks, that means a lot."

"I'm just sorry you had to brave Lara's angry dragon routine to talk to me about an uncomfortable working situation that shouldn't even exist in the first place."

Dani waved her concerns off. "It's fine. Is there anything you want to ask me about, from my reports?"

"Nope, they've all been clear and concise. Anything you care to share about the other day with Zed?"

Dani shook her head while pressing her lips together. "Nope. Absolutely not."

"Yeah, I should probably stop the teasing before harassment paperwork becomes involved. Then again, I'm the one who signs off on the complaints . . . so, yeah, this will never stop being funny."

8

ZED

After they'd made what Zed considered pretty epic love in the *faille* clearing, Dani had been quiet the whole drive back to her house and had barely offered a kiss or a handshake or '*Embrasse moi tchew*' before telling him, "Thanks!" and hopping out of the truck.

Zed couldn't figure out what the hell had happened. He'd never had a woman thank him for sex, put on her clothes, and walk away. And now Zed seemed incapable of having a conversation with Dani without coming off like a complete *couillion*. He didn't know what to say. He didn't know where to look now that he'd seen what she had going on under the llamas. He didn't know what to do with his hands. He spent their rare interactions just trying to figure out where to put his hands.

And so Zed sat in Bathtilda's Pie Shop on a Thursday morning, trying to drown his sorrows in pastry and figure out what had happened to his dignity.

The pie shop was a pre-Civil War wood structure that had been pressed into service when Bathtilda decided to open her sweet shop. Its pressed tin roof and walls were painted white and emerald green. But of course, a dragon couldn't have a space without gold. All of the art on the walls featured gold foil in some way, whether it was a landscape, a painting of a gray kitten, an old icon of a Russian orthodox saint, or a landscape of the Las Vegas skyline. The mismatched paintings added a sort of weird kitchiness to the classic diner arrangement, with the polished maple lunch counter and weathered green vinyl booths.

A dozen mismatched pie stands stood along the long maple counter, their clear homes displaying all of Siobhan's pie creations from lemon meringue to the apple-pear crumble. The house specialty, chocolate-rhubarb, had a special place on the back counter behind Siobhan, near a mirror veined with gold. Zed had never had a taste for it. It was just a bit too sour for him and he'd never liked the combination of chocolate and fruit. His favorite had always been blueberry. It was a taste of summer, of rolling in high grass, and fattening up for winter.

Bathtilda was smart enough to know that while she had a head for business, she was no baker. Decades before, she'd gone into partnership with Siobhan, who worked magic in the kitchen, and in the dining room. Bathtilda managed the inventory and the books while Siobhan determined what sort of pie the customers needed, and served it to them on Bathtilda's gold-rimmed plates.

But there was no blueberry goodness on Zed's plate this morning. So far, all he'd eaten was a big slice of humble pie, served by Bael Boone. Bael was sitting in the booth across from Zed, smirking into his coffee.

Bastard.

"And then what happened?"

"She said 'thanks' and hopped out of my truck! *Thanks*! Like I'd changed a flat tire for her. I'm telling you, man, I felt used and cheap." Zed frowned, looking every inch the pouty bear.

"What's your deal with her?" Bael asked. "I've never seen you so twisted up over a girl before. Usually you like a girl, and if she likes you back, awesome. And if not, you move along to somebody else. But you're spinning on Dani like a hamster wheel."

"I don't know," Zed admitted. "I've never met anybody like her. She doesn't make anything easy for me. She's not immune from my charms, exactly. But she leaves it at that. I'm throwing out my best woo and she just smiles and moves on in the conversation. I have no idea what she's thinking any time, ever. I mean, Pam was crazy, but she was predictable. If you talked during *Gray's Anatomy*, she broke your stuff. If she sees that her number is saved under 'Crazy Pam' on your phone, she throws a TV through your bathroom window. There were patterns. This girl, I just never know. The things that would make most girls go nuts? Not even a blip on her radar. But imply that I might like to take her out on a date, it's apparently the greatest insult to womanhood since strip aerobics."

"So, she's not falling all over herself to crawl into your love cave. Boo freaking hoo."

"Well, that's not the sympathetic response I was hoping for," Zed said.

"Oh, because for once, you're having to work to keep a lady's attention? That's called being a grown-ass man, being interested in a grown-ass woman. Because grown-ass women require more of you. You think it's easy trying to hold a conversation with a woman who has a Ph-damned-D? All of the words she uses have more than three syllables. You know what she talks about in her sleep? VENN DIAGRAMS. Because of her, I went out and bought a damn book on poverty and how it affects American communities. But it's worth it. Because grown-ass women are worth it. Yeah, these girls from the outside world are wily and unpredictable—Ow." He paused as Jillian slid into the booth and lightly punched his bicep.

"I am not wily or unpredictable," Jillian said, pointing a finger in his face. "I am a delicate fucking flower of guilelessness."

"You're right, *elskling*, You're practically made of spun sugar."

Bael pushed part of his pecan pie over toward Jillian's plate and she seemed slightly mollified.

Zed laughed. "Tell me again how it's all worth it."

"You make whipping sounds and I'll take you outside and beat your ass," said Bael.

Jillian shrugged and scooped pie into her mouth.

"I went through something similar with Jillian after we first got together, remember? I showed her my horde, which is as close to 'Will you go steady with me, check yes or no?' as dragons get. And she thought it was a research opportunity?" Bael reminded him. "We had weeks of miscommunication because she didn't get my culture. And that was with a woman who desperately wanted to understand and accommodate that culture."

"I said I was sorry about that," said Jillian. "There is literally no book about how to date a dragon."

Bael kissed her forehead. "I know, sweetheart."

"So, I have questions," said Jillian.

The men at the table chorused, "Of course, you do."

Jillian ignored them. "Don't bears tend to have a lot of partners? Bael said you dated around plenty before I got here."

"When we find the right woman, we give her the mating bite—after proposing—and that prepares her body to carry our young. Werewolves do something similar."

"But you don't mate for life?" Jillian asked.

Zed grinned. "Yes, unlike real bears, *we* mate for life. And we reach sexual maturity very early."

She lifted a brow. "Great, when will you reach emotional maturity?"

Zed waggled his hand back and forth. "Meh."

"So, here's my advice," Bael cut in. "Man-bear up and tell her that you'd like to date her and take her out for pie and spend a Sunday with your mama. But if she doesn't want that right now, that's fine. If she's who you want, you'll accept what she's willing to give, until she's willing to give more."

Zed shook his head. "And that doesn't make me sound like the saddest little sad-sack that ever sacked?"

"Do you want to be proud or do you want to be happy?" Bael asked.

Zed harrumphed. Just then, the woman herself walked in, wearing a blue t-shirt that read, "Save the Drama for Your Llama!"

"What's with all the llamas?" Bael asked.

"I have no clue. She even has them on her underwear," Zed said. "It's just the cutest thing you ever saw. When she walks around in them, it looks like they're jumping across her ass cheeks and—"

Jillian pursed her lips together and shook her head.

Zed paused. "Too much?"

Jillian nodded.

Behind Bael and Jillian's backs, Dani sat at the end of the counter and placed her order with an unsmiling Siobhan.

"Well, I like her," said Bael. "But because you tend to pick crazy women, I just need to know how far on the scale she is, so I know what sort of contingency plans to come up with—air, water or ground rescue? Will a drone be required? Does she have the means to shoot down my drone? I need to take all of these things into account and in order to do that, I need more information."

"You're an asshole," Zed told him.

Bael countered, "I'm prepared."

"To be an asshole," Zed shot back.

"Zed, the last time you went on a date, I had to interrupt a perfectly nice evening with Jillian to bring a box-cutter to your house, because Nina Pinion duct-taped you to your kitchen wall and left you like something out of a Stephen King book."

"To be fair, she'd just found out I had a date with her cousin the next day," Zed said. "And Dani's not crazy, at all. I don't think.

Most of the time that comes out in the first couple of conversations."

Bael pointed to his face. "Unimpressed."

"So, to change the subject to something only slightly less awkward," Jillian interjected. "Uh, what's going on with your mama and my honorary father figure?"

"What do you mean?" Zed asked.

"You haven't noticed that Clarisse has been spending an awful lot of time with Mel?" Jillian prompted. "At night? Alone?"

Zed scoffed. "That doesn't mean anything."

"She made him boudin and spatzel for dinner the other night."

"Aw, shit, she does like him," Zed sighed.

"And then they watched *The Bridges of Madison County*," Jillian added.

Zed gasped. "That's like *The Notebook* for old people!"

Zed remembered what happened the last time he and Pam Beulieu watched *The Notebook* together. And he gagged. He was not prepared for his *maman* to date. He knew she'd been alone since his Papa died, when Zed was just a cub. And he knew she deserved love and companionship more than anyone on Earth. He just didn't want to think about his mom being a sexual creature. In his mind, when she and Mel said goodnight, she pushed him out the door and went to bed alone on a mattress made of angel feathers.

"Your bear shifter mom is dating my river frogman dad," said Jillian. "It sounds like a bad sitcom set-up. How do you feel about that?"

Zed shuddered. "I don't know. I mean, if she's interested in him, he must be pretty great. And instead of threatening to bury his body somewhere in the swamp, I should probably respect her feelings and try to make things as easy as possible on both of them. I should get to know him and give him a fair chance and make him feel welcome in my loving family. Damn it."

"Being a grown-up sucks, huh?" said Jillian.

"It really does. And on that depressing note, I bid y'all good day."

Bael called over his shoulder. "Hey, Zed, remember all the shit you gave me about mooning over Jillian? Payback's a bitch."

Zed boomed, "Fuck you, Bael!"

And because his neighbors were used to this sort of exchange, none of them batted an eyelash—except of course for Bathtilda Boone, who poked her gray head out of her office and snapped at Zed, "Watch your mouth in my establishment, Mr. Mayor!"

Zed approached the counter as Siobhan slid Dani's pie in front of her with a side of thick-cut bacon. He crossed the dining room, barely stopping for the people who called greetings out to him. He sat at the counter seat on Dani's left.

"I'll have a piece of blueberry, Miss Siobhan," Zed called.

"This gal took the last piece," Siobhan said, nodding toward Dani, whose plate overran with fat blueberries seeping out of a thick shortbread crust.

"I'm not even sorry," she told him, forking a bite into her mouth.

Zed gasped and placed his hand over his chest. "You wound me with your coldness, *cher*."

Dani's dark brows drew together and Zed wondered if he'd hit a little too close to home. But the uncertain expression faded from her face as she chewed Siobhan's divine blueberry creation. The motion of Dani's glossed lips combined with the rich fruity smell of pie filling had Zed's mouth-watering.

"So, you get to order a specific pie?" asked Dani. "I thought the whole deal was that Siobhan is supposed to choose your pie for you. Jillian told me it's better that way. Everybody has told me it's better that way."

"Yes, but Siobhan has always chosen blueberry for me. Ever

since I was a cub. I'm a creature of habit. At least, when it comes to pie."

"So of all the magical soul healing available, you've needed the same thing since you were a cub?"

He shrugged. "I guess so."

He attempted to pluck a blueberry from her plate and she poked her fork none-too-lightly into the back of his hand.

"What in the fuck do you think you're doing?" she asked.

"I told you, blueberry was my favorite!" he exclaimed. "And you have the last piece."

"I have cut people for less," she said. "There is a guy wandering around Hurghada with half a thumb because he tried to take my kabob."

Zed raised his hand, grinning. "I respect that. So what are your plans for today?"

"I'm going to head over to the public library, do a little writing and some research."

"We have a whole office complex set up by the parish hall, you know," Zed told her. "You don't have to hide out at the library."

"I like it there," she told him. "There's a nice, calming atmosphere, from all of the books, all of the people who go there to learn. And Miss Bardie is so sweet. I like spending my breaks with her."

Zed frowned at the description of Miss Bardie as anything but an angry book-hoarding harpy, but didn't say anything.

With Bael's admonishments in mind, Zed cleared his throat and asked, "Dani, I like you, a lot. I think you're beautiful and funny and you sort of scare me sometimes, which I think is awesome. I would like to date you. I would like to take you to dinner, or even cook you dinner, if that's what you want. I would like to spend time with you and get to know you better. I would like it if some of that time was spent naked, but if that's not okay with you, that's fine, too. Anything you're comfortable with, that's what I want."

Dani's happy, relaxed expression sort of melted off her face and was replaced by discomfort.

Shit.

He had miscalculated.

Also, Bael was an idiot.

"I don't really date. Anyone," she said. "It's not you, it's me. If you want to get together for sex sometime, I'm okay with that. I mean, more than okay, I'd be thrilled. But I've got a job to do here and I don't really have time for distractions like dating and dinners."

"Wait, what?"

"Call me if you're up for it. I need to get to work," Dani said, hopping up from her seat. "You can eat the rest of the blueberry."

"I do not understand what is happening here," Zed replied.

Zed turned back to the booth where Bael and Jillian were sitting, both grimacing in the face of his rejection. Zed threw his arms up into the air.

Siobhan passed by on her way to refilling Earl Webster's coffee and put a stick of butter on the counter next to Dani's abandoned plate.

"I don't put butter on my pie, Miss Siobhan, that is morally wrong," said Zed.

Siobhan scoffed. "I know, it's to go on that sick burn that girl just gave you."

9

DANI

Gramma had always encouraged Dani to give people second
chances, even if they made bad first impressions, to grow
on her and possibly develop a friendship you might have otherwise
missed out on.

But the more Dani got to know Maureen, the more she did not
like Maureen. If anything, Dani's first impression of her had been
an understatement. Maureen inquired multiple times how Dani
managed to find hiking pants "in *your* size," with an insulting
emphasis on "your." Maureen constantly brought up techniques
and theories Dani had never heard of in an attempt to intimidate
her. She was condescending and insulting in that subtle, stinging
way that was supposed to make Dani feel inept and unprofessional.
Instead, it just pissed her off.

But she didn't want to risk her paycheck in the name of petty
revenge . . . or murder. So she tried to ignore the woman, which
was easier than one would think. She rarely saw Maureen in town.
The only place she had to deal with Maureen was the rift site, and
when Dani saw her there, she generally turned right around and
went back home to write. Dani didn't feel comfortable working on

the rift when someone else was already there working on it. It felt unsafe to let her work mingle with someone else's. She tried not to think of it as avoiding confrontation. She was trying to be gracious and professional . . . and remain un-jailed.

And so, she sat at her comfy space at a table near the reference section, reading about the history of Mystic Bayou and making notes. She wasn't lying to Zed about the atmosphere here. It was quiet, so much quieter than her office, and much more restful than her house, where Zed could show up any minute to work on her shower with his distracting toplessness. She felt at home in the surprisingly grand space in the Mystic Bayou Public Library, surrounded by golden walls and tall oak shelves, stocked with everything from mass market paperbacks to scrolls that looked like they came from the library at Alexandria. Stained glass windows throughout the building depicted famous dragons in literature, but in nearly every one, the story was flipped. St. George was slayed by the dragon. Smaug ate the Hobbit. The Jabberwocky chased Alice out of Wonderland. It was a little perverse. Dani loved it.

Over her shoulder, Dani heard Miss Bardie's low voice telling another patron, "We should have a book on Tibetan meditation practices just over here in the religion section. As you can imagine, with so many cultures represented here, the selection is quite extensive."

Dani glanced up, her lips already bent in a smile to greet Miss Bardie, but then saw that the patron Bardie was leading toward her was Maureen Sherman.

Dani grumbled. "Motherf—" She pasted on a fake pleasant expression and said quietly, "Maureen, how interesting to see you here."

"Yes, I've found your hiding spot," Maureen trilled. "I can't stand the noise and bustle of the office village, can you? I prefer my own little rental property outside of town."

"Yeah, I wonder why I would be hiding," Dani sighed.

"What brings you to the library?" Maureen asked.

"Books," Dani said, turning back to her work.

Bardie beamed at Dani, showing a full display of sharp, shiny white teeth. "Dani is a wonderfully thorough researcher, and never puts the books back damaged or out of order."

Dani grinned. "Your standards are very low, Miss Bardie."

"Have you read anything on focused attention meditations?" Maureen asked. "I'm afraid I've pushed myself beyond my instructor's experience and need to consult the great works of the masters. I was looking for Chodak's work on the subject."

"I'm sorry, I don't have any experience with focused attention meditations or books on the subject," said Dani.

"Oh, how strange. I couldn't get through the day without mine! Perhaps that's why you seem so . . . overwhelmed when I see you."

Dani's eyes narrowed. "Miss Bardie, would you excuse the two of us? I think Maureen and I need to have a discussion on polite, professional behavior and how we're going to define it from here."

Maureen waved her off. "Oh, no I'm afraid I don't have time to chat. I have to find my book and return to my work. The muse is being so demanding today!"

"Oh, what a shame that you have to leave," said Dani.

Bardie turned to Maureen. "Well, let's help you find that book then, shall we?"

"See you at the rift site, dear," Maureen trilled.

Dani rolled her eyes and returned to her work. Maureen Sherman was making Dani seriously reconsider her stance on not weaponizing her talent.

DANI COULDN'T RELAX BACK INTO HER CUSHY LIBRARY CHAIR until she heard Maureen checking out her precious book on meditation. It took her several hours of reading to finally quiet her mind, and then several hours of writing got her to unwind enough to stop grinding her teeth.

Dani worked well beyond the dinner hour. Bardie went on a break to go to the pie shop, offering to return a take-out meal to Dani, but Dani was so focused she politely refused. She was just grateful that Bardie trusted her enough to leave her alone in the library. It was locked, which meant that Dani was technically "chained" inside. But still, it was nice to be trusted.

Dani leaned back in her chair, skimming over a book she'd found on Mystic Bayou's founders. Zed's "great-great-great-great-great-great-great-grandaddy" was mentioned several times, as was his penchant for dropping his pants in public. It was interesting material, pants aside, but she was so tired, and the chair was so comfortable. And she felt so safe in this dragon-guarded building full of books. She propped her chin on her hand, her eyes growing heavier by the minute...

DANI STARTLED AWAKE. SHE HAD FALLEN ASLEEP, PROPPED against the table at the library. But something was wrong. She sniffed, wiping at her eyes. Why were the lights out? How long had she been asleep? Why hadn't Miss Bardie come back for her?

Dani scrubbed her hands over her face. She hadn't even felt tired that afternoon. What had made her pass out like that? Could working with the rift be draining her energy in ways she hadn't anticipated? She made a mental note to do a nice, restorative nap when she got back to the house. She couldn't be dropping unconscious around town at random times. It was super inconvenient.

Shaking off the heaviness of fatigue, she stood, squinting in the dark so she could gather her notebooks and laptop into her bag. She was pretty sure she could find her way out of the labyrinth of shelves between her and the exit, but the doors were chained. Maybe there was a fire exit? Surely Miss Bardie wasn't allowed to lock a fire exit. The town was run by supernatural beings, but there were still OSHA laws.

Miss Bardie didn't have a cell phone to call. Should Dani call Jillian or Zed to come get her? Maybe she should just bunk down in the children's section, where Miss Bardie had placed some awesome squashy green beanbags.

She pulled out her phone to use the flashlight function and figure out a path to the nearest fire exit. She was making good time, passing through the various sections, but a spiraling sense of dread crept up her spine. Though she'd spent time in some pretty eerie environments, the claustrophobic catacombs of Paris, the wild jungles of Peru, a particularly dodgy convenience store in Parsippany, New Jersey, the darkness definitely gave the usually cozy air of the library an edge. The bookshelves seemed to loom overhead, threatening to topple down on her.

In the dark, she heard a footstep.

Dani froze, craning her head to the right, where the noise had come from. She clicked off the flashlight. She bit down on the urge to call, "hello?" into the dark. That was how people died in horror movies. And if someone else was creeping around in the library, she didn't want them to know where she was.

Dani shoved her phone into her back pocket and hauled ass through the geography section. She stopped at the end of the aisle, listening. A few breaths, silently inhaled, and she heard a board creak. Dani backed away, tears gathering in her eyes. The creak came from the other side of the book shelf.

Gloved hands reached through the shelves, grabbing for her.

Dani threw her weight back against the shelf. "Shit!"

The hands tossed books off the shelf, as if they could tunnel through and grab her. Dani sprinted down the aisle, listening for footsteps. Just as she reached the open space of the reading area, someone or something barreled into her side, knocking the wind out of her as she landed.

Dani threw an elbow back, hoping to catch whoever had tackled her. She focused all of her strength on not being forced down on her face, occasionally making contact with a warm body with her feet and elbows. Her attacker groaned, but never stopped trying to grapple Dani to the floor. Dani gagged at some sickly sweet smell that seemed to be wafting off of her attacker.

Dani rolled out onto her back and shoved her assailant aside, throwing them into a nearby shelf. She pushed to her feet and ran toward a door marked with a neon "exit" sign. She ran past the checkout desk, so close she could see the red neon's glow on her hands as she reached for the push bar. Hands shoved at her shoulders, knocking Dani down on her knees on the carpet. Strong fingers closed around her throat, squeezing tight. Dani screamed for all she was worth, kicking and fighting against the person pinning her to the floor.

The hands at her throat were tightening and her strength was fading fast. Something was sucking away her very will to draw in her next breath, and it wasn't strangulation. She was being drained.

She was going to die in a library, drained of all of her energy, with some psycho's hands around her neck. She'd always assumed that she would die in a tragic balcony sex accident. This was going to be a short, shitty obituary.

Her poor Grandad. He'd always worried so much about her safety when she traveled overseas. He'd assumed she would be safe on American soil. She was so sorry she was leaving him. She hoped maybe Jillian could persuade the League to pay him some part of Dani's contract fee. Poor Trudy, being left holding the bag on all that debt. And Zed . . .

Suddenly, the stained-glass window exploded in shards of color as a huge brown bear leaped through the casing. The break allowed light from a nearby streetlight, just enough for Dani to see the bear knocking over the "Reading is FunDamental" book display and the audiobook racks. The weight against her back instantly relented. The bear roared, its fangs gleaming even in the low light of the room. Dani would have covered her ears with her hands if she'd had the muscle control to do so. After a few ragged breaths, sound rushed back into her ears like the returning tide.

The bear cantered past her, nudging her lightly with its nose before giving chase to the person running across the library. The bear knocked several bookshelves down in its pursuit, growling and snarling for all he was worth. Struggling to sit up, Dani heard a door slam and—if she wasn't mistaken—smack into a bear skull. The bear howled in frustration . . . and pain, probably.

Dani rubbed at her throat and coughed, wishing for a glass of water like she used to wish for her Gramma's apple butter. The bear cantered towards her, whuffling as he sniffed at her. He flopped his considerable weight down next to her and curved his paws around her body, pulling her toward him. She had to assume this was Zed. She didn't know of any other bears that would want to rescue and/or cuddle her.

Dani was finally able to focus on the sheer ridiculousness of a freaking bear cuddling her like she was a comfort toy. Holy hell, his head was the size of a car engine. She ran her fingers over his velvety nose, which prompted more sniffing. She gave a watery laugh, stroking the fur between his eyes.

"Okay," she sighed, rewarding him with a scratch behind the ears. "I'm okay."

The bear grumbled, nosing at her neck. His breathing evened out and Dani relaxed against him, taking the moment to appreciate being held by a creature of such immense size and strength. In this form, Zed could break her by sneezing too hard, and yet, he was curved around her like a wall of furry protection, like he needed her more than sleep or food or air. And it was nice, being wanted that much, to know she meant so much to Zed. If relationships could just be *this,* minus the fangs and fur, she might not run from them like they were emotional lava.

The bear, for a lack of a better term, melted away, easing back into Zed's human shape. His very naked human shape, which was cuddling her. "You sure you're okay? I probably should have gone after her, but it was a choice between her and checking on you . . . and my instincts were to stay with you."

"It was a she?" Dani asked, her voice gravelly.

"Definitely," Zed told her, sitting up and pulling Dani into his lap. "And she smelled weird. Did you notice that she smelled weird?"

Dani nodded. "I was a little more focused on drained, but yeah, she definitely smelled weird. Like industrial air-freshener. I've smelled something like it before, but I can't think of where or when."

Zed nuzzled her neck. Dani wrapped her arms around him. "Thank you, for saving me. I'm probably going to get pissed off later and insist that I could have taken care of this myself, but thank you."

"Any time. I know you're a strong, independent person, but it really pisses me off when people try to strangle girls I like."

"Reasonable," she told him, patting his bare chest. "Not that I'm complaining, but where are your pants?"

"I may have shredded them running toward the library when I heard you scream."

"How did you hear me scream?" Dani asked.

"I may have been waiting outside to make sure you get home safe."

Zed walked to the light switch and illuminated the room, which was in shambles. Shelves were listing to all sides, as if a confused tornado had run through, their contents piled haphazardly on the floor. Tables were broken and chairs splintered. Also, Zed was naked, which was always a spectacle.

Zed huffed. "Aw, man. Miss Bardie's gonna be pissed."

MISS BARDIE WAS, INDEED, QUITE PISSED. HER ALREADY THIN mouth was pinched into a very sour line as she handed Zed an envelope marked with the official Mystic Bayou Library seal, banning him permanently from the library. She did however, give Dani a bookmark woven from solid gold, set with peacock ore as an apology for leaving her locked in the library.

"I became very ill after my dinner at the pie shop," Bardie told her. "I'm sorry to say that I didn't have the presence of mind to send someone for you. I wouldn't have sent Zed, of course, but still. I should have sent someone. You have a dragon in your debt, Dani."

"Thank you, Miss Bardie."

"Zed, on the other hand, is in debt to a dragon, because I'm making him replace every single item he broke in his heroics."

"That seems fair," said Dani.

After answering a lot of questions for Bael, and signing a lot of release forms from Jillian, Dani came home, Bardie's bookmark heavy in her pocket, to find Zed packing up his tools. The porch had been swept free of debris and Dani was now the proud renter of a closet-sized wooden cubicle with a nice sturdy door. She assumed the shower was still inside somewhere.

"So is this monumental work of carpentry finally finished?" she asked.

Zed grinned at her. "I'm sorry. I know you've been patient with me."

"Well, you did incur a massive debt to a dragon to save my ass, so I guess I can't get too upset with you. I might just have to break something, so you have to come running right back."

"You wouldn't have to break anything."

"That's good to know," she said, shrugging out of her green t-shirt, revealing a bra imprinted with little blue llamas.

"Okay, as much as I appreciate the display. What's with all the llamas?" he asked.

"Llamas are my spirit animal."

Zed shook his head. "She said as if that was a completely normal thing to tell someone."

"Llamas work hard. They're curious. They carry burdens that other people can't carry themselves. They can adapt easily to new situations, and yet, they can occasionally be very stubborn. Does that sound like anyone you know?"

"I want to say no, but I'm a dude who becomes a bear when the mood strikes me, so I'm willing to keep an open mind," he said.

Dani opened the door to the shower stall and found a cozy space that offered a bit more room than the original shower foot-print had. She even had a dome light overhead. She turned the water on, waited for it to warm as it ran over her outstretched hand. "So, my shower is fixed."

Zed scratched the back of his neck. "Technically, it was fixed a while ago. It just didn't have any walls around it."

"Well, how do I know it works?" she asked.

"I can't guarantee it will stand another hundred years, but it will at least last through the fall."

Dani slid his t-shirt over his head. "I think I'm going to have to try it out."

She tucked her fingers into the waistband of his jeans and pulled him closer. He stopped her, putting his hand on her shoulders. "This isn't some gratitude thing, is it? Because I saved you?"

"No, this is an 'I enjoy having sex with you' thing. You're a nice person and an amazing partner."

"Thank you, that's true," he agreed.

She laughed. "That's very diplomatic of you. I know I'm not

giving as much as you're hoping for. I'm just not used to relationships."

"What are you used to?"

Dani shrugged. "Casual stuff. You know, you have sex, you both
put your clothes on, say thanks and part ways. No meals, or
romantic motorcycle rides or kissing under the spirit bottles on
my front porch. I haven't had a steady boyfriend since college. I'm
not good at being open with someone I'm having sex with, the
thought of starting that here, particularly with someone who has a
pretty heavy influence on whether I'm welcome here in town or
not, really freaked me out. And I sort of shrugged you off."

"I wouldn't ever do anything to keep you from being welcome
in town," he insisted. "Well, unless you threw a TV through my
bathroom window and then, yeah, people might judge you a little,
but I wouldn't do anything to rile people against you. I'm not a
creep."

She held up her finger as if raising a point in court. "That is
oddly specific."

"Long story, and a big reason I prefer baths."

"I know you're not a creep," she told him. "The problem here is
that I don't want to hurt you. In a few months, I'm going to move
on to the next job and I don't want things to be sad or weird
between us. And I thought maybe going back to treating you like
an acquaintance instead of someone who's O-face I'm pretty
desperate to see would make things easier. But I was wrong. And
I'm sorry."

"Why do you assume I'm going to be the one who's upset?

Dani pursed her lips. "Oh, honey."

"Okay, fine," Zed grumbled.

"I'm still not ready to date you. I feel I should make that clear."

"I am willing to meet you half-way," Zed said solemnly.

"Again, very diplomatic."

"Always accept romance advice from dragons," he murmured

against her mouth, making her giggle. She pulled at the button of his jeans, popping it open and shimmying them down his hips, revealing a sharp vee of muscle. Dani grinned at him, pushing the jeans down his thighs.

"And then, when we're done here, I'm going to take you upstairs, where I happen to have a bed that hangs from the ceiling."

Zed's expression went from hopeful to distinctly uncomfortable. "Um, I happen to know that Bael and Jillian spent quality time together in that bed. They put a new mattress on it before Jillian moved out, but ..."

Dani pursed her lips, thinking of the series of perfectly straight scrapes on the plaster, parallel to the frame of the bed. "That explains those marks on the walls."

"Yes, it does. I mean, I want to be close to my friends, but not that close."

"Well, then we're just going to have to content ourselves with multiple rounds in the shower." She pulled him into the shower stall under the hot spray. "If the wall falls over, we'll know you did a bad job."

10

DANI

Dani was sitting on the second story front porch, resting. She hated to admit that working with the rift, combined with the library ambush—also multiple rounds of shower sex—had left her pretty wiped out.

She tried not to let the fact that she'd been attacked and damn near strangled unnerve her, but she'd had a really difficult time sleeping since the attack. She would jerk awake in the middle of the night, absolutely sure that someone was lurking in the shadows of her house, waiting to hurt her again. And it would take her hours before she could relax enough to go back to sleep. Sometimes, she was still awake when the rising sun showed through her window.

The lack of sleep meant lack of focus, and it was messing with her ability to go to the rift site and work safely. A sleep-deprived dynakinetic was a dynakinetic that could end up turned inside out and pinched between dimensions.

Something was bothering Dani about the library attack, and not just the "strangulation" of it all. That over-sweet smell that had clung to Dani's skin all night afterwards. She knew she should be able to place it, but it was blocked from her memory.

Maybe if she got some sleep, she might remember.

Dani forced herself to relax back into her cane rocker. This was easily her favorite time of day on the bayou, when the light got all soft and the witch bottles started to fire up. The heat faded with the sun and you felt like you could take a deep breath without inhaling a mosquito. She was going to miss this, when she picked up and moved on to her next assignment. She would miss having her own space, as opposed to living in some soulless hotel room. She would miss the smells of honeysuckle drifting through her screen windows, and the chirping of birds and frogs.

She'd told her grandfather that the farm was the only home she'd ever known, but if she was honest with herself, this house—Mystic Bayou as a whole—had put her at ease in ways she hadn't felt in years. Yes, it was a strange place filled with stranger people, but she'd been accepted here. She didn't have to hide what she could do. She didn't have to worry about choosing her words carefully or coming up with a believable lie. Her skills made her part of something, instead of setting her apart. When she walked down Main Street, people knew her, they waved, called her by name. She had a place here.

And Zed.

She would definitely miss Zed in ways she didn't want to think about, particularly when she heard the rumbling of Clarissa's big rusty red pick-up truck that looked like it was produced in the 1940s . . . which was a little awkward. She hoped that Clarissa couldn't sniff out hormones and other bodily secretions, because she did not have the strength to deal with an angry bear mama.

Clarissa hopped out of the truck, reaching in the back and pulling out a large basket over-flowing with shiny red apples. "Hi there, *cher*!"

Dani jogged down the stairs to meet Clarissa at the door, pausing to spray on some perfume, just in case.

"I thought you might need a pick me up," Clarissa said, handing Dani the basket. "I thought you might appreciate some of the fruit from my trees."

"Oof!" Dani huffed under the weight of the basket. "Thank you, but I'd hate to take so much of your harvest. Do you want to come in?"

Clarissa took the basket back from Dani and bustled into the house. "I have more than I could ever eat. Are you feeling all right, sweetheart? You look like you're plumb ready to fall over."

"I've just had some trouble sleeping lately."

"Well, that's understandable, considering all you've been through." Clarissa patted Dani's cheek with her soft, warm hand. The gesture reminded Dani of her grandmother and she had to hold her breath to prevent her eyes from watering over.

Clarissa paused in front of the wall, where Dani had created a giant work board, drawing on the whitewashed plaster with chalk markers, pinning up maps, lists, notes and a list of names of people who had turned *magique* after being born human, including Jillian. This was the one thing she couldn't keep at the library or her office, for fear of people seeing it and misinterpreting half-done theories.

"Yeah, I know, it's a little intense," said Dani.

Clarissa shook her head. "Oh, no, honey, it makes a lot of sense . . . if you're a serial killer."

Dani laughed.

"These are beautiful," Dani told her, sniffing the sweet skin of the fruit. "I was surprised to find such a big local fruit selection at the store, empty as it was. I didn't realize you can grow apples this far south."

"Generally, they don't do well here, but with the various magics bouncing around the Bayou, my trees produce a nice crop."

Dani nodded toward the back of the house. "Join me in the kitchen?"

Clarissa followed Dani into the little dollhouse kitchen, where Dani washed the apples thoroughly. Then she took a paring knife from the drawer and peeled one in a single long strip.

"That's a neat trick," said Clarissa.

"Years of practice. Gramma wouldn't let you bake apple crumble if you couldn't clean an apple in one strip. My aunt Trudy could do it before she started kindergarten," Dani said, dropping the peel in the sink.

"I can't say I've had an apple crumble. We mostly stick to pie around here."

Dani grabbed another apple and began working her magic. "It's the same principle, but with a fancier topping. I don't have the ingredients right now. So I'm going to settle for some applesauce." Dani dropped the apple peeling into the trash.

"You can make your own applesauce?"

Dani searched the spice rack for cinnamon and nutmeg. "It was my 'home sick from school' food. Easy on the stomach, but still tasty."

Clarissa frowned. "Doesn't that take a long time?"

"If you want to can it, yeah, it can be a pain. But this will just take couple of hours," Dani told her, taking Miss Lottie's largest pot from a rack on the ceiling. "It settles my nerves."

Clarissa hummed. "Will you show me how?"

Dani nodded. "Sure, thing."

It took no time at all to get the sliced apples, spices, and brown sugar in Miss Lottie's big iron pot. Clarissa asked questions and made notes, but Dani noticed that she never brought Zed or their "relationship" up in the conversation. Dani appreciated that.

By the time she was done, Dani was yawning and nearly sagging against the counter. The meditative exercise of peeling apples and mixing spices had released some sort of blockage in her brain and she was suddenly so tired, she was almost nodding off on her feet. Or perhaps it was having Clarissa in the house. She knew with a literal mama bear watching her back, she would be safe as kittens.

Clarissa shooed her away from the stove. "How about you go upstairs and take a nap and I'll keep an eye on your apples. You might sleep a little better with someone else in the house. I have my Sudoku book to keep me busy. And Jillian downloaded some of those true crime podcast things on my phone. I am all set."

"You are full of surprises, Miss Clarissa."

"Well." Clarissa took a pencil out of her bag with a flourish and rifled through her sodoku book. "Zed said that my *Dateline* habit was starting to worry him."

Dani snickered. "Do you promise not to clean anything while I'm asleep?"

Clarissa's jaw dropped. She started to protest, but then her eyes narrowed and the corners of her mouth lifted. "Jillian warned you, didn't she?"

"Yes, she did. Keep your hands out of my towels and delicates."

"I fold laundry because I care!" Clarissa exclaimed.

"I can fold my own clothes, thank you. It's enough knowing that you're here and I can sleep..." Dani sighed, the weight of her fatigue dragging on her shoulders like a living thing. "That's a really difficult thing to admit, that you're afraid to sleep without a mama bear standing guard over you, to protect you from the scary things in the dark."

"Aw, *bebelle*. There's nothing wrong with asking for help. And there's nothing wrong with being scared, especially after what you've been through. It's normal, and healthy. If you weren't nervous about the dark, I'd be worried about what's going on in your head. Mama bears were made to guard against scary things." Clarissa paused to place one of her massive hands on Dani's shoulder. "Let me do this for you now, and in a while, you'll be strong enough to do it for someone else."

"Thanks, Clarissa."

"*Pas de tracas*, darling."

Dani sniffed. "Just leave the apples alone, except maybe to stir them every once in a while. And don't mess with the heat."

Clarissa sat down at the table and peered over her reading glasses at Dani. "You are bossy when you're tired."

"Yes, I am.

DANI SLEPT SOUNDLY FOR HOURS IN THE SWINGING BED, FINALLY catching up on the rest she needed to reset her brain. She woke to the smell of stewing apples and the sound of feminine laughter from her kitchen.

Pulling her heavy hair into a bun, off of her neck, Dani walked down her stairs and heard Jillian's voice say, "I always thought it was you that kept Zed's den all neat and compulsively tidy!"

"Oh, no, honey, ever since he was a cub, Zed has had a sort of obsessive compulsive need to organize everything. I never had to clean his room when he was little. He kept all of his toys lined up in perfect little lines."

"Zed?" Jillian asked.

"Have you ever seen his DVD collection? He has this massive selection of action movies and they're all categorized by genre and alphabetized by the last name of the lead actor. His Gerard Butler section is shameful." Clarissa clucked her tongue.

"For more reasons than one," Jillian muttered.

Dani paused at her kitchen door, taking in the sight of her boss and her . . . booty call's mother drinking tea at her table. "Are you like gremlins? I feed one of you and you multiply?"

Jillian flushed guiltily. "I just wanted to check on you. I know it's been a couple of days since you've been out to the rift and I wanted to make sure you still want to fulfill your contract. I would understand if you didn't..."

"No, no," said Dani. "I'm still on the job. I just needed to get everything recalibrated in my head. Otherwise it would be dangerous for me to work on the rift."

"Thank goodness," said Jillian. "I didn't want you to leave! You laugh at my jokes."

"Really? That's my qualifier?"

Jillian shrugged. Dani lifted the lid from the pot, pausing for a moment to enjoy the perfume of nearly liquefied apples. She suddenly wanted to call Trudy very badly. Since Lottie didn't have a potato masher, Dani took a heavy wooden spoon and stirred it with all of her might. The braised fruit broke down into a smooth spicy sauce.

"And I'd like to point out, you haven't fed me yet," said Clarissa.

"You know, gremlins get a bad rap," said Jillian. "They're actually pretty benevolent. Most of the time when people see them, they're trying to help fix the mechanical problem that's taking down the plane or train or whatever."

Dani pursed her lips. "Again, it's weird that you know that."

Jillian nodded primly. "I accept your premise."

Clarissa sighed as Dani dished up two piping hot bowls of applesauce. "This is very nice for me. I mean, I enjoy my time with my boys, but there's something to be said for the company of ladies."

"There's probably significantly less belching," Jillian said.

"It reminds me of nights in the kitchen with my grandmother and my aunt, when I was growing up," said Dani. "Grandad would fall asleep in his recliner while we were washing dishes and we would sit in the kitchen eating dessert and talking."

"That sounds nice," Clarissa said, patting Dani's hand. "Do you get to visit home very often? Your grandparents must miss you."

"Not as often as I like," Dani said, glancing toward Jillian's hand and spotting a rather large diamond ring set in a gold band etched with dragon scales. "What the hell is that?!"

"Oh, yes." Jillian stretched out her fingers, admiring her ring, and trying to sound casual. "Bael proposed."

Clarissa squealed. "Oh, honey, I'm so happy for you!"

"Thanks. It means a lot. Since Bael's family isn't really talking to him, you and Bael and Mel are going to be the only family we have at the wedding. It's not like I can invite my parents here. It's not like I would want to."

"Are you going to have the full dragon bonding ceremony?" Clarissa asked.

"I don't even know what that means. I think my wedding planning is going to involve more research than the average ceremony."

"Congratulations, Jillian," Dani said. "Was it one of those flash mob proposals with surprisingly organized singing and dancing?"

"No, he just took me out to the water and showed me the ring and..." Jillian's cheeks went pink. "Said some pretty mushy stuff. I'll spare you the details. And he asked me to marry him."

"What kind of stone is that?" Dani asked. "It's sort of gray for a diamond."

Jillian frowned. "You know, he didn't say..."

"I'm sorry we don't have champagne for a toast," said Dani.

"Homemade applesauce is a much cozier substitute," Jillian replied.

Clarissa moaned around her spoon. "It is really good."

"If you're nice to me, I'll make you an apple crumble." Dani scooped a spoonful of applesauce into her mouth.

"Does not mentioning the fact that you're banging my son count as nice?"

Dani coughed, splattering applesauce down the side of Jillian's face.

"Ew." Jillian wiped her face with a napkin as Clarissa cackled.

"Is this some sort of shifter congratulatory ritual I didn't know about?"

"Sorry. Not cool, Clarissa," Dani said.

Clarissa snickered as she took another bite of applesauce. "I'm so sorry, but your face!"

"Okay, you want to play that game?" Dani responded. "Let's talk about your sex life with Mel."

Clarissa spluttered, sending another mouthful of applesauce at Jillian, who shouted, "Oh, come on!"

11

ZED

Zed answered the door wrapped in a towel, holding a rubber fish.

It was his house and he would answer the door any way he pleased.

Of course, his house was more of a stone mound, a sturdy tin roof and a large steel door. But still, he would answer that steel door any way he pleased. And he found Dani waiting for him on the other side. He smiled at her, ridiculously happy to see his favorite girl on his porch.

"Um, did I interrupt something?" she asked.

"No, I just like wandering around my den wearing nothing but a towel."

She laughed, kissing him soundly. "Why don't you ever do that at my house?"

He dragged her into the house, thrilled to finally have Dani in his territory. The walls were stucco, painted in varying shades of gray, and unbroken by windows. There was a living room with a ridiculously large TV and a very large collection of DVDs. He led Dani through a door on the left where the bedroom floor sunk to a point in the middle of the room, like a burrow, and was lined with furs, pillows, and blankets. There were candles in hurricane shades on a lot of different surfaces, most of them lightly scented with honey and lemon. In the far corner of the room there was a sunken tub, already filled and churning with water.

"So I caught you in the middle of a bubble bath?"

Zed cleared his throat, striking a manly pose. "Do you see bubbles, *abeille?*"

She nodded toward the lip of the tub, at a bottle of bubble bath with a giant bee on it. "No, because you haven't added them yet."

Zed snatched the bottle of bubble bath and hid it behind his back. "I told you. I prefer baths to showers. For. Reasons."

"Do I even want to know what the rubber fish is for?"

"Bears don't have rubber duckies at bath time, we have fish. It's how cubs learn to catch," he said, his tone defensive.

"Aw, that's so sweet . . . and weird," she said, giggling.

"Do you want to take a bath?"

"Do I get the rubber fish?"

He shook his head. "No, Herr Scalesnstuff is mine, but I'll let you borrow Dr. Squeakenstein."

Dani snickered. "Of course, they have names."

"You are far too overdressed for a bath. Let me help with that."

Smiling, he stripped her out of her clothes, tossing them aside in a trail leading to the tub. She yanked at his towel, dropping it next to her clothes, and he felt a good portion of his blood head southward.

They slid into the tub, the hot water taking their bodies. Dani sighed, dipping her head back to wet her hair. He gathered her into his arms, sliding his hands down her wet skin. She was sleek as a seal, her breasts bobbing delightfully in the currents.

Zed bit lightly at the curve of her jaw, lifting her arm so he could watch the water paint rivulets against her skin. His hands mapped the curves of her, soft and rounded and all his for the taking. He kissed every bit of her, from her ears to the tips of her toes.

Her lips were wet, warm and soft as they finally closed over his, and he groaned into her mouth. They played and splashed like a couple of cubs, kissing and touching and laughing. He found he didn't mind drawing things out a bit, rather than getting to the main event. He could spend all day, warm and naked and clean with Dani, especially if her breasts continued to move in the water like that.

Dani swam into his lap, settling her knees on the little rock bench where he was seated. She looped her arms around his neck, kissing him deeply. She fit against his body like no other woman had, without worries of crushing her and hurting her. His Dani was strong in ways that should probably have terrified him, but all he wanted to do was test that strength.

He slid his fingers between her thighs, finding her wet and ready. He rubbed his fingers against her in small circles, his thumb searching for the firm little button of flesh that could help him produce such absolutely charming noises from her long white throat. He caressed and kneaded, feeling her slick against the fingers he pressed inside her.

Her hands scrabbled against his chest and she bucked her hips. She cried out, mouth pink and rounded, as he pumped those fingers in and out. He caught her nipples between his blunt teeth, worrying them with his tongue. And when those first flutters spasmed around his fingers, her howl was music to his ears. He pushed her through the orgasm, relishing each ripple around his digits, and hoped he might be able to spark another one right after. But then her body felt oddly weightless as he lifted her against the hard stone edge of the tub.

She kissed him, long and hard, leaving him short of breath. "Thank you."

"Thank you?" he repeated, chuckling.

"I have lovely sex manners."

Zed kissed her while she laughed. "Well, of course, you do."

He pressed his forehead against hers, pushed forward slowly, filling her, making her gasp. She was hot and wet and so very tight and he stayed brick still to keep from losing himself right there.

His arms braced against the rim and she gripped them for leverage. She whimpered, rolling her hips against his straining, still form. The water splashed over the edge of the tub with every movement, but the clean up later would be worth it. He would mop the whole damn house gladly. She wrapped an arm around his neck, pulling herself up so she could kiss him and roll her hips against him. He couldn't tell where her wetness began and the water ended and all he could think about was *more more more*. She crossed her ankles at the small of his back and pulled him closer and he welcomed it.

He reached down with his free hand, and traced the lines of her body from her collarbone, between her breasts, over the curve of her belly and dipping between her thighs to bring her to the edge again.

"I think you might kill me," she moaned.

"But it will be a fun way to go," he told her, snapping his hips.

She nodded and he could feel her tightening around him once more. A coil of pleasure sparked to life at the base of his spine, and he could feel it building, echoing the ripples of the water around them. Knowing he was close, his rubbing became even more frantic, because he was not going to leave her unsatisfied. He plucked and soothed and stroked, until he felt her slide into one last good climax. She screamed, her nails digging into his arms. He bent and propped his forehead against hers, his hips stuttering to their conclusion.

They stayed, joined together under the water, breathing heavily, waiting for their hearts to stop pounding. Zed carefully slid out of her, cradling her against his chest while her feet floated freely. As her breathing returned to normal, he poured his honey-and-milk shampoo into his hand and working it through her hair. She was practically purring by the time he worked the lather all the way down to the tips.

"You are the very best person to have water sex with."

"Thank you, it's true," he agreed.

She snorted.

He formed her hair into a thick, foamy coil on top of her head, and then tried to make it stand up like the Eiffel Tower. That was what you did in adult relationships, right?

"So that thing you said about your urge to publish being hereditary, what did that mean?" he asked.

"You picked up on that one little detail weeks ago and held on to it? And chose to bring it up now?"

"You don't hold still long enough for me to ask you questions most of the time!"

She conceded, "This is also true."

"Come on. Tell me something real." Zed took the cup that he used for his own hair-washing and filled it with water, rinsing out her hair.

"Okay, so, I originally studied physics in college, which is how I got interested in my talent in the first place, kinetic energy and all that. But I knew that I wasn't interested in getting my PhD. My mom has several of them, and they don't seem to have made her any happier. But I do like to write academic papers, which is why I'm working on the book. You know, publish or perish, that whole thing."

Zed stared at her, remembering the process Jillian had described in getting her own PhD. "Your mother has *several* doctorates?"

She jerked her shoulders. "Yeah, she's this Cannon Award-winning astronomer, who has spent her entire life studying neutron stars. She went out to the desert so she could watch some sort of meteor shower and she met my dad, a hippie who renamed himself Journey. They spent three days having sex under the open sky and nine months later my mother named me for the morning star."

"Well, considering your dad's name is Journey, it could have been worse."

"Oh, he wasn't around for my birth. He wasn't around for the first two years, really. My parents never married, thank God. That would have been the real nightmare. But my mom handed me over when I was almost three. I sort of bounced as a toddler, between dad and my grandparents. Dad spent a lot of time traveling, and found it very convenient to leave me in Wisconsin with them."

"You never stayed with your mom?" Zed asked.

"Well, astronomy labs aren't exactly child-friendly. The expensive equipment, the extremely sensitive telescopes. And she moved around a lot, depending on who was funding her research. My grandparents wanted me to have some stability. And she really preferred quiet, stress-free home environments, so she could focus. That Nobel prize isn't going to win itself, you know."

"Do you still talk to her?"

She nodded. "Oh, sure, once or twice a year on the phone. She's not a bad person, just very self-centered. She wasn't and never will be ready to be a parent. I was lucky that she chose to leave me with people who were prepared to raise me.

Zed wrapped an arm around her. "And your dad?"

"I traveled around with him a bit when I was a teenager, during the summers. I saw a lot more of the world than most kids at my high school. But eventually, my grandparents stopped agreeing to his trips. You can only tolerate your granddaughter being questioned by customs authorities in Amsterdam so many times before you have to draw a line. Dad's a bit of a hot mess," she admitted. "I haven't seen Journey much since, which is fine, because he's not someone I enjoy spending time with. You would think I would have weird abandonment issues, considering that both my parents left me behind. But I'm pretty well adjusted, except for this little thing where I run from emotional intimacy like my hair is on fire."

"Oh, really? I hadn't noticed."

Dani slung a wet wash cloth at him. Zed caught the wet terrycloth before it smacked him in the face, twining his fingers through hers.

"So you grew up in Wisconsin?"

Dani grinned. "On an apple farm, of all things. It's really beautiful there."

"Never took you for a farm girl."

"There's plenty of physics to study when milking a cow, plowing a field, calculating how hard you have to throw an apple to hit your smartass aunt in the back of the head, while she's driving away on a tractor."

Zed peered down at her, so Dani added. "The answer is 'pretty hard.'"

"What does your family make of your gift?"

Dani sighed. "They don't know much about it. No one else in my family has gifts. I thought I was either going crazy or seeing ghosts when I was a kid, because I could see and feel all this energy swirling around the house—streaks of green and blue light dancing down the hallway, sheets of yellow warmth hovering over the orchard. And I was afraid to say anything to my grandparents because they were already watching me for all these signs of psychological trauma because of my parents' general jackassery. I was afraid they would send me to a mental health facility, which would have really hindered my middle school social life. So I did some research, ended up in some rather weird internet forums, read some books and I realized that nothing I was seeing fit the pattern of hauntings or ghosts. I was just reading the energy currents surrounding my grandparents' house. It was a lot less scary than thinking the ghost of apple pickers' past were hanging around outside my window."

"I would imagine," he said, nodding. "But you still haven't told your family what you can do?"

"I don't try to *hide* it from them, but I don't flaunt it either. You forget, living in a town where almost everybody is something special, that not everybody believes in this sort of thing. My mom doesn't believe in anything she can't quantify through a lens. My dad wouldn't believe me, but that wouldn't keep him from trying to turn it into some sort of business opportunity . . . for himself. Grandad and my aunt Tru know that I'm a freelance photographer. That's all they need to know. I don't want to see them hurt."

"I would like to go see the farm someday," he said, carefully, eying her for some sort of panic response. "Once we get all this rift stuff settled, I'd like to see your grandpa's farm, meet Trudy, all that."

"Have you ever left the state of Louisiana?"

"Yes, and I'm sure the town will be okay for a week or so without me around. It would be important to me, to meet your family. You've already met most of mine. It's only fair," he told her.

He expected her to object. He expected her to remind him that they weren't in a relationship. But instead, she just smiled and let him pull her close, and said, "I think I would like that."

12

DANI

Dani parked her rental car on Main Street, bobbling her covered Pyrex dish as she closed the driver side door behind her. The dish was just hot enough that she needed hot pads to carry it. If she had Bael's dragon powers, she wouldn't need them. Of course, he could probably bake by breathing on the Pyrex.

It was so weird to think those things about her friends, and for them to be true. She'd really expanded her weird quotient, living here in the Bayou.

"Miss Teel!"

Dani turned to see Maureen Sherman trotting down the sidewalk in sensible loafers and an even more sensible beige pantsuit. Dani blew an irritated breath out of her nose. *Shit*. Why did Maureen Sherman always show up when Dani least expected her? She was like the snotty redheaded Spanish Inquisition.

Dani sighed. "Hi, Maureen, how are you?"

"Just brilliant, dear. My book is really coming along. I was just at the library, doing a little research. I was just speaking with

Bardie Boone. I was so sorry to hear about your difficulties. Were you really attacked while sleeping at your table? How very odd."

Maureen didn't seem sorry about her difficulties. She seemed very smug about her difficulties. And not just in that "if you hadn't been there in the first place you wouldn't have been attacked" kind of way.

"It wasn't that big of a deal."

Maureen sniffed. "Well, research isn't for everyone. I would say perhaps you're better suited for field-work, but you don't seem to excel there, either. Don't worry, dear, I'm sure you'll find your strong suit soon enough. Perhaps it's baking! That smells delicious!"

Dani's jaw dropped. "Oh, Maureen, I'm sure I could never find anything as 'strong' as that pantsuit."

Maureen's tinkly laugh echoed off the buildings. "Well, I really must run, I'm simply bursting with ideas. Have to get home and let the muse take over!"

Maureen waggled her fingers as she trotted down the street toward a blue sedan.

"I hope you do burst..." Dani muttered through a faked smile while waving. "Into flames."

Dani sighed. "I do not like that woman."

Still murmuring ill wishes against Maureen, Dani ducked into the pie shop. There was a rare lull in store traffic, with only a few older Mystic Bayou citizens drinking coffee and chatting in the booths—Jimmy Hickens, Earl Webster, Jeb Cho, and Karl Bruhl. Zed said this was all the retirement some of the seniors would tolerate, because they couldn't stand sitting at home all day doing nothing. So they sat at the diner, doing a little more than nothing.

"We don't allow outside food," Siobhan called from behind the counter.

"I know that, Miss Siobhan," Dani said, carefully placing the warm dish between glass cake stands. "I made something for you as a thank you for all the pie."

"People usually don't bake for me."

Dani chirped, "I know, that's why I thought you might enjoy it. The novelty of it."

Siobhan frowned.

"What's wrong?" Dani asked.

"I'm trying to remember if I've said anything salty enough to warrant you trying to poison me."

Dani rolled her eyes and took out the second part of her offering, which she poured in one of the pie shop's glasses. "This is a bottle of fresh whole milk I got from the Hickens family's farm on the way over here."

"Thank you for your business!" Jimmy called from the booth.

"The milk is unpasteurized and un-messed-around-with," said Dani. "Which I find terrifying on a microbial level, but I understand that's how you prefer it. I would leave it out in a wooden bowl, but I don't have one handy."

Siobhan lifted her scraggly gray brow.

"This is as close as I get to leaving out a traditional fairy gift of bread and milk. I can't bake a decent loaf of bread to save my life. My Gramma's was amazing, but mine always turns out all chewy. The yeast just doesn't seem to like me."

Siohhan lifted the glass lid of her baking dish. "Is your Gramma the one who taught you to bake?"

"I grew up on an apple farm. We always had extra, getting ready to go bad. Gramma was constantly coming up with ways to make sure they weren't wasted. Apple butter, apple pies, apple jelly, cider. We sold some in the farm store, but our poor next-door neighbor got so sick of applesauce that he went into a panic if he saw her carrying a jar. And this is her famous apple crumble."

Siobhan took a fork out of a nearby napkin roll and dug into the sugary topping.

"No slicing, huh?" said Dani. "Just going to dig right in . . . nope, I respect that. I wouldn't share, either."

The brownie lifted a forkful of baked apples and cinnamon to her mouth, chewing thoughtfully, like an epicure tasting wine. She tilted her head and seemed to stare off into the distance. And then Siobhan did something Dani never expected. She wept—not just gentle tears rolling down her wizened cheeks, but deep wracking sobs of grief that shook her bony shoulders. The regulars sprang up from their booth, clearly unsure of what to do in the face of the unprecedented spectacle of Siobhan crying and reaching across the counter to clutch Dani's hand.

Siobhan waved the older men off, hiccupping softly. "Oh, don't fuss, I'm fine! I'm fine!"

The regulars returned to their seats, giving Dani a mild case of stink-eye. Dani stood stock-still, not quite sure if it was safe to move. Siobhan squeezed her hand gently. "You must have missed your grandmother very much when you were making this."

Dani laughed, though tears sprang to her eyes. "Yeah, I was missing her. I always do. It's probably a sense-memory thing with the cinnamon and nutmeg. Gramma sort of set me up to mourn her every Thanksgiving for the rest of my life."

Earl cleared his throat. "You know, my son Ash is still single. If you can bake like that..."

"Don't try to bust up a good thing with her and Zed," Siobhan told him. "If Ash is meant to find somebody around here, he will."

"That and even with Ash's phoenix fire, Zed would squash him like a bug," Jeb Cho told him.

"My boy is no lightweight!" Earl boomed.

"What would you have done to somebody who got between you and your mate?" Karl shot back.

Earl winced. "Never mind, honey, stay away from my son. He needs all his teeth."

Eating a bit more of the crumble, Siobhan took a long drink

from her glass of milk and Dani tried not to visibly shudder. Siobhan stood a bit straighter. Her wrinkles smoothed out ever so slightly, her cheeks blooming pink and bright. Her hair unfrizzed and fell around her face in smoother, gray waves. Her dark blue eyes actually twinkled. She grasped Dani's free hand and pulled her closer to the counter, looking deep in her eyes.

"Thank you for offering me this gift from your table. From now on, you are blessed. Your kitchen will be a place of strength and joy in your house. Your food will never rot. Your larder will always be full. Any bread you make will be light as a feather, fluffy as a cloud."

Dani almost objected to the silliness of Siobhan's statement—a loaf of her bread was once used as a door stopper for Grandad's barn—but a warm, pleasant sensation blossomed in her chest and she knew that Siobhan had just laid down some serious fairy mojo.

"Thank you, Siobhan."

"Of course, I have some thoughts about you using a little orange zest," Siobhan said, scooping another bite on her fork.

Dani moved the dish back across the counter toward her. "I will take it back."

Siobhan grabbed at the dish, quick as a snake, dragging it towards her. "It's perfect!"

"Damn straight," Dani told her.

Siobhan smirked at her and whipped an index card from her apron pocket. "I'm going to give you my blueberry pie recipe. It's your Zed's favorite."

Given the gasps of the regulars, Dani deduced that this was a considerable gesture from the cranky little brownie. Dani wasn't sure if she was ready to try baking one of Siobhan's recipes. Her own pie crusts were adequate, but they were nothing compared to the light, flaky miracles that Siobhan created. However, knowing how her Gramma would have reacted if someone had turned down an offered recipe, she simply said, "Thank you, ma'am."

While Siobhan was scribbling the exact ratio of fruit to filling in her blueberry pie, Jimmy Hickens assured her that Siobhan *never* shared recipes.

"She says she doesn't trust anybody else with her kitchen magic. My Alma has been trying to weedle the lemon meringue recipe out of her since the 1970s," Jimmy told Dani solemnly. "Siobhan's never given her a single ingredient."

"Because your Alma could burn water!" Earl cackled.

Dani had expected Jimmy to object in his wife's defense, but he jerked his shoulder. "It's true. I love the woman something awful, but I've suffered through more holidays with food poisoning than any man alive."

"And that's why I won't give her my recipe," Siobhan told him. "It's for the greater good. Besides, this girl's got the touch. You don't bake like that without knowing how to put the right sort of strength into people."

Dani's brow crinkled with confusion. "What do you mean?"

"The work you're doing out there in Afarpiece Swamp. You're moving energy around, right? Taking one form of it, making it into another. That's all cooking is, taking one thing, making it into another." Siobhan paused to write her name at the bottom of the recipe. "But in my kitchen, it happens to be something that will give another person strength, make them healthy, ease their heartache, get them fired up. And you? Well, missy, you do it without even thinking about it, which is a great gift. Which is why you're getting my recipe and Alma never ever will."

"I'd never thought of it that way," Dani said. "Thank you."

Dani was still somewhat skeptical of her ability to produce Siobhan-level results, but she supposed with Siobhan's blessing, she might be able to pull it off. She wasn't going to make it for Zed any time soon, because if she combined her already amazing sexual prowess with making his favorite dessert, he might never let her leave his cave.

IT WAS NICE TO HIKE OUT TO THE RIFT SITE ALONE, WITH HER own thoughts. As much as she liked staying nights with Zed, she also appreciated having some space for her own thoughts. Of course, the things she normally devoted that time to, were giving her relatively little trouble. Work was . . . complicated. Her progress with the rift was starting to feel like one step forward, two steps back. She suspected that having two dynakinetics working on the rift at once was, for a lack of a better word, "confusing" it. If she continued to feel this sort of resistance, she was going to have to have a difficult "I can't work like this, It's her or me" conversation.

Then again, there was the possibility that someone besides Maureen was messing around with the rift, someone with fledgling skills who didn't really know what they were doing, and was causing more trouble rather than helping. Sort of like the hobby astronomers who drove her mother crazy with oversized telescopes and loud, light-polluting camping equipment that disrupted Susan's field observations.

Something about the way Siobhan described her kitchen magic was gnawing at the corner of her mind. Siobhan had basically described energy work in her cooking. She'd referenced Dani's work directly. What if Siobhan had decided to expand her repertoire to "dabbling" at the rift? Dani doubted that the woman who had spent decades soothing the souls of Mystic Bayou with pie would suddenly turn into a rift-ripping supervillain.

Dani sighed, pausing for a breather, as she still couldn't get through the fern ocean without a fight. Maybe this job was making her too suspicious.

Work worries aside, Dani was enjoying her growing friendships around the Bayou. Her grandad's situation seemed to have stabilized somewhat, since Trudy had made the initial payments to the creditors. Her father, well, she didn't want to waste a nice walk through a sunny swamp thinking about Journey and his bullshit.

And then there was Zed.

Zed. Zed. Zed. Zed.

As much as she wanted to deny it, she was in a relationship with the man. A real relationship, with feelings, and expectations. She wasn't sure when the transition happened, probably when he shared his rubber fish with her, which was a super weird way to mark the beginning of a romance. But that night in his tub was the first time she shared something real with a partner, something from her past. She shared actual intimacy with Zed. And it was freaking her out more than just a little bit.

But even with his demands for her to be open and honest with him, he wasn't pushing her for a commitment or to tie herself down in the Bayou. And she appreciated that.

If she was going to stay anywhere, with anyone, she could very easily see herself making a life here in the Bayou with someone like Zed—someone who made her laugh and understood her weird quirks because he had plenty of his own. Someone who appreciated the contents of her head as much as he did the contents of her bra. But after making such a big deal about not defining what they had, Dani would have to approach that conversation carefully—because the potential for Zed gloating was pretty epic.

Dani was relieved when she arrived at the rift site and didn't find Maureen Sherman lurking around in her judge-y pressed khakis. But the atmosphere around the clearing seemed heavier somehow, thicker to walk through. The colors that normally danced on the air were spread out much further than they were even on Dani's first visit. The split in the air was almost visible, its aura leaking in thick ropes from the frayed edges.

Dani walked to her rock, took her stance and prepared herself for opening to the rift. But before her internal shields could come down, Dani stumbled back with the force of the energy against her mind and landed on her butt with an "oof."

Her ears were ringing and she laid back on the grass to catch her breath.

Something was wrong here. Something was very wrong.

Panting, Dani took the time to scan the rift carefully. This wasn't a rift, it was a gash, an intentional rip in the energetic fabric of the sky. And it was going to get bigger by the day, if left unchecked.

Dani pictured the very ends of the rip healing, the tendrils of energy winding together and knitting into a smooth scar. There were several stops and starts. Dani actually had to stop for a water-and-granola break about an hour into her efforts.

But finally, Dani felt like she'd managed to repair the worst of the leakage. The seepage was only slightly worse than it had been on Dani's first day. She was exhausted and drenched in sweat by the time she was finished. But all she could think of was getting to town, warning Jillian and Zed.

All of her work, all of Maureen's work, if she'd really done any, had been undone. How much of the rift's mojo had oozed into the Bayou, wreaking who knows what sort of havoc on human genetics and the powers that the *magique* already had.

Dread, cold and heavy, settled into her chest. She was definitely going to have a difficult conversation with Jillian about Maureen Sherman. There was no way someone with a "dabbler" level of talent had ripped open the rift like a cheap can of tuna. Maureen was the only other dynakinetic in town who was capable of that sort of damage—though Dani had no clue why Maureen would want to do such a thing. She had to be stopped and she had to be stopped now.

13

ZED

Having an amazing office was one of the few perks of being Mystic Bayou's mayor. Unlike Bael's one-room sheriff's department across the open floor-plan, Zed got an office all to himself instead of having to sit outside in the common area with the other departments. As much as he liked his coworkers, being able to shut his door on them when they were annoying him was probably what kept their working relationship friendly.

He'd hoped to be in a much more impressive stance than leaned back in his chair with a napkin tucked into his collar when Dani saw his "seat of power" for the first time. But Jillian and Bael had brought by lunch and he wasn't about to say no to Jillian's grilled cheese sandwiches. She couldn't cook much, but her grilled cheese was a work of carb-y art.

Dani strode into the office with purpose, and Zed's feet dropped off his desk. He straightened in his chair as Dani skidded to a halt.

"Wow, you certainly have a lot of pictures of yourself," she noted.

Zed's only response was to grin. He'd devoted his office to all things awesome: pictures of Zed on his Harley, pictures of Zed fishing bare-handed, pictures of Zed's *maman*, pictures of Zed with Bael and Jillian. He'd even crafted his own desk out of a huge live oak that had been struck by lightning out by his *maman's* house. He carved the repeating pattern of Germanic runes into the face of the desk and its drawers with his own claws. He'd once even tried to refer to himself as "Zed Oakendesk" after watching *The Hobbit* one too many times. But Bael had vetoed his suggestion, based on some Draconian prohibition against grown men picking their own nicknames.

Shaking off her brief distraction, Dani turned to Zed. "You've got a problem."

"You know, my mechanic uses the same tone of voice when he tells me I've got an oil leak."

"Well, it's an interesting comparison because that's exactly what's going on," she said.

Bael swallowed the last of the sandwich and raised his hand. "I don't follow."

Jillian set aside her lunch plate and sat at attention, in full League supervisor mode. "What's going on, Dani?"

"The rift is wider since the last time I saw it, since just a few days ago," Dani said. "Someone has been pulling at it. Like when you worry a loose string on a sweater? I thought maybe I was imagining things, but it's becoming less stable as I work with it, not more. If this continues, the birth rates you're seeing of *magique* in human families? Think double or triple. Same with the adult humans suddenly sprouting antlers and previously unknown mojo. The born *magique* will experience big spikes in their talents, which sounds pretty good at first, except that eventually, they'll start spiraling out of control like Carrie at the prom and even people born with those powers won't be able to handle them. I am, of course, speculating, and not basing this on any sort of math like Dr. Aspern could apply."

Zed growled softly, making Dani's brows rise.

"This is going to sound like an accusation, which is not my intention, but are you sure it's not your work de-stabilizing the rift?" Jillian asked.

Dani shook her head. "I think it might be that other energy witch in town, Maureen Sherman? She's the only person I can imagine would be capable of doing this kind of damage. But I've never stayed at the site while she was working, so I can't say what she's been doing."

"What? Why would the League send another consultant to work on the rift?" Zed asked, turning to Jillian.

"Maureen Sherman?" Jillian shook her head, a line of confusion crinkling her eyebrows. "I don't know who that is."

"Maureen Sherman?" Dani repeated. "She got to town about two weeks after I did?"

Jillian's expression was equal parts confusion and alarm. "I haven't met her, Dani. I swear, I've never even heard the name."

"But when I was asking you about League contracts, you told me you were sorry about the redhead horning in on my territory!"

Jillian's jaw dropped. "I meant your office space. I was talking about the redheaded socioeconomics guy who thinks that no one can smell him microwaving fish if he vents the window."

Dani's face scrunched into a shape of "instant regret." Her legs seemed to sag under her. Zed stood and caught her elbow, supporting her weight. "Oh my God, I just ended the conversation as quickly as possible because I didn't want to endanger my job by complaining about a coworker. I needed the money so badly that I just wanted to do my work and get paid."

"Oh, shit," Jillian said through gritted teeth, leaning back in her chair.

"I'm so sorry, Jillian," said Dani.

"It's not entirely your fault." Jillian turned to Bael and Zed.

"Guys, how could we not notice a stranger wandering around town, poking around in the rift?"

Bael shrugged. "There have been so many strangers moving through town with the League, it wouldn't seem strange to see unfamiliar faces."

"Is it possible the League sent someone to Mystic Bayou without telling you?" Dani asked.

"It doesn't seem likely," said Jillian. "But we're talking about the same people who have had garden gnome spies in the White House for ten administrations and counting."

Jillian pulled her cell phone from her pocket and said, "Siri, call Goddess of Secrets." She kept it on speakerphone while Siri dialed, propping it up on Zed's desk.

A melodic alto filled the office. "Sweetie! Is this a work call or a 'you missed me so much because I'm amazing' call?"

"A little of both, Sonja," replied Jillian. "I've got Bael, Zed, and Dani here with me on speakerphone, just as a warning."

"I always appreciate your dedication to speakerphone etiquette. What's up?" Sonja asked.

"Sonja, do we have a Maureen Sherman on the rolls as a League employee? And if she is, did the League send her down here as a consultant without telling me about it? Because it's causing some confusion. And hurt feelings."

Dani chewed at her thumbnail while the office echoed with the sound of clacking keys. Zed rubbed circles on her back, making what he hoped were soothing chuffing sounds.

"Uh, sweetie, I don't know what exotic fern Ms. Sherman is smoking, but the League has no idea who she is," said Sonja. "We have no records of any version of a Maureen Sherman working for us. As a consultant or otherwise.

Dani buried her face in her hands. "That's a problem."

"How old would you say she is?" Sonja asked, her tone no-nonsense. "Physical description?"

"Um, I'd say late forties, early fifties, red hair, fine features. Big blue eyes," said Dani.

A few seconds later, Sonja added "And I'm not seeing any social media presence for a Maureen Sherman matching that description. I'm getting a few hits on Social Security Numbers in the right age range, but the individuals they pertain to seem to be actively employed in full-time jobs in California, Idaho, and Wisconsin."

Dani's grip on her chair tightened. The window rattled as if some earthquake was focused solely on Zed's office. She took a deep labored breath and the phone signal crackled and several glass panes in the photo frames split. Zed moved to her side, stroking his warm hand between her shoulder blades. "Um, I don't know what's going on right now, but you need to stop. Breathe, come on, honey. Breathe."

Zed shot an alarmed look toward Bael. He'd never seen Dani show "outward" signs of her gift that way. Was she changing, like all *magique* seemed to change in Mystic Bayou?

"Sorry," Dani wheezed. Bael ever so subtly shifted his body between Dani and Jillian. And because it seemed to make Dani feel worse, Zed glowered at Bael. While Zed understood the need to protect his mate, he couldn't help but be highly annoyed by additional distress on Dani.

Jillian snapped her fingers. "Okay, so priorities, we stop Maureen from doing further damage. And Dani goes out to the rift to do damage control and repair."

"Agreed," said Bael. "Where do you think she could be now?"

Dani straightened and took a deep breath. "She said she had a rental place outside of town. How many rental properties are there outside of town?"

"The Warburton place comes to mind," Zed said. "They weren't able to sell it, because the front yard is basically a big mud hole. Mace Warbuton mentioned renting it out on Airbnb."

"Really?" Jillian asked.

Zed shrugged.

"Maureen seemed too high maintenance to live in a house in a mud hole, but sure, let's give it a shot. I'll go with you. I can ID her," Dani said.

Bael put his hands on her shoulders and turned her away from the door. "You're not going with me."

"What? Why?"

"Because I need to follow procedure and I can't do that if I'm busy trying to keep you from whippin' her ass," Bael said. "Once she's in custody, you can ID her here."

"I wouldn't—okay, yeah, that's fair," Dani said.

Bael's tone gentled, and his arm curved around her, nudging her toward Zed. "You're going to stay right here and rest because Jillian says that using the force takes a lot out of you and you're going to need every bit of your strength over the next few days to get things back in order."

"I don't think I employed the phrase, 'use the force,'" said Jillian.

"If Dani had said the words, 'use the force' when she was explaining her gift, I probably would have understood it a lot faster," said Zed.

Dani sighed.

"We'll be back," Jillian told them. "You stay here. Zed, keep her safe."

As the door clicked behind them, Zed wrapped his arms around Dani and pulled her close. She was shaking. Dani never shook. She was always so resolute and steady in what she did, that it made him afraid for her. And yet, at the same time, a low-simmering anger was churning through his gut. She hadn't lied to him, but she'd put herself in danger through her stiff-necked pride and doubt. He had the urge to take her over his knee or lock her away in his cave, but he was sure either instinct would earn him one of those light balls up his ass.

"I feel so stupid," she sighed into Zed's chest. "I just let her hang around while I worked because I assumed she had a place there. Because she had a lot of authority in her voice. This isn't like me. I don't let people push me around. Why did I let her get away with it?"

"You're new to working on this scale," Zed answered. "The League was asking a lot of you. It's natural not to want to make waves when you have a lot at stake. And on that note, we need to talk."

Dani scrubbed a hand over her face. "Nothing good ever followed those words."

"Well, you have it coming, so get ready. What the hell has been going on inside your head? Why wouldn't you mention some creepy older lady following you around town when you've been attacked? What do you need money for so badly that you're willing to put yourself in danger—more danger than usual?"

Dani bristled a bit, the first emotion she'd displayed beyond anxiety since she'd walked in. "I don't see how it's any of your business."

"It's my business if you get yourself hurt because of it. And it's my business if people I love get hurt."

"Dammit, that is some really sound logic," Dani grumbled.

Zed slid his arms around her and tucked his face into her hair. "Come on, sweetheart. Tell me."

"I told you that my grandparents basically raised me at their place in Wisconsin," she said. "And that my dad is a selfish waste of space who disappears for parts unknown for months or years at a time?"

Zed released her, letting her sit in one of his office chairs while he balanced an asscheek on his desk.

Dani pinched her nose. "Well, dear old dad has disappeared to some ashram in India with a shit-ton of cash in his pocket. Most of that cash came from mortgaging my grandparents' farm, twice. He took out home equity loans, lines of credit, all without me or my grandfather knowing, all with my grandmother's cooperation, because she didn't realize what was going on. Gramma's dementia was more serious than we thought toward the end. She had developed a lot of little coping mechanisms to hide how bad off she was, pretending she hadn't heard us correctly when we asked her a question or pretending she'd left her car keys in the freezer as a joke. Journey had figured it out, I'm sure, and if my dad told her she was just signing some papers to give her son a little 'help,' I'm sure she would put her initials on anything he handed her."

"Holy shit." Zed sat back on his desk. He couldn't imagine what he would do if his own mother's livelihood, her home, was threatened. He couldn't imagine the strain of knowing that his own parent had put someone he loved in danger. And that Dani had been going through this alone, instead of sharing her burdens with him? Hurt blended in to that simmering anger soup, making for a stomach-churning mix.

Dani nodded. "Yep. With the fee I'm earning from this job, combined with my savings, I'll be able to pay off the debt, keep the creditors at bay."

"So, knowing what you've been worrying over, I can sort of understand why you freaked out at the idea of losing this job," he offered.

"Thank you."

"What I don't get is why you wouldn't tell me about this so I could lighten the load a little bit for you?" he asked.

She shook her head, looking so very angry and helpless that Zed wanted to take her back to his cave and keep her far away from anything that could possibly hurt her feelings. "I don't have an answer for you. I don't know why I didn't feel comfortable telling you. I don't know why I wouldn't trust you to help me. I don't know why I do a lot of things. I'm sorry. I know you wouldn't judge me for it. I know you wouldn't shy away. I'm just used to handling things on my own. That's my first instinct, so that's what I did."

Zed leaned forward and kissed her. "Okay."

"That's it?"

He nodded. "Yep. What's the ashram called?"

"It's not called anything. It's known as The Place With No Name, which is really difficult to track down, no matter how good your Google skills are—"

He pressed a solemn kiss to her lips. "Let me get this one."

"I don't understand?"

"I'm still annoyed at you," Zed answered. "And we're going to spend a lot of time talking about you taking too much on yourself. But I am very close to loving you and I'm going to take care of this one thing for you, okay? Let me get your father off of your back."

"I don't see how you're going to do—"

He kissed her again.

"Stop kissing me to shut me up!" she protested.

"You got a more fun way to do it?"

Dani sighed. "Fine. You can have this one."

"Awesome. Eat this." Zed handed her a still-warm sandwich and a bottle of water. He pulled his cell phone out of his pocket and dialed a number. Rajesh picked up on the second ring.

"Zed! How are you, my friend?"

Zed cleared his throat. "Hey, Rajesh, how's it going?"

Winking at Dani, Zed walked out of his office and shut the door gently behind him.

"Very well! We just found out that Analah is expecting our first child," Rajesh said, his tone proud.

Zed hooted into the phone, grateful for some good news during what had been a really shitty day. "Really? Congratulations, buddy! When's she due?"

"Thank you. We're very excited. And in about six months. We hope that by then, the medical staff will have moved into town. I can't exactly take her to a human doctor's office for an ultrasound of our baby big cat cub."

"Any day now, Rajesh, I promise. Dr. Ramsay has had a little bit of trouble tracking down a doctor willing to move to the Bayou permanently."

"I suppose that's reasonable. If you've spent that much on medical school, you probably don't want to end up in a town with two stoplights," Rajesh said.

Zed snorted. "Hey, man, we're going to have the third stoplight installed in a couple of weeks."

"Now, what can I do for you?" asked Rajesh. "You normally don't call me in the middle of the day."

"Yeah, I know. I just have a quick question—how often do you get over to India?"

14

DANI

D ani sat alone in Zed's office, feeling the full weight of her stupidity. She'd been tricked. This woman Maureen fed her a pack of lies and she'd just bought it, without asking. If she'd just said something earlier, instead of being so paranoid about keeping her job that she'd put up an entirely unnecessary front, a lot of this might have been avoided. If she hadn't been so determined to keep Zed at a distance, he wouldn't be quite righteously pissed at her. If she had said something to Jillian, the rift wouldn't be in such bad shape.

And Zed? Instead of yelling or telling her off, he'd been so understanding about the whole thing. Which just made her feel worse. As someone who didn't suffer this sort of crisis of conscience very often, she told herself this was a feeling she would learn from and never repeat again.

She pushed the sandwich aside, too nauseated to eat, but drank the bottle of water. She tipped her head back against the chair. And it was possible that she'd nodded off because in what felt like no time at all, Zed was marching back into his office with Bael and Jillian in tow.

"Did you find her?" Dani asked. "Did you question her? Tell me it involved a phone book and a hose."

Bael grimaced and took a step back from her. "Maureen Sherman won't be answering any questions. She's dead."

Dani slumped in her seat. "I immediately regret the phone book comment. Am I a suspect?"

"No, it looks like she had a heart attack in her kitchen. There was a bottle of heart medication on the counter. I think she was trying to get to it. Ivy Portenoy will be able to give us some test results in a few days to help us figure out what happened. The ID in her purse and the label on her meds both said 'Maureen Sherman,' but Ivy should be able to confirm that with dental records. Once we figure out cause of death, we'll know whether this is a murder or if it's just a weird problem that resolved itself with tachycardia." Bael shot Zed a wry look. "And that's why we need a coroner."

Zed shuddered. "She's still creepy."

"Did Maureen ever say anything to you about having a heart condition?" Bael asked.

"Not really," Dani replied. "But she'd been hiking through heavy terrain a couple times a week. And if she's been working with the rift a lot, she probably felt drained. It wouldn't be out of the question for her to just collapse."

Jillian placed a white banker's box on Zed's desk. "I found a bunch of journals and stuff in her house. I thought you might help me look through them. I haven't read much, but it looks like she really was conducting her own research. She wanted to write her own book about the rift, and part of her research was determining whether the rift could be expanded."

"Does it say anything in her notes about trying to kill me in the library?" Dani asked.

Jillian shook her head and handed Dani the brown, leather-bound diary. "Nope. I don't see a section about 'planned assaults.' But I haven't read very far, maybe it's more toward the end."

"Is there any way of knowing how much damage she inflicted on the rift?" Zed asked.

"Not really. I can say that I feel more energy leaking out of the rift than I did before, but I don't exactly have a scale for this sort of thing," Dani said. "I just don't understand why. Why would someone do this?"

"Because they want to cause a panic and sabotage the League's efforts to gently integrate *magique* into the world," said Jillian.

"Or because they're trying to create more *magique*," Zed suggested. "It could feed into the whole panic motive. Or it could be another Simon Malfater, trying to get magical powers for ordinary people."

"Is there any way to fix what was done?" Bael asked.

"Sure, it could take me a few months, but I can do it. Of course, every single human in Mystic Bayou could be a *magique* by then," Dani said.

"We should warn people," Bael told Zed. "Give them the choice."

Zed nodded, a grim expression on his face.

"I'm sorry. I wish I'd said something sooner," said Dani.

"Well, yeah, that would have been handy, but no use getting upset over it. It's not like we can go back and fix it." Jillian paused and glanced at Bael. "We don't have anyone who can go back in time to fix it, right?"

Zed and Bael shook their heads. "No."

Jillian frowned. "The one magical power we don't have around here."

15

DANI

D ani slid a freshly baked apple crumble out of Zed's oven and set it on a cooling rack. The man had become downright pouty about the fact that she'd baked one for everybody in town except him, so she'd finally broken down and crumbled a bunch of apples. The contemplative exercise of peeling, slicing, and mixing had been good for Dani's mental clarity. Everything felt so jumbled up since Maureen had been found dead, she couldn't seem to think one thought at a time.

Tox results on Maureen hadn't come back yet, but Ivy reported that nothing about her body seemed abnormal. It was more than likely Maureen's body had simply succumbed to the effects of working with the rift. Still, her death nagged at Dani, in terms of its lack of logic and why Dani had believed her bullshit story in the first place. Dani liked to think she was a better judge of character than that, but clearly, she needed to up her cynicism quotient.

Why would Maureen go to these lengths to manipulate the rift? Why manipulate the rift at all? Dani had never met another dynakinetic who wanted to *open* a rift. They were too unpredictable, too dangerous. Maureen pretended to have experience, but how much of *that* was a lie?

And when she thought about the attack at the library, really thought it out, did Maureen have the strength to wrestle Dani to the floor? Could it be that Maureen wasn't working alone? Could there be someone else out there, looking to unravel Dani's work and hurt Mystic Bayou?

Dani had worked extensively at the rift site in the week since she'd made her confession about her "coworker" to Jillian, and never alone. Zed had accompanied her to the site every day, watching her back. She'd managed to repair most of the damage to the rift, convincing Zed that maybe an emergency warning to the Bayou's citizens was unnecessary for the moment. But the work left her so exhausted that Zed had to practically carry her home every night.

And so, Zed would come home to his own apple crumble.

Watching the steam rise off her perfect brown and bubbly creation, Dani realized, she was baking for a man. And waiting for him to come home to their cave. She glanced down at the apron she was wearing to protect her favorite sundress.

Dani sighed. "I'm sorry, feminism."

She wondered if feminism would forgive her if she explained that magical thing Zed could do with his tongue?

She took off the apron and checked the time. She'd planned on dropping by Jillian's office and then coming right back to the cave for an early dinner and a thorough oral workout for Zed. She liked to think she was striking a healthy work-life balance.

Just as she picked up her purse, an unknown number from an international area code she certainly didn't recognize lit up Dani's phone screen. Frowning, Dani swiped her thumb across the screen and pressed it to her ear. "Hello?"

Her father's rich baritone filled Zed's kitchen. "I don't know what you're up to Danica, but you can't send people here to the ashram looking for me, disrupting our peace. You really upset the guru. I'm on kitchen duty for a month. Do you know badly you've upset my community?"

Dani blinked rapidly, trying to process what the hell her father was talking about. She hadn't sent anyone to India. She didn't really know that many people from India, much less *in* India—

Wait.

She suddenly remembered Zed calling Rajesh Agarwal from his office and shutting the door behind him before the conversation got interesting. Had Zed sent some friend of Rajesh's to the Unnamed Ashram to look for her dad?

Yeah, sorry feminism, Zed deserved this crumble.

"You know, Journey, I really could not care less," Dani said, slapping her apron against the counter.

"I don't care what negativity you've spread in that backward country you call home," Journey seethed. "I'm not leaving India. I haven't reached my enlightenment yet. I need more time."

"More time? How much more time? A few weeks, a year? Just enough time for the statute of limitations to run out?" Dani scoffed.

"Statute—what are you talking about?"

"I know, Journey. I know all about the loans and the mortgages you took out on the farm. I can't believe you would do that—strike that, actually, I can completely believe you've done this, because as far as I can tell you have the moral compass of a brick."

"I didn't take anything my own mother didn't offer me freely, out of love," Journey insisted, his tone becoming reedier and shrill. "Because that's what family does for each other. That money was my birthright and I'm putting it to much better use than any good it might do in *Elkhorn*."

He spat the word "Elkhorn" like it was a mortal insult. Asshole.

"It's funny that you were so strong in your convictions that you couldn't tell Grandad what you were doing," Dani shot back.

"Because it wasn't any of his business. I can't believe you're so focused on something as fleeting as *money*. You're focused on *the past*. I'm focused on the eternal."

"The past? As in primordial 2016?" she snorted.

"Why can't you just forgive? Why do you have to be so negative?" he whined. "Why can't you remember all of the things I've done for you instead of all the things you think I did wrong?"

Dani groaned. "You know, you should record the things you say and play them back, so you can hear the same level of dumbass that I do."

"I won't accept this abusive language from my own child."

"Here's something you need to accept. Despite all your fuckery, I found a way to keep the farm in the family," she growled. "You didn't manage to accomplish whatever sad, adolescent revenge you were trying to get against Grandad. And another thing—I *will* find a way to get you back home. For once in your life, you're going to be held accountable for your actions."

Journey gasped. "Who do you think you're talking to? I'm your father!"

"No, you're my sperm donor. You've never been my father."

Over Journey's tirade about "family" and "forgiveness," Dani ended the call and buried her face in her hands. The whole episode reminded her so much of her last interaction with Journey, after he'd come home for Gramma's funeral. During the private viewing, he had spent a lot of time trying to convince Grandad that it was a waste to bury Gramma with her wedding ring. He tried to argue that Dani would like to have it, but Dani knew if Journey got his way, he would be driving away from the farm with the ring in his pocket. Grandad was determined that his wife would be buried with the ring. So Dani spent most of the visitation planted between Journey and the casket.

It had taken hours to distract her father with some other shiny object and when her self-appointed guard duty was over, she ran down the hallway and threw up in a wastebasket near the "process-ing" area. She would never forget the way that hallway smelled, like overblown roses and antiseptic and—

Dani's head shot up so hard she whacked it on a cabinet. That smell. She knew what the over-sweet chemical perfume smell was. Formaldehyde. Who in town would smell like—

Aw, hell.

Ivy Portenoy.

Ivy Portenoy had attacked her in the library. Ivy Portenoy had tried to strangle her.

But why?

Personal resentment? Dani couldn't think of any way she'd harmed Ivy, other than turning down her invitation to join the weekend card games. And no one took *Magic: The Gathering* that seriously. Well, some people did, but still, trying to smash Dani's head over the rejection seemed like an overreaction.

Professional rivalry? Ivy had nothing to do with the rift. She worked in a completely different department and didn't seem to know anything about Dani's work.

Maybe Ivy was secretly in love with Zed?

Zed had made his preference for Dani pretty clear to anyone in the Bayou with eyes, and he wasn't exactly subtle in his disdain for the "creepy little Wednesday Addams girl." But if Ivy had feelings for Zed, that would definitely make Dani a target.

Before Dani could contemplate it further, she grabbed her purse and ran for the door. Ultimately, the library attack didn't matter nearly as much as more important questions—did Ivy have something to do with the damage to the rift? Or with Maureen Sherman's death? What if the person investigating Maureen's "heart attack" was the person who caused it?

Dani jogged toward her car, dialing Zed's number. Before the call could connect, a glowing orange sphere, like a small sun, came flying over the lawn and struck Dani right in the belly. Dani's legs flopped forward as she slammed into the ground like a rag doll, her breath knocked clear out of her lungs. Her hand hit the ground with a *thwack* and Dani heard the crunch of breaking glass. She assumed that was her cell phone, which wasn't good.

"Ow . . . Fuck." Dani wheezed, attempting to force breath into her lungs. Lara Gershwin's face floated over her. The weirdly focused receptionist from Jillian's office grinned down at Dani, waggling her fingers. She stomped on Dani's phone, shattering it completely.

"Shit," Dani mumbled before losing consciousness.

DANI WOKE IN A WHEEL-BARROW, HER LEGS FLOPPED OVER THE sides, ferns smacking her in the face as Lara pushed her through the underbrush. She wasn't sure why, but being hauled through the swamp in the same conveyance her Grandad used for cow manure was incredibly insulting to her wobbly sensibilities.

"What in the fuck!" Dani attempted to sit up, but found she didn't have the motor functions to make that happen. Her central nervous system seemed to have yelled "nope" and shut down. "What in the hell did you hit me with?"

"Oh, just a little construct I've been saving, just for you." Lara chirped.

Dani flopped back into the metal bucket, watching the foliage pass overhead. The smell of honeysuckle was unmistakable. "I'm assuming you're taking me out to the rift?"

"This can be the one time that you don't make an ass out of you for assuming!"

"Why? Why would you do this?" Dani asked.

"Same reason as you. I'm being paid to. Not by the League, of course, but by outside parties invested in opening up the rift for their own purposes."

"What outside parties?"

Lara shrugged. "I'll be honest. I don't really know. They'd heard of my work, sent me a deposit, instructed me in how to apply for a job with the League. It was easy enough once I was hired. Once my reputation for being competent was established, I just had to wait for my opportunity to get assigned to the Mystic Bayou project. Not that many League employees were fighting for the chance to move down here."

"Why would outside parties be interested in opening the rift?" Dani asked.

"Again, I don't know. I don't care. They were willing to pay handsomely and their checks cleared. That's good enough for me."

"Were you working with Maureen?"

"Not exactly. I mean, I'd heard of her from her deluded posts on the internet where she pretended to understand our talent," Lara said, rolling her eyes. "And I lured her here, offered her money for private research on the rift, but told her to pretend to be with the League in order to fly under the radar around town. I told her there would be fewer questions that way."

"For plausible deniability?" Dani guessed.

Lara's smile was downright evil in its glee. "It never hurts to have a scapegoat. I get to do my work behind the scenes as she flings her half-assed work around accomplishing nothing. And if anything went wrong, I'd pretend not to know who she was and call League security on her. We never met in person after all. She couldn't prove I was the one corresponding with her."

"I'm assuming something went wrong? What with her being dead and all?" Dani suggested.

"The pompous bitch wanted an appointment with Jillian," Lara said, all indignity. "Just strolled into my office and demanded to see Jillian, because she was *sure* that Dr. Ramsay would want to know all about her breakthroughs with the rift. She wouldn't take no for an answer! She told me she was going to report me to the League for 'impeding the progress of science!' She tried to approach Jillian away from the office!"

"The nerve," Dani muttered.

"So I did the only thing I could do. I went to that grubby little house she was renting and offered a slice of your apple crumble as an 'apology.' Jillian has been hoarding it in her mini-fridge for a week. Maureen swore she never ate sweets, but she wolfed it down quick enough. She didn't even ask about the secret ingredient I'd sprinkled on top. A little powdered foxglove, right out of that awful Clarissa Berend's garden. Just enough to set off that nasty heart condition of hers. All I had to do was keep her meds out of reach and the digitalis did all the work." Lara reached into her shirt pocket and removed a tiny glass vial filled with a fine gray powder.

Dani gasped. "You used my Gramma's crumble recipe to murder someone? That's it, stop the wheelbarrow, I'm kicking your ass."

"I don't think so. I think you're probably just going to sit there in that wheelbarrow, trying to breathe properly, until I take you out to the rift site and kill you. I'll make it look like an accident. You were just so upset over your failure to contain the rift that you spent too much time out here. You took on too much and your poor heart couldn't take it. I mean, you are carrying around a few extra pounds, your heart's probably pretty strained already."

"Fuck. Off," Dani shot back.

"Any more questions?" Lara asked.

"Why in the hell do you smell like formaldehyde?"

Lara laughed. "Film processing. It's part of the final wash. Call me a purist but I just don't think you can call yourself a real photographer unless you print from your own film. The problem is that no matter how many times you wash your hands, you can still smell it for days."

"Well, that explains it. I've only used a digital camera."

Lara glowered at her, as if this was a grievous offense, worth killing Dani over as a matter of principal.

"I owe that creepy little girl at the morgue a big apology," Dani said. "Did you use digitalis on Bardie Boone? To make her sick the night you tried to strangle me at the library?"

"No, dragons don't respond to digitalis, so I had to use some good old-fashioned arsenic. She metabolized it quickly and with only a little bit of stomach trouble, but it was enough to take her out of commission for the night," she said. "And before you ask, yes, I tried to kill you. Because you were annoying me and I have occasional snaps of temper just like everybody else."

"Most people have snaps of temper than don't involve attempted murder, you psycho."

"Well, fortunately for you, I'm over it," Lara said. "But unfortunately, you stumbled into my plans like a chubbier version of Scooby Doo—

"Fuck you, I'm awesome."

Lara ignored her. "And now you know everything and there's no way you'll keep your fat mouth shut."

"I'm thinking you're projecting some pretty serious body-image issues, Lara. Along with being a murderous psycho."

"So I'm going to have to kill you. I'll drain you dry, and dump you here, and make it look like you just crumpled under the pressure from the rift," Lara said casually, as if she was discussing grocery shopping. "You'd been struggling lately, keeping up with the demands of the rift and I doubt your skills have ever really been what you claimed they were."

"Again, fuck you, because I'm awesome."

Dani could feel that they'd reached the rift, even before Lara dumped her out of the wheelbarrow like garbage. She flopped to the ground, dead weight, unable to so much as raise her arms to break her fall.

Lara nudged her with her boot, flipping Dani onto her back.

Dani wheezed, "Are we done with the crazy supervillain monologue portion of the proceedings?"

Lara hissed and slapped Dani across the cheek, which stung, but then followed by holding her palm inches away from Dani's face. A look of angry concentration twisted Lara's features and Dani could feel her strength being sucked away, like water down a drain. She could see it being pulled out of her body in a thick golden thread, and into Lara's hand.

"You're not better than me. You don't know what's coming."

Lara stopped the drain, shaking off her hand as if it burned. Dani panted, attempting to prop herself up on her elbow, only to flop back on the ground. "Oh, you're right, you're not even a supervilllain. I only warrant a half-competent minion to bump me off. I think that hurts my feelings."

Lara growled and subjected Dani to another painful bleeding of her life's energy. Dani sagged to the grass, rasping out a breath. Dani had never been subjected to anything like it. She could feel her will to live, her very soul, being sucked away. She didn't even know it was possible. Was Lara going to use what she was taking from Dani to rip the rift even further? Was she going to weaponize Dani's life force?

Panic turned Dani's insides to ice. She couldn't move to stop Lara as she gathered more and more from Dani's body. Tears leaked out the corners of Dani's eyes and onto the grass. Her whole body hurt, even her hair. She wasn't going to make it out of this clearing. She would never see Zed again or tell him she was sorry and that of all the people she'd ever met, she loved him best. She wouldn't get to say goodbye to her family or Jillian or Clarissa. She'd never get to apologize to Ivy Portenoy for suspecting her of murder.

And she was going to have to accept that very soon. Because Lara couldn't take fuel from a dead battery.

If Dani had a hard time moving before, now, the effort to force air through her vocal cords to speak seemed Herculean. And yet, this bitch had fat shamed her, so it was worth it.

"Your work is shit," Dani panted. "If it was any good, I wouldn't have been able to fix it so quickly. You need to stop working so hard to be flashy and put some intent behind what you're doing, you weak ass wannabe."

"You shut your mouth."

Dani propped herself up on her elbows, sweating with the effort. "Was mommy a real witch? Is that why you're so pissed off at the world? Is she disappointed in the mediocre party trick you call 'work?' What are you going to pull out next? Fancy card tricks? The dismembered thumb bit?"

"Shut. Up," Lara growled.

"If you're gonna kill me, go ahead and do it. Just don't subject me to any more of your bullshit about how fucking clever you are. If you manage to do any real damage to the rift, it's because you're stealing the means from me, you half-assed, half-wit joke—"

Lara hissed an angry breath, creating a small orange sphere the size of a tennis ball. She didn't bother throwing it, simply slammed it into Dani's face. As Dani slipped out of consciousness, she thought perhaps she'd made an error in judgement.

Because OW.

16

ZED

Zed jogged up the stairs to Jillian's office in Building One. He'd been feeling uneasy all afternoon, that weird nagging tension that pulled at the corner of his mind when he thought maybe he'd left the stove on. But it felt bigger and worse. Something was wrong in Zed's territory, and he wasn't going to rest until he laid eyes on Dani and knew that she was safe.

He noted that Lara, the scary receptionist was not at her desk, which was odd in itself. That girl was always glued to her desk. But he also noticed that he didn't smell Dani anywhere in the office, despite her plans to meet with Jillian that afternoon. And that only made his discomfort worse.

"Jillian?" he called.

"I'm back here!" she yelled.

Zed leaned against Jillian's door frame, frowning over the office's single occupancy. "Hey, where's Dani?"

Jillian lifted a brow. "I don't know . . . because she's an adult woman. And she objected when I tried to put a bell on her."

"She said she was going to meet with you this afternoon."

Zed frowned at her, which was enough to make Jillian sit up

and put her serious face on. "I, honestly, don't know, Zed. How did you get back here, anyway? Lara usually throws herself bodily at anyone who tries to cross my threshold without her written permission."

Zed waved his arms toward the unoccupied waiting room. "She wasn't out there."

"What?" Jillian stood, walking toward the lobby. "She's not off until four. And Lara never takes breaks. Ever. She's basically Batman with better typing skills."

"So Lara *and* Dani are missing now?"

"We don't know that they're missing," Jillian said, her expression concerned. "They're just . . . misplaced."

"So you haven't seen her at all?"

"Zed. I haven't seen Dani since yesterday. And Lara was at her desk like ten minutes ago. I heard her berating the copy repair guy for stepping too close to our machine without an appointment. I don't know where either of them could be."

Zed pulled his phone out of his pocket and dialed Dani's phone number. It went straight to voicemail. "She's not picking up her phone."

"Okay, well, that's no reason to panic," Jillian said, though her tone was becoming more serious. "Maybe she just can't get it at the bottom of her bag. Or her phone battery died. Or she's meditating."

Grumbling, Zed dialed Clarissa's phone number. She picked up on the first ring. "Hello, my *bebe*."

"Have you seen Dani today?" he demanded. "Or Jillian's uptight assistant?"

"No, and I'm assuming that from the tone you're using with your *maman* that this is an emergency of some sort," Clarissa said.

"I'm sorry, *maman*. It's just Dani's not where she says she would be and she's not picking up her phone and I've been uneasy all day and no one has seen her and—"

"Okay, okay, settle down. Now, I drove past Dani's place this afternoon and her car wasn't there. And I'm not even sure what Jillian's assistant looks like. But I can go check at your place to see if Dani's there."

"Thanks, *maman*." Zed chewed his lip, panic rising in his chest. Dani wasn't where she said she would be. She wasn't with Jillian. She wasn't at the *maison*.

"Right." Zed turned on his heel and ran toward the front door.

"Hold on!" called Jillian. "Where are you running off to? She could be anywhere."

"Exactly! She could be anywhere!" Zed yanked open the front door and spotted a heavy-set redheaded man walking toward the parking lot. "YOU! GINGER FISH MICROWAVER!"

The man stopped in his tracks and turned his head toward Zed, his expression terrified.

"You work in Building Eleven?"

The man nodded.

"Have you seen Danica Teel? Is she in her office?" Zed asked.

The man shook his head. "I haven't seen her in days."

Zed roared . . . and the redheaded man took off running. Dani was missing. His mate was somewhere out there, hurt, and he didn't know what to do. He almost launched himself out the front door, but he stopped, sniffing the air. He closed the door and crossed to Lara's desk, sniffing all the way. He tossed aside paperwork and manila folders until he found the source of the sickly-sweet odor he was picking up. It was a copy of Popular Photography. He could feel crinkly, stiff patches on the cover, as if Lara had spilled something on the page and then it dried. He ran his nose along the glossy paper. Formaldehyde. The magazine smelled like formaldehyde. Dani mentioned a sickly-sweet odor on the person who'd attacked her in the library.

Lara. He'd noticed the intense way she'd stared at Dani, but he'd thought it was just Lara's personality. What had she been plotting?

"Zed, honey, what are you doing?"

Jillian's voice was the only thing that kept him tethered to reality.

"It was Lara," Zed growled, his fangs elongated. Jillian pushed a button under Lara's desk and Zed heard the click of a lock in the building's front door.

"What was that?" Zed asked.

"Automatic locks. I just don't want you to run off half-cocked and get yourself hurt. Just hold on for one second," Jillian said, pushing a couple of buttons on her cell phone, and setting it to speakerphone.

Jillian's robot friend's voice sounded from the phone. "What's up, sweetie?"

"Sonja, I need to use your evil computer mojo to access some employment records you're not supposed to read."

"Ooh, my favorite!" Sonja said.

"You're wasting time," Zed grumbled.

Jillian held up the "wait a minute" finger. The sound of clacking keys filled the room while Zed's panicked rage bloomed. "Okay, I've got HR's secret files open. What do you need?"

"Lara Gershwin." Jillian replied. "When was she hired by the League?"

"About six months ago," Sonja said. "A little bit before you got sent to the Bayou. Dr. Montes recommended her to the board, based on a paper she wrote on 'Dynakinesis and Human Potential.'"

"Dr. Montes recommended a receptionist, based on a paper she wrote on a completely unrelated subject in experimental physics?" Jillian asked.

"Yeah...Oh, no." Sonja replied.

Jillian pinched the bridge of her nose. "Dr. Montes's fuckery strikes again. So it would seem that my receptionist is the one

who's been tampering with the rift. I'll fill the appropriate paperwork out after I handle the extremely angry bear shifter in my—
Zed, no!!"

By that time, Zed had done the only thing he could think of,
running at the office door at full speed, leaving a Zed-shaped hole
in the door as he ran toward his motorcycle.

As he fired up his engine, he heard Jillian yell, "Dammit, Zed!"

ZED DROVE THROUGH TOWN ON HIS MOTORCYCLE WELL BEYOND
the legal speed limit. He scented the wind, trying to find some hint
of Dani, some whiff of formaldehyde. He followed traces of that
warm, floral scent he loved, swerving around corners and, in some
cases, through fields. He realized after a few miles that he was
being led toward the rift, and sped toward Afarpiece Swamp.

At the edge of the swamp, he ditched the bike without bothering to use the kickstand, leaping off the seat and landing on four
paws. He bounded through the woods, ripping through underbrush and bowling over trees. He didn't even take the time to
appreciate the comfortable rightness of his other form. He only
gloried in the ability to run at top speed to get to his mate faster.

His ursine brain wasn't capable of producing much in the way
of connected rational thought, beyond, *mate, mine, unsafe,*
DANGER. But he knew he had to get to the rift as quickly as he
could. He refused a life without Dani. Refused. He would get her
back and he would destroy all threats to her forever.

Right, good plan.

He barreled into the clearing, shaking off the ear-popping
unpleasantness of being near the rift. Even without Dani's talent,
he could see it now, a riotous living vortex of color that made him
dizzy and nauseous to look at. He spotted a figure hunched near
Dani's rock marker. Lara was bent over Dani's prone body, holding

her hand over Dani's heart. Lara's hand seemed to be drawing a river of golden light from Dani's body.

As he transformed to two feet, slipping into his small human shape, Zed hollered. "DANI!"

Lara turned, her lovely features twisting into an ugly smirk. "Oh, sure, move closer, make me work faster to drain her life away. That will be good for her."

Zed howled, "You let her go, you evil bitch!"

Lara clicked her tongue. "What would your *maman* say about you using such foul language in a lady's presence?"

"You're no lady," he growled.

Dani was barely breathing, and he could only see the imperceptible movement of her chest. She was so pale, just a shadow of a person against the vibrant green of the grass. And it made his heart ache to see her so still, to see her face without life or color, no hint of that smile he loved so.

Enraged, he threw himself at the barrier, launching his body past the rock circle limit for *magique*. He groaned as the bone-buckling pressure ground down on him. Every step was agony. It felt like an ocean of pressure crashing down on his body. His head throbbed. His ear drums felt like they might burst. He could barely breathe.

But he had to get to Dani, had to make her safe.

Lara's grin was downright nasty and Zed wanted very badly to wipe it from her face. "You're too late. I've got what I want from her. She's just a shell now. She didn't even know what hit her, that was the sad part. She never even considered weaponizing her powers did she? Silly hippie bitch. That's what pacifism gets you."

"Shut up," he growled, a berserker's rage filling his chest as he inched closer.

Lara was struggling to stay on her feet and now it was his turn to smirk.

"You took too much from her, didn't you? You can barely

stand?" he asked, inching closer. "Dani says that's dangerous, taking too much in without an outlet. You should have thought of that."

Dani's head jerked, just barely, toward the sound of Zed's voice. He buried the urge to crow. *Come on, baby,* he thought, *come on, concentrate on my voice and wake up. Be my self-rescuing princess. Come on.*

Lara rolled her eyes. "God, you're worse than the rest of the assholes in this town, do you know that? You think you're smarter than everybody, which is really easy when you're surrounded by idiots. You all think you're so damn special because you managed to make a life here in this backwater shithole. Do you know what it's like being stuck here when you're used to living in civilization?"

Lara turned away from Dani completely to focus on Zed, and he welcomed it. Dani's eyes fluttered open behind Lara's back, and he nodded to her while Lara ranted about how difficult it had been to live in Mystic Bayou. Dani frowned up at her captor, making what Zed could only describe as her "cut a bitch" face.

"Look, lady, I don't give a shit how much you hate it here. I'm taking my Dani back," he told her. "And if that means throwing your ass in the swamp, that's what I'll do."

Dani's eyes drifted closed again but her hands began to move in a circular motion over her chest. Lara was so caught up in yelling at Zed, she didn't notice Dani's movements.

"You want this empty sack of skin?" Lara snorted. "Fine. She's basically a vegetable. No more scintillating conversations you barely understand."

"Shut your filthy mouth before I close it for you."

Lara sneered. "You would never hit a woman. Your stupid redneck code of honor would never allow it.

"I'm not gonna hit you," Zed told her, nodding toward his gal. "But she will. And she is *pissed.*"

Lara's head whipped toward Dani. Dani rolled, her hands

clenched around a glowing ball of light that crackled with lightning. She heaved a breath and flung her arm, sending that angry ball of intent straight at Lara's face. Lara screamed and attempted to dodge, but the ball hit her in the back. The sheer force of it sent her muscles into seizure. She sagged to the ground, writhing in pain as Dani's weapon did its work.

Keeping an eye on Lara, Zed knelt next to Dani. He slid his arms under her legs and shoulders, scooping her off of the ground. "Come on, baby."

Zed stumbled back to the *magique* safe line as fast as his legs would carry him. Dani's nose was bleeding freely, but her heart rate, while fast, was steady.

"Ow," she murmured as he set her on the ground. "I can taste blood and . . . artichokes. Is that bad?"

Zed burst out laughing, bumping his head against hers. "Nah. I'd say that's to be expected."

"Pretty sure I love you. I'm so sorry," she murmured, kissing his mouth, despite the nosebleed.

"Pretty sure I love you, too. Now, you just stay right here. I'll be right back, okay?"

"Yep." Dani let the "p" pop and she let her head drop to the ground.

Zed struggled back over the *magique* line, forcing himself toward Lara's crumpled body, step-by-step. And when he finally reached her, he picked her up by the arms. This woman had nearly taken Dani from him. She'd hurt his woman. She'd put his people in danger. And he could not allow that to stand.

She sniffed, waking from unconsciousness and blinking warily at him. She snarled. "You won't hurt me. You don't have the balls. What would your *maman* say? She'd be so disappointed in you, betraying your redneck roots and hurting a woman."

Zed bared his teeth at her and using all of his upper body strength, he tossed her like a rag doll toward the shimmering color.

She screamed, disappearing into the tornado of light with a sizzle. To his surprise, the rift simply danced on without so much as a blip, as if Lara had never been there.

"My *maman* would have kicked your ass and then tossed you," he muttered.

Zed shuffled back to Dani, eager to put distance between them and the rift. He lifted her gently, tucking her head against his chest. "Just sleep, *abeille*."

As he carried her back to where he'd left his motorcycle, he called Bael's number. Bael picked up without a greeting. "What in the fuck are you doing, Zed? You have Jillian completely freaked out. She can't find Dani and she's gone all flame-y over it and—you ran through her front door like a damn cartoon character!"

"Yeah . . . uh, I'm going to need to meet you at the parish hall," she said. "I need to turn myself in. I kind of murdered someone. I'm not particularly sorry about it, but I feel like it's going to result in a lot of paperwork for you. And Jillian."

Bael sputtered. "I'm sorry, what?"

ZED DID, INDEED, TURN HIMSELF IN TO BAEL OFFICIALLY AT THE parish hall. Jillian and Bael met them there, with Clarissa, who had blankets, brandy and blueberry pie. Zed draped Dani in his office chair and put a bottle of water to her lips. Dani had managed to hold on to Zed's back on the motorcycle, but he could tell it had taxed what physical strength she had left. He covered her with the quilt Clarissa brought.

"Are you going to spoon feed me next?" Dani asked, raising her eyebrows.

Zed nodded. "If that's what it takes."

Clarissa shooed him away. "Here, let me fuss over her. You go talk to Bael. He's about to chew through his desk."

Bael was, indeed, sitting at his desk, wearing his official uniform, including the hat. Zed supposed this was meant to convey that he was acting officially as sheriff of Mystic Bayou, not as Zed's friend. Jillian was wringing her hands in her lap, struggling to keep her cool. It took Dani shuffling into Bael's office, still wrapped in the quilt, to get Jillian to stop glancing across the complex anxiously.

"I thought I told you to rest," Zed said.

"It's cute you thought that would work," Dani replied.

Zed grumbled, but settled Dani on his lap.

"If you'll recall, I was semi-conscious for most of this, and I'd like to know what happened," Dani said, then she went through what she remembered, starting with her abduction from Zed's house and concluding with Lara's snarky gloating over her murder of Maureen and tampering with the rift. Zed carefully relayed his version of events from that afternoon, including Dani's heroics with her lightning ball and Zed's throwing Lara into the rift, and then he waited for Bael to hand him his ass for taking justice into his own hands.

"So you tossed her into the rift and she just—*ttthhhp*—disappeared?" Bael asked.

"Yes," Zed said. "I don't regret it. She was a danger to our community and to my mate."

"Last time I checked, you were elected mayor, not judge, jury, and executioner," Bael reminded her.

"When Simon Malfater took Jillian, you attacked him in dragon form and tried to burn him alive," Zed said.

Bael shrugged. "Yeah, but I missed, so it doesn't count."

"So am I going to be charged with murder? That's probably going to get me impeached," Zed muttered.

"Not if our current political climate is any indication," Dani said.

"Technically, we can't determine that you committed murder,"

Dani told him. "I mean, we don't know what's on the other side of that rift. Sure, her very cells could have been ripped apart into nothing because people were not meant to be thrown through interdimensional tears. But it's also possible that she's stuck in a dimension where dinosaurs are in charge of the government or the only fruit available is kiwi."

"I think no cells is better than the 'kiwi only' thing," Zed stated.

Clarissa, who had been hanging on every word from the doorway, shot a curious look at Zed. He shrugged. "I don't like the seeds."

Bael pinched the bridge of his nose, and seemed to be praying.

"So am I in trouble or not?" Zed asked. "Keeping in mind that if I end up serving time and get separated from Dani for an extended period of time, I will tell her where you got the stone for her engagement ring."

Jillian frowned. "What?"

"I'm going to list Lara's disappearance as an 'unknown accident,'" Bael said, glaring at Zed. "But this is a one-time pass. You cannot use the rift as your go-to disposal for people who piss you off."

"Fine," Zed mumbled, though he was smiling.

"Can we go back to the engagement ring thing?" Jillian asked.

"I'll tell you later," Bael promised.

"You'll tell me now. Am I wearing some sort of murder diamond on my finger?"

"Only if you consider burning books 'murder,'" Zed said as Bael made threatening faces at him.

"I kind of do," Jillian said.

"Oh, good grief," Bael sighed. "Jillian, I took the ashes from burning your report and compressed them into a diamond. I thought it would appeal to your love of books and my love of dragon fire. It was meant to be a thoughtful gesture. If you hate it, we can go through the hoard and find something you like better."

Jillian's expression was a strange mix of touched and horrified. "No one in the world will have a ring like it?" she squeaked.

Bael's shoulders slumped in relief. "Exactly."

"And it is very pretty," Jillian admitted. "Thank you for making me something . . . special."

Bael gave her a quick kiss. "You're welcome."

"Do me a favor, don't burn something I love to make me a present," Dani whispered to Zed.

Zed nodded.

Jillian sighed and scrubbed a hand over her face. "So there's a mysterious outside group who is hiring whackaloons to infiltrate my staff and mess with the very thing that brought me to Mystic Bayou, potentially bringing about some mass *magique* transition."

"That was what I gathered from Lara's rantings, yes," Dani agreed.

"That is going to mean so much paperwork," Jillian said, turning to Dani. "And I think your assignment just got long-term. We're going to need you to watch the rift, repair it and keep us updated on any changes."

Dani nodded. "That works for me. I don't feel like leaving anytime anyway."

"I'll throw in a raise," Jillian offered.

"That will be nice." Dani chuckled a little. "Why are you sweetening the pot? I already said 'yes.'"

"And a bonus for discovering the sabotage."

Dani threw up her hands. "Seriously, I'm already agreeing to it."

"And you only have to bake apple crumble for me once a week," Jillian added, her tone suspiciously casual.

Dani scrunched her face into a scowl. "This is starting to feel like a trick."

17

DANI

Dani sat on the gazebo swing on the town square, watching her new neighbors mill about, going on with their daily lives. None of them seemed to know how close they'd come to losing everything. They hadn't seen the rift, felt its intent. They didn't know what Lara had planned. The knowledge in her head made her feel isolated and separate from almost every man, woman and child in Mystic Bayou.

And yet, it was much better that way, she knew. The last thing the League wanted to do was cause a panic, and there was wisdom in that.

Still she feared what was to come. She was going to be staying in Mystic Bayou for the foreseeable future. She couldn't leave until she determined what sort of damage Lara had done to the rift. She didn't know how much energy was leaking through to their side. Not to mention, Lara hadn't been working alone and whoever had directed her to the bayou was out there somewhere, waiting for another opportunity to tear at the rift. And the scary part was that Dani had no idea why someone would want to do that. It certainly didn't strike her as something someone would do if they were remotely interested in people being safe or healthy. It seemed about as smart as using a nuclear warhead as a hammer.

Dani couldn't leave, knowing that what was on the other side of *la faille* was bleeding through to Mystic Bayou, changing its citizens, spreading to other areas. She definitely couldn't leave knowing some mystery dynakinetic could come along and rip open the repairs she made.

She was going to be the self-appointed Guardian of La Faille.

She should definitely get some sort of name tag made up.

"You look like you're thinking some pretty heavy thoughts."

Dani grinned up at Zed. He leaned down and butted his head gently against hers. She pressed a warm kiss to his mouth.

"So, since you're going to be here for a while, I was thinking that you might bring some things over to my cave for when you stay over. Toothbrush, extra socks, your whole body," he said.

Dani snickered. "Subtle."

"I will not rush you. But I want to love you and be with you for the rest of my life."

"Oh, good, thanks, no pressure."

He added, "Also, my *maman* says you can't leave until you make her, oh, a dozen or so apple crumbles."

Dani grinned, and pulled Zed toward her by his belt loops. "If you're very nice to me, I'll give her the recipe."

"Wait, if I'm nice to you, *she* gets the recipe? What's in it for me?"

"I'll be nice to *you*." Dani kissed his mouth soundly and then gave him a little peck on the end of his nose.

"Zed, I'm really glad you found your mate and all." Bael scrubbed his hand over his face. "It's still gross to see you do that. Like watching your siblings make out."

Zed winkled his nose. "Ew."

"You're telling me," Bael retorted.

Dani peered around Zed's massive form to see Bael and Jillian standing on the steps of the gazebo. Jillian was holding a small gift box wrapped in silver and blue paper.

"Sorry your satellite phone got smashed," Jillian said, handing her the gift box. Smiling, Dani ripped open the box to find a smart phone model she'd never seen before. She turned it on and saw that a picture of Zed grinning at the camera, shirtless, was her wallpaper.

"It's a satellite-powered smart phone," Jillian explained. "You'll have all the range of your old phone, but with all the same functions as a smart phone, email, FaceTime, internet and all that. It's the newest perk for League higher-ups. I only just got one this month. So I pulled some strings and got one for you too, as a 'sorry you almost got drained of all your life-force because I made a bad hiring decision.'"

"Forgiven." Dani scrolled her thumb across the screen and saw that her email, social media and contacts were already logged in and ready to go on the new phone. "I don't want to know how the IT department knew all of my usernames and passwords, do I?"

"No, you do not," Jillian said. "But you should be able to use all of the functions no matter where you are, which is maybe enough to make up for the creep factor, there."

Pursing her lips, Dani opened her Facetime account and dialed Trudy's number. Zed opened his mouth as if to object, but Trudy picked up on the first ring. Tru's rounded face appeared on the screen with her youngest son, Jackson, dancing around like a monkey behind her shoulder.

"Oh, hey hon! This is a surprise!" Trudy exclaimed.

"Hi, Trudy! It's really good to see your face."

Dani thought maybe she might tear up for a second. When she'd thought she was dying, Trudy's was among the faces she knew she'd miss the most. Sensing her distress, Zed ran his hand along Dani's thigh, squeezing it gently. Dani sniffed and gave Trudy a watery smile.

"Oh, hon, don't be upset. I got the transfer you sent and started the payments. We should have everything taken care of within a week." Trudy practically yelled over the sound of Jackson's monkey noises. "Cheese and *rice*, Jack, go find your grandpa and tell him Aunt Dani's calling before I lose my ever-loving mind."

Zed laughed and that made Trudy's face freeze on screen. "We're not alone, are we?"

"No." Dani glanced at Zed. He leaned into the camera's frame and waggled one of his ham-sized hands at Dani's aunt. "Trudy Gustafsson, this is Zed Berend. Zed, this is my aunt-but-more-like-a-sister-but-basically-my-best-friend, Trudy."

Zed waved. "It's really nice to meet you."

"Oh good gosh! *That's* the guy you've been 'not dating' this whole time? You could have mentioned he was—" Trudy's green eyes went even wider and her cheeks turned pink.

Dani asked cheekily, "Could have mentioned what?"

Trudy shot her an annoyed look, though there was no real heat in it. "So tall."

"But we're sitting down, Tru," Dani said, her tone too innocent to be genuine.

Trudy slapped a hand over her face.

"And if makes you feel any better, I finally got her to admit that we're dating." Zed piped in.

"That's amazing progress. You have no idea."

Jillian snickered, but tried to cover the sound with a cough.

"Oh, come on, are there other people there, too? Just show me to everybody so I know what I'm dealing with and stop sticking my foot in my mouth," Trudy cried.

Dani motioned for Jillian to move around the back of the swing. Bael hesitated slightly, but followed along when Jillian pulled on his uniform shirt.

"Trudy, this is Jillian Ramsay, who is uh, head of the tourist commission here, but has become a really good friend. And this is

Bael Boone, who is the sheriff in these parts. Guys, this is my aunt Trudy."

"It's really lovely to put a face to the name," said Jillian.

Bael followed Zed's example and waved. "Hi, there."

If it was possible, Trudy's cheeks got even more red. "Are all of the men in Mystic Bayou so..."

"Tall?" Jillian supplied helpfully. "Not quite, but we do have a higher than average rate of 'really tall' men around here."

Trudy chewed on her lip. "The kids get out of school for two weeks in December. We could probably come down for a holiday visit..."

Grandad's voice boomed off camera. "Why's your face so red, Trudy?"

Trudy was now fanning said cheeks. "Dani called, Dad. She wanted to talk to you."

"Well, hot dog! Hand me the phone." Suddenly, the image on the screen blurred and the four of them were presented with a picture of a wrinkled ear, complete with a little tuft of white hair on the lobe.

They could hear the muffled voice of Trudy saying, "No, Dad, it's just like calling on the laptop. You hold the phone in front of your face."

"This is why we never introduce my *farfar* to technology," Bael muttered to Jillian.

Dani nodded. "Probably the right idea."

Trudy must have pulled the phone out of Grandad's ear and positioned it in front of his face. His eyes lit up at the sight of his granddaughter. "Well, hey there, Dani-Girl! . . . And a bunch of other folks. Who are your friends?"

"Dani-Girl?" Zed whispered, only to have Dani elbow him in the belly.

The introductions were made again, and once Grandad realized that Zed had his arm around Dani's shoulders, the questions began.

Grandad asked, "How old are you, son?"

Jillian grimaced, glancing at the two shifters, who sometimes forgot that humans didn't live well into their two hundreds. But Zed answered smoothly, "Just a few years older than Dani."

"And how long have you been dating my Dani?"

Zed, suddenly realizing this was the equivalent to a relationship job interview straightened up his posture and began speaking in a much more serious tone of voice. "Long enough to know I'm not going to let her go any time soon."

Grandad nodded in what could be mistaken for approval, but his eyes narrowed and he asked, "Do you have a job, with all that hair flying everywhere?"

"Yes, sir, I'm the mayor of Mystic Bayou, have been for almost two years. Our budget is small, but balanced. Our high school graduation rates are high and we keep our taxes low."

Grandad raised a fluffy gray eyebrow. "The mayor? With a beard that long?"

"You should have seen the other guy," Zed offered.

Grandad stared at the screen incredulously for a half a beat, threw his head back and laughed. "That's a good one. All right, boy, good for you for not letting an old man push you around. So I take it that you might be staying on in this town for a while, Dani?"

"For the foreseeable future. I'm thinking about taking a permanent job with the," Dani paused and added, "tourist commission here in town."

"Well, it will be nice to know where we can find you for a while. Even if it is far away, at least it's in the same country."

Dani checked the surrounding sidewalks to make sure everybody was in human form and behaving relatively "normal" for Mystic Bayou. "Do you want to see it?"

Grandad nodded. "Sure!"

Dani hit the button to turn the camera around, panning slowly across the town square to show him Main Street, the shops, the fountain, the parish hall.

Grandad whistled. "Well, lookee there."

Trudy exclaimed, "What a cute little town! No wonder you're pushing tourism. People should be lining up in droves to visit."

Bael shuddered, visibly.

"Is that a dragon on your city hall?" Grandad asked.

"Our town founders were really...whimsical." Zed answered.

"Well, it's nice that you keep up the traditions then. Dani-Girl, I'm glad you found a nice place to live for a while. And it seems like you've found some good friends, too. I'm really happy for you, that you've found home."

Rather than protesting, Dani just smiled at her grandfather. "Yes, I did. Thank you, Grandad."

Just then, a white unmarked van parked in front of the parish hall and entered into the camera's frame. The panel door opened and Jillian shrieked like a banshee, making Grandad startle. Jillian took off running toward a tall, dark-haired woman climbing out of the van. The newcomer was wearing a sleek black suit and heels with red soles and yet, she was knocking over several League personnel to get to the anthropologist.

Dani turned the camera so it was focused on her face again.

"Is your friend all right?" Grandad asked.

Dani said, "I'm not entirely sure."

"Sonja!" Jillian screeched, practically scooping the woman off her feet with a hug. Sonja squealed, wrapping her arms around Jillian's neck and sobbing.

"I'm not sure how I feel about the fact that she only showed that much enthusiasm for my coming home when I brought her Siobhan's cherry blondies," Bael commented.

Zed shrugged. "It's kinda hot."

Grandad snorted on the other end of the line. "Son, if I've learned anything about female friendships, it's that you better just sit back and try not to get in the way. Women can be downright terrifying when crossed."

"Trust me when I say I'm familiar with the concept," Bael said.

"Dani, you bring that boy up to the farm sometime, for me to meet him proper."

Trudy was heard giggling hysterically in the background.

Dani chuckled. "I think I'll do just that. Probably around Christmas. Talk to you soon, guys. I love you."

Grandad nodded. "And you tell that nice dragon boy that sprinkling a little vetiver and poppyseed around the entrance to his horde will make it much harder for other people to find. Oldest and simplest magic there is."

Dani's jaw dropped low. "What?"

Bael looked vaguely offended, as if he couldn't believe someone had seen through his cover. "But I didn't . . . dragon."

Grandad scoffed. "I'm a Nilsson, Dani-Girl, one of the oldest families in Sweden. My ancestors were responsible for carving the dragons for the ships that crossed the great sea. You don't think I recognize a dragon when I see one?"

Dani spluttered, "But we're not . . . you never . . . you could have . . . What?"

"Way to go, Dad, you broke her brain." Trudy cackled.

"There's a lot more to the world than you or I could ever see, Dani-Girl. Hell, your great-great-great-grandmother on Abbigail's side could make little balls of light with her hands and toss them around like a hot potato. She used to do it as a party game at Christmas."

"WHAT?!" Dani shouted.

"Granny Newtsund said it was the oddest thing you ever saw." Grandad's train of thought was interrupted by a crash from the background of Trudy's kitchen, followed by Trudy sighing and telling Jackson to get the mop. "Whoops. I better go clean that up. Jackson's knocked over the maple syrup jug again. Love you, Dani-Girl."

Dani stared, still open-mouthed at her screen, then turned to Zed and cried, "What the hell?"

EPILOGUE

DANI

D ani carried a shipping box through the entrance of Zed's
tidy stone house, and gave Zed a smooch as he took it out
of her hands and carried it to the spare room.

"Last one?" he called.

"Last one!" she assured him.

Dani's moving into Zed's house-slash-cave had taken all of
fifteen minutes. She had a total of five bags, including her
purse, and six boxes. After he answered *several* questions about
Dani's great-great-great-grandmother, the light ball tosser,
Grandad had been happy to ship some of her things from
home, the little knickknacks and bits of nostalgia that she
hadn't been able to pack around with her while she traveled—
her yearbooks and the little wooden llama figurines she'd
collected since she'd received one as a birthday present from a
Peruvian shaman named Alois. Grandad had also included
several framed photos of himself and Gram, Trudy, and her
family. There were no photos of Journey and she was fine with
that.

She hadn't heard from her father since his whiny call from the ashram. She suspected Zed had something to do with his lack of contact. She was also fine with that.

She scooched the bowl of keys just a little left of center on Zed's little foyer table. She also moved the table just a little bit closer to the nearby outlet, so she could plug in her phone charger there. She kicked off her shoes and left them in the shoe basket on the floor, meant to keep them from tracking bayou mud all over the house. She put her purse on the table and her key, situated on the little silver bee keychain Zed had given her, in the bowl. She stood back, observing the concrete evidence that she was now a resident of the cave, and gave a happy little sigh.

"Well, it's not like you had a lot of boxes," Zed said. And no furniture. This is way better than the time Bael asked me to use my truck to help him move a gold statue of a hippo. A life-size statue, mind you, with ruby eyes the size of my fist. The thing was creepy. Dragons get very weird birthday presents."

Dani noted that during this little anecdote, Zed had glanced at the foyer table no less than three times.

"I moved the table."

Zed cleared his throat. "Oh, no, no, no, no, it looks great . . . way over there, really. I was just admiring it."

"You literally just said 'no' four times," Dani said, laughing lightly. "You know that if I'm living here, I'm going to have to occasionally touch your stuff, right?"

Zed closed his eyes. "I'm trying not to be weird about this, but it's challenging every one of my compulsive housekeeping nerves."

"If this is too much too fast, I can ask about renewing my lease at the maison," Dani insisted.

Zed's eyes snapped open and went wide in alarm. "No!"

He opened his arms and slung them around Dani, holding her close. "I definitely want you here. I don't want you anywhere else. I've just been on my own for so long, it's going to take a little time to get used to sharing my space."

"OK," she said, kissing him. "I promise not to do anything permanent without talking to you first."

"Thank you. Besides, I'm sure there will be plenty of distractions to keep me from thinking on it too hard," he kissed her, snaking a hand around her waist and giving her ass a little pat.

Dani peered up at him and asked, "Like the fact that Mel is moving into your mom's place this weekend?"

"Yeah, like that."

Dani immediately regretted putting that frown on his face. It was, admittedly, a low blow. Zed was trying to be supportive of his mother's relationship with the adorable little frogman. He didn't begrudge his mother her happiness. He just didn't want to think about it too hard.

"He makes her eyes all gooey and her voice go giggly," he sighed, hitching Dani over his shoulder fireman style and carrying her to the big granite-colored couch. "And he makes her salmon however she wants. And then he does the dishes."

Dani smacked his ass for treating her like a moving box, though she thoroughly enjoyed the novelty of a man who could pick her up like she was made of dandelion fluff. "Are you telling me or reminding yourself?"

Zed gently dropped her on the couch, so she could lean her head back on the arm rest. "A little of both."

He flopped onto the opposite side of the couch and toed off his boots and socks. He took her bare foot in hand and pressed his thumbs into the ball of her foot. She made a noise that was positively indecent.

"Ooh," he said, pressing that spot again. "I'll have to remember that one."

"If you keep that up, I'll never leave," she promised.

"All part of my plan, darlin.'"

She snickered and took his left foot into her hands, to return the foot rub favor. It was weird that for a guy who frequently ran around barefoot and occasionally sported four-inch talons on his paws, he had absolutely beautiful feet. They were long and narrow with a high arch and perfect little square nails. And he clearly knew about pumice stones, because his heels were soft as a baby's butt.

Except.

Dani lifted Zed's foot, so it was closer to her face. "Is that a birthmark?"

She squinted at the small dark mark on the sole of his foot, just below his big toe. It looked like a Nordic rune, though definitely not one that she'd seen before, written in dark blue ink. It looked like an hourglass that had been squished and filled with tiny triangles. "Do you have a tattoo on the bottom of your foot?"

Zed bit his lip. "Yeah, that was something I was going to show you eventually. Probably after we'd both recovered from the shock of moving in together."

"To show me how well you can withstand a crazy amount of pain?"

Zed laughed. "No, it's a bear-shifter thing, *abeille*. That is my secret tattoo."

"Meaning your mom has never seen it?"

Zed snorted. "No, meaning, my uncle is the only one who has ever seen it. It's the family sigil. He inked it himself after I was officially judged a man."

"I'm guessing you had a full beard when you were ten," she said.

Zed nodded. "I had a respectable amount of peach fuzz. Normally, a boy's father would ink the sigil on his foot, but my own daddy had passed on."

"So how is this tattoo different from the many other tattoos you have?"

Zed pressed his thumbs into her foot to make her moan again. "Because the only other person allowed to see that mark, besides my patriarch, is my chosen mate. The person I'm going to be with for life. Bear clans are very secretive about their sigils, you know. We take this very seriously. Even more seriously than dragons and their 'true name' craziness."

"Oh." She glanced back at the little squashed hourglass, and to her surprise, the idea of forever with Zed didn't scare her. Zed was home now, just like Mystic Bayou was home.

Zed grinned. "And now that you've seen it, that means you have to make an honest man out of me."

"You get through a sentence without looking over at the foyer table and we'll talk about making an honest man out of you," she told him.

"Fair enough."

"And you'll have to tell me what the other tattoos mean," she demanded.

"I can do that."

Dani started giggling without warning, and was soon wiping at her eyes, leaving her bear shifter confused.

"What's so funny?"

"It's just . . . it's on your foot," she sniffed, her cheeks flushed. "How have you kept it hidden all these years? If you were unsure about a girl, did you wear socks to bed?"

He nodded. "Yes."

And she giggled even harder. "Well, thank you, for being vulnerable enough to share your foot with me."

"It was all a ruse to trap you into marriage."

"Worth it," she wheezed, wiping at her eyes.

She pressed the heel of her hand over the sigil and rubbed at it. He grinned and burrowed down into the couch. "So do you have any other secret tattoos I don't know about?"

Zed smirked at her. "You'll find them eventually."

Dani tweaked his toe. "I look forward to it."

DANI'S COMFORT APPLESAUCE RECIPE

And if you'd like to make Dani's family applesauce recipe:

Comfort Applesauce
12 Granny Smith Apples
6 Gala apples or red apples of your choice
2 tablespoons of ground cinnamon
½ teaspoon ground ginger
½ teaspoon ground nutmeg
½ teaspoon ground allspice
½ cup light brown sugar

These measurements are all subjective. Honestly, I don't measure most of the time. I'll just add enough brown sugar and cinnamon until it "looks right," and then add a dash of each of the spices. But I thought that might make first-timers nervous. This recipe is very difficult to mess up, so just find the mix that works for you.

Instructions

1. Peel apples. (You don't have to do it in one strip, just keep all of your fingertips and I'll be happy.)
2. Core and slice apples.
3. Place apples in slow cooker and top with brown sugar and spices. Stir the mixture until the sugar forms a glaze over the fruit.
4. Heat fruit on low for three hours. Stir occasionally. The fruit should puff up and reach what I call the "perfume" stage, where you lift the lid and the scent of the bubbly apple liquid hits you right in the face. (In a good way. It will smell better than any fancy candle you could ever buy.)
5. Once the fruit has hit the puffy, perfume stage, it's ready to eat. If you like chunky apple sauce, eat it as is. My kids don't like chunky, so I attack it with a potato masher until it's relatively smooth.

This is really good by itself, but I like to serve it over vanilla ice cream!

DISCOVER THE SOUTHERN ECLECTIC SERIES

From beloved author Molly Harper comes a romantic comedy and women's fiction series featuring the lives, losses, and loves of the McCready family as they manage their family's generational funeral home and bait shop (you read that correctly) on the shore of picturesque Lake Sackett, Georgia.

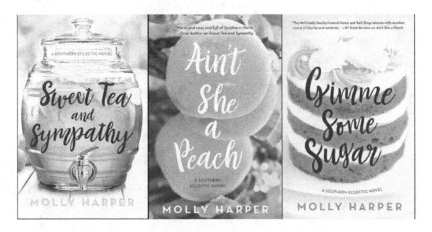

Read on for excerpts from each book!

SWEET TEA AND SYMPATHY EXCERPT

Praise for the Southern Eclectic Series

"This sweet tale of the city girl finding a home in the country launches Harper's latest series and will go down as easy as honey on a deep-fried Twinkie." (*Library Journal*)

"Harper writes characters you can't help but fall in love with." (*RT Book Reviews*)

"This book is funny and the characters engaging....Finished it in 24 hours and already looking forward to the next in the Southern Eclectic series." (*BookRiot*)

Chapter 1

MARGOT CARY LEANED her forehead against the warm truck window as it bounced along the pitted Georgia highway.

She closed her eyes against the picturesque landscape as it rolled by. Green, green, green. Everything was so effing green here.

***

GREEN WAS NOT her lucky color. It certainly hadn't blessed the opening of the botanical garden's newly completed Wesmoreland Tropical Greenhouse. Maybe it had been a mistake to carry the green theme so far. Green table linens, green lanterns strung through the trees, down to emerald-green bow ties for the catering staff. Weeks later, she still remembered the terrified expression on one waiter's face when she caught him by the arm before he carried his tray of crudités into the party space.

Despite her glacial blond beauty, the younger man practically flinched away from her touch as she adjusted his tie. Margot would admit that she'd been a bit . . . demanding in organizing this event. She had taken every precaution to make sure that this evening's black-tie opening was as smooth as Rosaline Hewitt's recently Botoxed brow. She'd commissioned a silk-leaf embroidered canopy stretching from the valet station to the entrance to prevent the guests' hairstyles and gowns from being ruined by the summer rain. She'd researched each invitee meticulously to find out who was gluten-free or vegan and adjusted the menu accordingly. She'd arranged for two dozen species of exotic South American parrots to be humanely displayed among orchids and pitcher plants and a flock of flamingos to wade through the manufactured waterfall's rocky lagoon.

She was not about to have all of that preparation undone by a cater waiter who didn't know how to keep a bow tie on straight. "Go," Margot said, nodding toward the warm, humid air of the false tropical jungle. He moved silently away from her, into the opulently lit space.

Margot turned and tried to survey the greenhouse as it would appear to the guests, the earliest of which were already filtering into the garden, *ooh*ing and *aah*ing. Calling it a greenhouse seemed like an understatement. The glass-paneled dome reached four stories into the sky, allowing the tropical plant specimens inside plenty of space to stretch. Carefully plotted stone paths wound through the flowerbeds, giving the visitor the impression of wandering through paradise. But knowing how much Chicago's *riche*-est of the *riche* enjoyed a nice soiree, the conservators had been smart enough to add a nice open space in the middle of the greenhouse to allow for a dance floor. She'd arranged elbow-high tables around the perimeter, covered in jewel-tone silk cloths. Gold LED lights cast a hazy sunset glow over the room, occasionally projecting animated fireflies against the foliage. And since society's ladies would never do something so inelegant as visit a buffet, the waiters had been informed to constantly circulate with their trays of canapés in a nonobvious, serpentine pattern around the enormous shrimp tower in the middle of—

Wait.

"No," Margot murmured, shaking her head. "No, no, no."

She snagged the next waiter to walk through the entrance and took his tray. The sweet-faced college kid seemed startled and alarmed to have the chief planner for this event grabbing him by the arm. "You, get two of your coworkers and very quickly, very quietly, very *discreetly* get that shrimp tower out of here. If anyone asks, just tell them that you're taking it back to the kitchen to be refilled."

The poor boy blanched at the brisk clip to her tone and said, "But—but Chef Jean was very specific about—"

"I don't care what Chef Jean was specific about," she said. "Get it out of here *now*."

The waiter nodded and pulled away from her into the gathering crowd.

Margot stepped forward into the fragrant warmth of the greenhouse, careful to keep her expression and body language relaxed. She was aware that, while professionally dressed in her black power suit, she was not nearly as festive as the guests in their tuxedos and haute couture gowns, but she was perfectly comfortable. She'd attended hundreds of events like this growing up. She would not be intimidated by some plants and a pretentious wannabe Frenchman. She pressed the button of her earbud-size Bluetooth and whispered, "This is Margot. I need to speak to Jean."

She could tell by the way her words were echoing in her own ear that the head chef of Fete Portable had taken his earpiece out —despite Margot's repeated requests to keep a line of communication open with her—and set it on the stainless steel counter in the makeshift kitchen. She blew out a frustrated breath. Jean LeDille was not her preferred caterer for high-profile events, but the de facto hostess of tonight's opening—Melissa Sutter, first lady of Chicago and head of the botanical garden conservators' board— had insisted on using him. So far he'd been temperamental, resistant to the most basic instruction, and a pain in Margot's Calvin Klein–clad ass. And when she was done with this event and had secured her partnership at Elite Elegance, she would have Jean blacklisted from every Chicago party planner's contact list. Theirs was a close-knit and gossip-driven circle.

Someone in the kitchen picked up the earbud and said, "Ms. Cary, he says to tell you he's unavailable."

Margot gritted her perfect white teeth but managed a polite smile to the head of the opera board and his wife as they passed. Jean wouldn't be able to get a job making a clown-shaped birthday cake by the time she was done with him.

"So I guess I'll just have to make myself available to him, then." Margot's assistant, Mandy, a sleek brunette who reminded Margot of a Russian wolfhound in four-inch heels, fell in step behind her. "Make sure that tower is gone. You have two minutes."

"On it," Mandy snapped, and peeled off after the hapless waiters.

Margot pushed through the heavy plastic curtain that separated the greenhouse from the kitchen tent. Far from the muted music and golden-green light of the greenhouse, the tent was ruthlessly lit with fluorescents and heating lamps. Jean's shouts filled the air, demanding that the canapé trays be restocked tout de suite.

Jean was a stocky, balding man with thick, dark eyebrows and an unfortunate mustache. His chef whites were splattered with various sauces and he sneered—actually sneered—at Margot as she walked into his kitchen.

"What are you doing in ma' kitchen?" he demanded in an exaggerated French accent. "I tell you before. No outside staff when I am *creating*."

"Jean, would you explain to me why there is a shrimp tower in the middle of my venue?"

"I was overcome by the muse this morning. I decide to build you a shrimp tower. Only four hundred dollars extra. I do you favor, eh?"

"Wait. Is that shrimp salad on the crostini?" Margot asked, stopping a waiter before he left with his tray of appetizers. "Because we agreed on poached quail eggs. Mrs. Sutter, the hostess of tonight's event, whom you've cooked for on several occasions, is allergic to shrimp. As in, she can't even be around people who are eating shrimp because she might come into contact with the proteins. I wrote it on everything. *Everything*."

Margot motioned to the field refrigeration unit where she had taped a neon-green sign that read please remember that Mrs. Sutter is highly allergic to shrimp.

Jean waved her off. "I do not read the cards. My sous chef reads the cards."

"Jean. Drop the French accent that we both know is about as

real as that ridiculous hairpiece and tell me what you are feeding the mayor's wife."

The chef, whose real name was John Dill, shrugged and in his natural, Midwestern voice said, "The market didn't have enough quail eggs, so I took the shrimp. It's not a big deal. If she's allergic, she'll know not to touch it. People make too much of their food allergies anyway."

"It's just lovely to know that someone with that attitude is making food for innocent bystanders," Margot snapped. She called out loud enough for the entire kitchen staff to hear, "Eighty-six the shrimp crostini. Throw them out and take the bags out of the tent. All of you wash your hands—twice—and any utensils that have touched the shrimp—also twice. I need one uncontaminated staff member to make a special shrimp- free plate of food for Mrs. Sutter so we can feed her tonight without poisoning her. Get it done, now."

Jean was seething, but Margot didn't give a single damn. Mandy popped through the plastic curtain, a stricken expression on her angular face.

"There's a problem with the tower," she said. "It's too heavy to move. But they're working on disassembling the shrimp trays to bring them back in before people notice."

"I don't care if it's made of concrete. I need it—" Margot's response was cut short by a strange honking ruckus from the greenhouse, followed by screams and crashing . . . and running?

One of Margot's golden eyebrows rose. "What is that?" Mandy grimaced. "Don't flamingos eat shrimp?"

Margot dropped her clipboard and her headset to the ground and scrambled through the plastic curtain. "Oh, no."

The flamingos were making a run at the shrimp tower, pink wings flapping, pecking at the waiters who were attempting to remove the shellfish. The guests were falling all over one another trying to get away from the shrimp-frenzied birds and in the process had knocked over several cocktail tables and the votive candles on top. Those candles had set fire to the tablecloths, which set off the greenhouse's sprinklers and alarms. The parrots did not appreciate the clanging alarms or the sudden scramble of people. They broke free from their perches and were flying around the greenhouse, leaving "deposits" on the guests in protest. Oh, and Mrs. Sutter was purple and covered in hives.

Margot gave herself ten seconds to surrender to the panic. She let her stomach churn. She let her ice-cold hands shake. She allowed herself to hear everything and nothing all at once. In her head, she saw her career going up in flames with the tablecloths. The promotion and partnership she'd worked for were disappearing before her eyes in puffs of smoke. Everything she'd planned, everything she wanted in life, was slipping out of her fingers because of some misplaced shellfish.

And then Margot put a lid on her anxiety and did what she did best. She put out fires metaphorical and literal. She called an ambulance and the fire department, grabbed the EpiPen from Mrs. Sutter's purse, and jabbed her in the thigh. Hell, she even took off her pumps and wrangled the shrimp-seeking flamingos back into the lagoon.

But the damage was done. The news photographers who'd prepared themselves for a boring evening shooting glamour poses gleefully snapped photos of society matrons in soaked designer gowns and runny makeup dashing for shelter from the sprinklers. A guest who happened to be a member of PETA started screaming at Margot for mistreating the flamingos while trying to herd them away from (attacking) the guests. And a conservators' board member handed her an invoice for the thou- sands of dollars in rare orchid species that had been trampled in the melee.

The next morning, an exhausted Margot sat slumped in the offices of Elite Elegance as her boss, Carrington Carter-Shaw, slapped newspapers with headlines like **FLORAL FIASCO AND**

REAL-LIFE ANGRY BIRDS! on her desk. One particularly cheeky tabloid had printed a picture of Margot beating the smoldering remains of a matron's hairpiece with a wet napkin under the head-line FLOWER POWER F***UP!

"How could you let this happen?" Carrington cried, her care-fully blown-out dark hair dancing around her heart-shaped face. "We're the laughingstock of the Chicago social scene. Guests from last night are trying to stick us with dry-cleaning bills, medical bills —Michelle Biederman claims a parrot flew off with her two-karat diamond earring! The mayor's office has contacted us—twice—to call our business license into question. I had to move three guys from the mailroom just to handle the incoming phone calls. Margot, you're my star! My rock! You can make a backyard potluck birthday party look like a black-tie gala. You're the planner I call when it's clear in the first meeting that the client is absolutely batshit insane. What happened?"

Margot wanted to blame the untested Chef Jean and his "inspired" impromptu shrimp, but ultimately the fault rested with her. She'd lost control of the party. She'd lost control of the food. She'd lost control of two dozen species of birds.

"I don't know," Margot mumbled, shaking her head. She took a prepackaged stain wipe out of her Prada clutch and dabbed at a questionable blotch on her lapel. "It all happened so quickly. I—I know, at this point, the partnership is off the table—"

"Partnership?" Carrington scoffed. "Honey, I can't even keep you on staff. You're professional poison. I'm going to have to fire you and do it in a very public manner—I mean, picture the polite urban equivalent of putting you in stocks in the town square and pelting you with rotten fruit—so people know that our company is safe to use again."

Margot let loose a breath she didn't know she'd been holding. She nodded. In some way, she'd been expecting this. She knew it would be rough for a while and she would have to put off some bullet points in her five-year plan, but she could handle this. She had contingency funds and a secret contact list of important people who owed her favors.

Margot cleared her throat and tried to straighten her rum- pled suit jacket. "And what, you'll shuffle me out to one of the branch offices in the suburbs and I'll organize bar mitzvahs until this all blows over?"

Carrington frowned. "No, Margot. *Fired.* As in employment permanently terminated. The partners are willing to give you a three-week severance in recognition of the work you've done for us. And I'll write you a positive recommendation letter. But that's it."

"But I've worked here for almost ten years. I've put in eighty-hour weeks. Ninety during the holiday party season. I don't have a social life because I'm always here. I haven't been on a date in more than eight months."

"Yes, I know. That's why you get the third week of severance pay. Really, Margot, I think we're being more than generous here, considering the fallout from this fiasco."

As Margot walked out of Elite Elegance's plush offices with a banker's box full of her belongings and a severance check in hand, she told herself that it would be okay, that this was what backup plans were for, that this situation couldn't possibly get worse.

It got worse.

Stage one of Margot's plan had been to retreat to her apart-ment to regroup, polish up her résumé, and compose a list of companies she could apply to, but her unit's new tenants kept stopping by to measure for new flooring and curtains. Just a week before the "Floral Fiasco," she'd given up her lease in preparation to move to a newly purchased condo in Wicker Park. Between the down payment she'd saved and the raise she was supposed to get with her promotion, she would have been able to afford it. But the day after she was fired, she'd gotten a call from the mortgage officer handling her condo loan. Mrs. Meade had seen the news about the greenhouse incident and her firing, and informed Margot that without a job, the mortgage company could not guarantee her loan. The only good news was that the mortgage company was willing to return 70 percent of her down payment. So now, with her lease running out and her condo being sold to someone else, Margot was effectively homeless.

And still, it got worse.

Without a job, she couldn't get an apartment in a decent building. And the buildings where she could get an apartment were not places where she wanted to live. And she could not find a job. Anywhere. Receptionists laughed and hung up when she called the best event-planning companies in Chicago. Receptionists from second- and third-tier event-planning companies in Chicago also laughed at her. She couldn't get the companies in New York or Los Angeles to call back. Hell, she couldn't get companies in St. Louis to return her calls. She still had her savings, but thanks to MasterCard and her monthly expenses, they were dwindling quickly.

Her friends weren't returning her calls or messages, either. And she couldn't turn to her adoptive father for help. Gerald hadn't spoken to her since her mother's funeral three years before. And she'd promised herself that she wouldn't take a dime after her parents made their last tuition payment. She still had the shreds of her pride.

The shreds were costing her. She was three days away from living in the storage unit where she'd moved her stuff, sitting at her breakfast bar—because it was the only table space she had left— actually filling in a JobLink profile, when a Skype notification popped up on her laptop. The message said it was from "hotsy-totsy45."

Margot frowned. She used this account for after-hours and long-distance consultations with clients. She definitely would have remembered a client nicknamed hotsy-totsy45. Leaning back from the screen, she clicked *decline*.

Blowing a long breath out through her nose, Margot continued to fill out the JobLink form. Another notification from hotsy-totsy popped up.

"Still a 'no,' creep," she muttered, clicking *decline* again.

But hotsy-totsy would not be denied. And given the amount of chardonnay Margot had consumed just for the sake of not having to move it out of her apartment, it wasn't surprising that her hand slipped a bit and she clicked *accept*.

"Damn it!" she grunted, trying to close the chat window before it opened. She did not want to witness the latest in creative junk shots currently being embraced by the Internet's weirdos. But instead of the expected random nudity, Margot's screen was filled with the face of an adorable little granny lady with a cloud of snow-white hair and Dalmatian-print reading glasses balanced on the tip of her nose.

"Hello?"

A brilliant smile lit up the granny lady's face, showing teeth too white and too even to be original parts. "Well, hello there! It took me a little while to track you down, but here you are!" the lady crowed in a Southern drawl so pronounced that Margot had trouble processing what she was saying at first. "You look just like I thought you would. A lot like your mama, mind, but you got a bit of your daddy in there, too. Of course, I thought you'd be a little more polished up, but I'm guessing you haven't left your house in a while."

Margot caught sight of her appearance in the little preview window in the corner of the screen and winced. She looked like someone who was unemployed. She was wearing a grubby North-western sweatshirt. Her carefully highlighted blond hair was piled into a haphazard topknot. She was wearing her thick-rimmed black glasses, making her hazel eyes look owlish and too big for her face. She hadn't worn makeup in days, so her skin had taken on a cheesy appearance in the blue light of the computer screen. "I'm sorry, do you know my parents?" she asked. As friendly as this lady might be, she didn't exactly look to be Linda and Gerald's speed. Linda McCready, a nobody from nowhere with traces of a Low Country accent and a toddler daughter in tow, had managed to snag Gerald Cary, MD, while she was working as the records clerk in the hospital where the handsome British expat practiced surgery. She had spent considerable time and energy clawing her way into the upper middle circles of Chicago society. Linda Cary would have gone blind before she wore Dalmatian reading glasses.

"Well, your mama and I were never close, but your daddy is my nephew, so I guess you could say I know that sad-sack face of his pretty well," the woman said with a chuckle.

Margot's jaw dropped. Her stepfather had adopted her when she was four years old. But considering that he was from just outside London, it was unlikely he had relatives in Georgia. "You know Gerald?"

"No, honey, your *daddy*. What do you young people call it— your 'biological father.' Stan McCready. I'm your great-aunt Tootie."

"Beg pardon?" Even Margot couldn't be sure which part she was questioning—the "biological" bit or the ridiculous nickname. Even in the South, people knew better than to name their children Tootie, right?

"I'm Stanley McCready's aunt, honey."

Stanley McCready. Margot slumped on her bar stool. She'd never met her father's family. Linda had made no secret of her "unfortunate" first marriage to a man named McCready, but she'd referred to it as a youthful mistake she'd corrected when Margot was barely three years old. Stanley was a heavy drinker, Linda had insisted, a trainwreck of a man who couldn't provide for them.

After Linda left, he'd almost immediately given up his rights to his daughter without so much as a court motion.

Margot didn't know where he lived. She couldn't remember what he looked like. Her mother had never even shown her a picture, insisting that it would be disloyal to Gerald. Neither Mr. McCready nor his family tried to contact her in thirty years, which was fine with Margot. She didn't have room in her life for an irresponsible drunk who couldn't be bothered to send so much as a birthday card. And frankly, she resented the idea that her father's family only reached out now, when she was at her lowest.

And it wasn't even her father, just some wacky great-aunt with a ridiculous name.

"You know, I thought you'd have that nasal-sounding Chicago accent, but you sound like you should be having tea with the queen. So proper and prim. I suppose that's your mama in ya. Did she make you take those diction lessons?"

"No, I just like using all the letter sounds."

The woman snorted a bit and said, "My point is, honey, I've been looking for you for weeks now, after I saw the video of your party on YouTube. I spotted you and knew you had to be Linda's daughter."

"YouTube?" Margot winced. "How many hits did it get?"

"Hundreds of thousands! Honey, you're your own meme!" Tootie exclaimed. Suddenly, a window popped up in the corner of Margot's screen, showing one of the press photos of Margot herding the flamingos away from the shrimp tower with giant print reading NO CAN HAZ SHRIMP, FLAMINGOZ! NO CAN HAZ!

Margot buried her face in her hands. She'd spent most of her twenties carefully policing her own social media posts so as not to damage her professional reputation. And now this. Also, her great-aunt seemed to be awfully tech savvy for a woman who looked to be in her eighties.

"Well, thanks for contacting me and mocking me with age-appropriate Internet humor . . . and dredging up a bunch of unre-solved emotional issues," Margot muttered. "But I'm going to have to sign off now."

"Oh, sure, honey, I'm sure you're busy with your job search. How's that going?"

"I've submitted quite a lot of résumés," Margot said, trying to sound casual.

"Any interviews yet?" Tootie pressed.

Margot floundered a bit while searching for an answer. "It's still early. You don't want people to think you're too eager."

"Not one callback, huh?"

Margot pursed her lips. "Not one."

"Well, that's just fine, because I have a proposition for you." Margot's instinct to say no right that second was quelled when the bank paperwork that showed her checking account balance caught her eye. "What sort of proposition?"

"We need an event planner here at the family business. We'd be willing to provide room, board, and a generous salary."

"How generous?"

"Well, now, you've got to remember that the cost of living is much lower here as opposed to the big city," Tootie cautioned.

"How generous?" Margot asked again, and Tootie's blue eyes sparkled behind those reading glasses.

"Here, I'll send you the compensation package the family put together."

Another box popped up on Margot's screen. She clicked on the file and grimaced at the salary, which was about one-quarter of what she'd made at Elite Elegance. "How *much* lower is the cost of living there? Also, where is 'there'?"

"Did you notice that the package includes health insurance?" Tootie asked. "When does your coverage run out?"

"Soon," Margot grumbled. "Also, I noticed you didn't answer the question about location."

"And I'm guessin' from the packing boxes in the background that your lease runs out pretty soon, too. So really, I could see why you would want to stay where you would be homeless and at risk of huge medical bills, in a city where you could be mugged or run down by a taxi or have a windowpane fall on you from twenty stories up. That's far preferable to coming down to Georgia, to a town where the crime rate is next to zero."

Margot had never passed the Mason-Dixon Line, not even to Florida. Her mother had always insisted on family vacations to Lake Geneva, to New York, to France. Anyone could go to Disney World, she'd told Margot; Linda was trying to give Margot the *world*. Margot didn't know how well she would function in a rural environment, much less a place where she would constantly hear the banjo music from *Deliverance* in the back of her head.

"But my life is here. My friends are here. I need to stay where the jobs are. And right now, that's in Chicago."

"So you lay low for a few months in God's country, get to know your kinfolk, get that city air out of your lungs, and then relaunch yourself at people who will have forgotten your foul-up once someone else messes up worse. It will be good for you," Tootie told her.

Margot stared at the offer. Tootie had thought of everything: financial compensation, meals covered, a clothing allowance, and health insurance. She'd even attached a picture of a small cabin on the edge of a lake, labeled *housing*. And another photo of a huge family posed in front of a lakeside dock. Tootie stood with an older man, holding his hand. Two couples in their fifties stood behind them next to a man with deep frown furrows barely touched by his lopsided smirk. His arm was thrown around a twentyish girl with purple-streaked hair in pigtails wearing a black T-shirt with a pink radiation symbol on it. Another couple stood on the far left, a man in his thirties with curly reddish-blond hair hugging a laughing blonde. The sun was setting behind the family and they looked so happy together, so at ease with one another. And it felt like a punch to the chest. These people didn't miss her at all. They didn't feel a Margot-shaped hole in their family, they'd just moved on without her. It shouldn't have hurt as much as it did. She'd spent a lot of time on visualization exercises so it wouldn't hurt. And yet . . .

She cleared her throat. "The whole family put this together? Even my . . . even Stan?"

"Everybody," Tootie said emphatically.

Margot skimmed the top of the document and caught sight of the letterhead, which read *McCready Family Funeral Home and Bait Shop*.

"Funeral home? Wait, you run a funeral home? And a bait shop?"

"Well, it's more of a full-service marina, but yes! For four generations now! You're part of a Lake Sackett institution, hon."

"Why would a funeral home-slash-bait shop need an event planner?"

"Well, the baby boomer generation is dropping like flies around here, so we've got more business than we can handle. We've needed to add another planning consultant for a while now, and when I saw your video and looked up your background, I knew you'd be perfect."

"I'm an event planner. For major society parties, galas, charity balls, that sort of thing."

"Well, a funeral is a kind of event. And some of the considerations are the same—timing, speeches, music, food, and such."

"Oh, I just don't think I could—"

Suddenly, the lights flickered out and her refrigerator died with a whine. Because she'd shut off utilities in preparation for the move to the condo that was supposed to have taken place the week before. But she had nowhere to go. And no health insurance.

She pursed her lips. "When can I start?"

***

AUNT TOOTIE—MARGOT was still refusing to call her that out loud, on principle—had been very helpful in organizing her immediate move to Lake Sackett. Using her above-generational-average tech skills, Tootie arranged for a local company to ship the few belongings Margot was bringing to Georgia. Tootie booked a flight from Chicago to Atlanta and then assured her that she'd have a car pick her up at the airport and drive her the two and a half hours to the lake country.

Tootie was just *so* efficient.

Three days later, Margot's flight was taxiing down the runway at Hartsfield-Jackson Atlanta International Airport and she was clutching her cell phone to her chest. Margot had no idea what she'd face when she deplaned. She'd intentionally avoided reading up on the funeral home or her new base of operations because she was afraid that additional information would convince her to cancel the whole agreement.

Margot managed to find her bags without problems, but she couldn't find the car service at the arrivals terminal. She scanned the little signs held by the handful of drivers near the exit. Not one of them said *Cary*. Maybe Tootie hadn't sent anyone, she thought. Maybe she could take the airport transit system to the departures terminal and book a flight back to Chicago. She didn't believe in signs, but maybe this was an omen. Maybe she wasn't meant to meet her father's family. Maybe she wasn't supposed to live in Georgia. Maybe she should step back on the sidewalk before that enormous green truck barreling through the pickup area squashed her flat.

The battered early-model truck skidded to a stop in front of her. The side door was marked **McCready Family Funeral Home and Bait Shop—Lake Sackett, Ga** in bold gold print.

Margot murmured, "Oh . . . no."

Tootie hadn't arranged for a car service. She'd sent a family member to pick Margot up. A stranger in a pickup truck. Everything inside of Margot seemed to tense at once. She'd thought she'd have at least a few more hours to pep-talk herself into the right frame of mind to meet any of her extended family—not to mention the little bottle of vodka she'd purchased on the plane to help prepare her to meet her father. But here it was, spewing exhaust at her, while the driver's-side door opened. The windows were tinted too darkly to allow her to see the driver. Would it be Stan McCready? Was she ready for that? Was it too late to run back into the airport and hide behind the baggage carousel?

A man in his thirties—the man with curly reddish-blond hair from the family photo she'd studied relentlessly for the last three days— popped his head over the truck frame and grinned at her. His eyes, the same ocean blue as Tootie's, glowed with amusement as he held up a poster-board sign that read **Welcome Home, Cousin Margot**! in bright red glitter letters. The sign had been decorated with balloons and glittery star stickers. He waved it madly and yelled, "Hey!"

Definitely *not* her father, then. Margot stepped back, eyes wide, and in a move natural to someone who spent most of her life in a major city, pulled her purse closer to her body.

The bearded man scampered around the front of the truck and threw his arms around her. "Hey, cuz!"

"Who . . . are you?" Margot whispered as he squeezed her tight. His T-shirt smelled of citronella and sunscreen, a pleasant combination, but she generally liked her personal space bubble to be a little more . . . bubbly.

"Oh, I'm sorry! I'm Duffy McCready, your cousin. Well, my grandpa is your grandpa's cousin, which always muddies the waters with third cousin and once-removed and all that. So we'll just keep it simple and say 'cousin.' "

"And Tootie McCready sent you?" she asked, just in case there was some other half-wild McCready picking up his long-lost cousin at the domestic arrivals terminal.

"We're so excited that you're here," he drawled in his heavy Georgian accent. "I'm sorry I'm late. I had this nightmare customer, refused to give up the search for Billy the Mythic Largemouth Bass. And then Atlanta traffic is always awful."

"You're still hugging me," she noted.

"Sorry," he said, detaching himself from her. He was a pleasant-enough-looking guy, thin but nicely muscled, with a cheerful face. He was dressed in well-worn jeans, work boots, and a plaid shirt over a forest-green T-shirt that read **McCready Family Funeral Home and Bait Shop**.

He attempted to take her Vuitton suitcase from her and she held firm to the handle, shaking her head. "I've got it."

After he realized that she was not, in fact, going to let go of her luggage, he raised his hands in surrender. "Suit yourself. I just can't believe I'm finally getting to meet you," Duffy said, opening the passenger door for her. "Everybody's excited that you're comin' back home."

"Everybody?" Margot whimpered.

Chapter 2

THE MCCREADY FAMILY had a compound.

An honest-to-God backwoods compound.

Duffy had called it that with absolutely no irony.

The ride to Lake Sackett started optimistically enough. Atlanta was a bustling metropolis, almost comparable to Chicago. Margot recognized various department stores and clothing shops, so at least she wasn't stuck in a fashion desert. But then the buildings got a little less polished and fewer and farther between. Pretty soon, all she could see whizzing by were scrubby pines and sunbaked red clay, broken up by the occasional run-down gas station or pecan stand.

She had never been this far away from any city. She'd never felt so alone or out of place. And she wasn't entirely sure this whole Aunt Tootie job offer wasn't some sort of ruse to lure her into the middle of nowhere so her paternal family could sacrifice her to Lake Sackett's forest god like something out of *The Wicker Man*.

While she was suffering this crisis of identity, Duffy continued to chatter to fill the silence. Where was her father? Duffy seemed nice enough, but there was this unspoken distance between them, the strange knowledge that they *should* know each other better but didn't, for reasons beyond either of their control.

"We didn't want to crowd you. Tootie said you weren't used to a big family fuss. We figured it would already be pretty over-whelming for ya, new state, new place, and all. Everybody's at Mr. Allanson's visitation—working as usual—so you have some time to settle in, get some sleep before you go through the full McCready roll call."

Some small part of Margot would admit that she was relieved. She didn't think she'd be able to handle meeting the entire family en masse at the moment. She'd barely handled meeting Duffy, and he'd been insistently sweet. She also noted that he hadn't mentioned where Stan was, that he hadn't even made an excuse for her father not being present. What did that mean? Had her father not even tried to make it to see her for the first time in almost thirty years?

Margot realized Duffy was staring at her with an expression both troubled and expectant. She tried to muster some semblance of a polite smile and said, "Thank you, that's very considerate."

"You'll meet 'em all soon enough. Grandpa E.J.J. couldn't be more pleased. He wanted to add you to the company letterhead right away, but we convinced him that might be jumping the gun a little."

"Grandpa E.J.J.?"

"Technically, he's Earl Edward McCready the Third, but everybody called him Earl Junior Junior. E.J.J. My dad was called Junior. And my mom said the whole damn thing was becoming too confusin' so they named me after her side of the family, the McDuffs."

"So my grandfather's name is Earl?"

"No, E.J.J. is *my* grandpa. *Your* grandpa was his cousin, Jack. He and Grandpa E.J.J. were the ones who really got the business thrivin'."

"I think I'm going to need a chart," she muttered.

"It's actually not that hard to remember. McCreadys have lived in Sackett County since before there was a lake. Our branch comes from a pair of brothers, John and Earl Jr. Now, back in 1916, Earl came home from World War I minus several toes and half an ass cheek and built a little bait shop on the shore of the lake selling night crawlers, plus homemade lemonade and sandwiches that his wife, Kate, made. Now, John never had much interest in fishing, but he could make the sturdiest cabinets you ever saw. The Spanish flu epidemic hit Lake Sackett real hard. John had to stop makin' cabinets and start makin' coffins. And it turned out he was an even better coffin maker than he was a cabinetmaker. With all the coffins the town needed—"

"Due to a plague decimating the town's population?"

Duffy smiled brightly—perhaps too brightly, in light of the pandemic discussion. "Yep. With all the extra orders, John had to have more space to work and Earl let him use the back of his store as a workshop. They'd always gotten along real well and liked having each other nearby as they worked. The bait shop grew, because people loved Kate's sandwiches and Earl's fishing stories. And the coffin business took off, because, well, everybody dies eventually. Earl and Kate had E.J.J. John and Ellie had Jack. They all added to the business over time, offering full funeral services and guided fishing tours and such. And they added their own kids with Sarah and Tootie—my dad, Junior, came from E.J.J., obviously. Your dad, Stan, and Uncle Bob came from Jack, who passed on years ago. Bob and his wife have our cousin, Frankie. My parents have my sister, Marianne, and me—clearly the better child. My dad passed away about five years ago. Mom's still a bit touchy on the subject. Marianne's the only one of our generation to get married and have kids, so far. She and her husband, Carl, have two boys, Nate and Aiden."

"I will definitely need a chart," she said.

"Marianne already made you one. She hung it up in your cabin." Duffy gave her a goofy half smile. "It's a lot to take in, but you'll get it. The most important thing to remember: Nate's a biter."

"I will try to remember that," she promised. "So I noticed that you didn't mention Stan with a second wife or more kids. Um, I guess my father never remarried?"

"No." For the first time in their acquaintance, Duffy's expression was not the picture of boyish excitement. He looked almost offended on Stan's behalf that Margot was questioning her father's loyalty. "He never even looked at another woman after your mama left."

Margot frowned. She'd been counting on some sort of story about a cruel stepmother who wouldn't let her father contact his only daughter. As a child, she'd spent a lot of nights coming up with elaborate reasons why her father never called or wrote. He was a spy. He was an amnesiac prince. He was in the Witness Protection Program. Gerald was a decent man who had always treated her civilly, if a bit coldly. But she'd needed some reason to excuse Stan's silence. And then her mother had given her the full awful explanation about Stan's drinking. Margot had spent years in therapy—sessions starting in college that she'd never told her mother about—working through those excuses. And to find that there was no story, no spies, no amnesia, no evil step- mother? It was more than a little deflating, especially when he'd failed to come pick her up. He'd finally had the chance to start making up for years of absence and he hadn't shown up.

"He's been sober for a long time, you know," Duffy added. "We had a big party for his twenty-year chip and everything. Mama said he was a real mess when we were little. Hell, nobody really blamed your mama all that much for takin' off. I mean, it sucked she never let us see you, but Stan was in no shape to be a daddy to you. We understood that. We just wish she woulda told us where she was goin' with you so we knew you were all right. And it still took years after that for him to clean up. But once he got on the path, he stayed on it. Hasn't had a drink since."

"Good for him," Margot said blandly. "So, is there a reason my father isn't here to pick me up?"

Duffy glanced into the rearview mirror and switched lanes, as if he was stalling. "Uh, well, I think he's seein' to Barbara Lynn Grady. He got called to pick her up a couple of hours ago. It's a bit of an occupational hazard. Death doesn't stop for holidays or airport pickups. He probably won't be home until late tonight."

Margot nodded. While she was hurt that she wouldn't see her father that day, she was also oddly relieved. And then she felt guilty for being impossible to please. To distract herself from these rapidly realigning feelings, she pulled out her iPhone and checked her messages.

"Oh, you're gonna have a hard time gettin' much of a signal up here," Duffy said, waving his large, calloused hands at her smartphone. "It's better closer to town, but the hills between us and Atlanta make it pretty hard for the towers to get through."

She dropped her phone in her carry-on bag. "Of course."

"So, Grandma Tootie says that you're going to start tomorrow. She said you didn't seem the type to want to take time off to rest after your move. E.J.J. is going to do his best to teach you all he knows about the 'people' side of the business. Uncle Bob is a dab hand at handlin' the logistics: paperwork for the coffins, the cremations, arranging the burials, workin' with the police on traffic arrangements, and all that. But he's all thumbs with non-McCready people, even if he's known 'em all his life. If you're not family, he just blurts out the most accidentally offensive things you can think of, because he doesn't know what to say. And that is not the guy you want talkin' you through one of the roughest times in your life."

Margot swallowed heavily. She hadn't thought that part of the job through, dealing with those who were handling the deaths of their loved ones. She'd thought her job would mostly involve ordering flowers and discussing casket linings. She was used to guiding clients through happy occasions. She'd been to only a handful of funerals herself.

No, no doubts. Margot could do this. It wasn't as if she knew these people. She didn't have to worry about what they thought of her handling of their grief. Hell, she'd gotten Miriam Schram through two "thank God the divorce is final" parties, including a custom piñata made to look like her soon to be ex-husband. Margot could handle funerals.

"How does that work, exactly?" she asked, watching as the trees became thicker and the roads seemed to get steeper. "The two businesses together. Don't the bereaved bring down the festive vacation mood for the boaters? Aren't the mourners offended by coolers and pool noodles being carted through the parking lot?"

"The way your grandpa Jack set up the parking lot, they come in through totally different entrances, plus the boaters tend to stick to the lake side of the building anyway. And people seem to like the novelty of it, the tradition. Knowing that yeah, today might suck and you're going through something hard, but better days are coming, and eventually, you're going to be back to living. And Frankie likes to think the funerals help remind the boaters not to be jackasses about wearin' their life vests."

"Does it?"

Duffy pulled a frown. "Not particularly. No."

Duffy easily guided the truck around a bend in the road and a huge glittering blue-green lakefront came into view. For the first time in about a week, Margot's smile was genuine. Lake Sackett seemed to be shaped like a fern, all irregular inlets with the occasional tiny island breaking up the glassy expanse of water. The water was teeming with sailboats and speedboats towing water-skiers and inner tubes full of screaming kids.

"Crowded," Margot observed, searching the shoreline for resorts and hotels. But she could find only small clusters of cabins here and there along those oddly shaped bays.

"Nah, this is nothin'," he said. "You should have seen it a few years ago, when the tourists were really flockin' in. This is the dregs. It's drivin' Uncle Bob just about nuts. Him and the town council, they're pullin' out what little hair they've got left trying to figure out how to get them back."

"Why? Where did they go?"

"Here we are." Duffy ignored the question and nodded his head toward two stone columns that seemed to pop up from out of nowhere. The neatly masoned columns, each with *McCREADY* carved into the rock in bold letters, flanked a gravel drive nearly hidden by the thick trees.

"The old family compound," Duffy said, steering the truck over bumps and craters in the drive as if they were nothing. Meanwhile, Margot bounced her head off the passenger-side window hard enough to make her teeth rattle. "McCreadys first cleared it as a homestead back in the 1840s. Barely held on to it over the years, to be honest. Turns out we're good at fishing and burying people—we are not great at farming. It wasn't lakefront back then, mind you. We were lucky that the water stopped short of the houses when they dammed up the river in the fifties to make the lake. A lot of people were 'encouraged' by the Corps of Engineers to move along.

It's made for what you might call a historically ingrained distrust of outsiders."

"Oh, good." The corners of Margot's mouth tilted up, but by the time she'd finished forming the expression, it was enough to make Duffy recoil.

"Hey, now, you're not an outsider. You're a McCready. Even if people in town don't know you, they're gonna know you. Know what I mean?"

Margot drew back against her seat. This was a mistake. She needed to tell Duffy to turn the truck around and take her right back to the airport because there was no way she could plan funerals and be some sort of minor redneck celebrity.

And she was about to tell him just that when they drove over another rut and she whacked her head against the window again. She opened her eyes just as they topped a rise in the gravel. The trees seemed to melt away to reveal a chain of log cabins grouped along the lakeshore, centering around one large two-story cabin. Each one seemed to have its own personality while sticking to the rustic aesthetic. There was just enough space between so the occupants would have some privacy but still be able to shout for help when the bands of roving rednecks inevitably raided the countryside. Each cabin had flower boxes blooming with yellow and purple Johnny-jump-ups and trailing fuchsias. The cabins had obviously spread out, with new ones added over time, from a huge log structure with a wraparound porch and three-eaved windows springing from the roof. Each was recently painted and neatly kept, except for a slightly dingy-looking yellow cottage with a peeling green shingle roof at the end of the road.

Duffy eased the truck past the main house and parked in front of an adorable specimen with a bright blue door. He reached behind the seat to pick up her suitcase, but she opened the back door and grabbed it. "I've got it, thank you."

"You have trust issues in relation to your luggage, huh?" Duffy observed.

"I don't mean any offense," she told him. "I just . . . This is so sad, but I don't have much left in the world. I sold a lot of my things before the move."

Duffy grinned. "Well, this place is all yours. It's one of the newer additions, used to be my sister's until she and Carl got married."

He opened the cabin door and ushered her through. The cabin was basically an overgrown dollhouse, like one of those trendy tiny homes without the pretentious storage solutions. There was one room divided into kitchen and living space, with one bedroom off to the left. A folding privacy screen, painted like the green mountains surrounding the lake, separated the bathroom from the bedroom. Margot got a look at the fairly new soaking tub, with its handheld showerhead but no shower curtain. She suspected it had been chosen because it was the only thing that would fit into the tiny plumbing footprint. "That is going to be an adjustment."

At this point, she was just glad there was a functioning toilet. A few of the things she'd shipped here were already arranged around the cabin. Some of her clothes hung in the wardrobe.

Her Northwestern mugs were washed and ready on the counter of the kitchenette.

"Tootie put the linens and towels out for ya. You should be all set." Duffy backed toward the door. "Well, I'll leave you to your unpacking. Get plenty of sleep tonight. You'll start your training first thing tomorrow. No worries. Bob's real patient. Hardly ever gets ruffled, not even when both of Curtis Taggerty's wives showed up to make his arrangements."

"Ex-wife versus current wife drama?" Margot asked with a yawn.

"No, they were both his current wives," Duffy said, shaking his head. "They just didn't know it."

"I would give that the reaction it deserves if I wasn't so tired," Margot said as she hung her suit bag in the tiny closet. Some- how, leaving a few things in her suitcase helped her feel like this wasn't a long-term situation, like she could throw her stuff in her bag at any time and use her open-ended ticket back to Chicago. "Also, I've meant to ask: what grown adult woman allows people to call her 'Tootie'?"

Duffy snorted, his big blue eyes twinkling. "Her real name is Eloise. When she was little, she took these tap-dancing lessons and that was one of the songs they learned the basics to. 'A tootie-tah, a tootie-tah, a tootie-tah-tah.' And she would just drive her whole family nuts, tapping up and down the hallway, up and down the stairs, up and down the sidewalk. 'A tootie-tah, a tootie- tah, a tootie-tah-tah.' They started calling her 'Tootie' to try to tease her out of it. But she's so stubborn, the name-calling just made her do it more. And eventually the name just stuck. Heck, we don't even call her 'grandma.' She's always been Tootie."

"Well, when your name is Tootie, what other qualifiers do you need?"

"That about covers it," Duffy said. "The spare key's on your nightstand there. And if you hear something that sounds like two rocks being banged together, don't panic. It's mostly harmless, just . . . don't go outside on your own. Really, it would be better if you just waited for one of us to come get you in the morning."

"Okay," Margot said, flopping down onto the mattress, making the springs squeal. The sheets smelled freshly laundered, that airy clean scent that came only from drying on a line in the sun. She'd smelled it once that she could remember, when her mother's Whirlpool dryer broke down and the appliance store took two whole days to deliver an upgraded replacement. The blue-and-green quilt was handmade, she could tell from the irregularity of the fabrics and the stitching. And she tried not to be touched that these strangers had taken the time to make her bed with sun-bleached sheets and an heirloom coverlet, but she was.

Her great-aunt had put a much-loved quilt on her bed, but her father hadn't even bothered to pick her up at the airport. That helped squelch the warm fuzzy feeling spreading across her chest. He didn't want to see her. After all this time, when he finally had the chance, he still didn't want to see her. Why did that hurt so much? She was a grown woman. She didn't need her "real" daddy to hug her and kiss her boo-boos. So why did the rejection leave an acidic burn that made her rub the heel of her hand against her sternum in the search for a deep breath?

Eyes watering with exhaustion and unshed tears, Margot buried her face into her pillow and inhaled the spring-fresh smell of linens dried in the sun.

Until her head popped up from the pillow. "Duffy! What do you mean 'mostly harmless?' . . . Duffy!"

***

Sweet Tea and Sympathy is available for purchase in stores everywhere.

AIN'T SHE A PEACH EXCERPT

Chapter 1

FRANKIE McCREADY CAREFULLY dusted Maybelline blush in Light Rose on the curve of Eula Buckinerny's cheek.

"Now, Miss Eula, I know you've never been one for makeup.

You've always been blessed with such a nice complexion, you've never needed it," Frankie murmured over the strains of the Mount Olive Gospel Singers' rendition of "How Great Thou Art." She liked to play her customers' favorite music in the background while she made them up, so they would feel at home. "But every now and again, a girl needs some help from a good foundation and blush.

"Do ya think I wake up every morning with this fabulous Elizabeth Taylor lash already in place?" Frankie gestured to her own carefully framed violet-blue eyes. "No, this is the result of a steady hand and some indecently expensive mascara that I splurge on every six months. But don't tell my mama. You know her. She gets downright indignant at the idea of spendin' more than ten dollars on anything you're just going to wash off your face every night."

Frankie studied her makeup kit and chose a lip color that, while just a bit pinker than beige, was still more risqué than anything Miss Eula had ever worn, even at the annual Sackett County Homemaker Society Awards Dinner. She painted a thin, careful coat across Eula's lips. "This will be our little secret."

Frankie dipped a smaller brush in a dark brown contouring powder called Hot Chocolate that would give Eula's features shadow and dimension. After a few strokes, Frankie leaned back and admired her handiwork.

"There. You look beautiful. And I really think that lipstick pops with your pretty pink suit. Trudy Darnell will spend the month trying to figure out how ya managed to go out looking better than her, even in your casket."

Smiling down at Eula one last time, Frankie bowed her head in a solemn gesture of farewell. She closed the frosted pink casket lid just as a loud knock sounded on the mortuary room door. "Frankie! Is it all clear?"

"Sure, Margot, I'm all finished up with Miss Eula." Frankie's cousin stuck her blond head through the door.

Margot Cary was just as sleek and polished as she'd been the day she stepped off the plane from Chicago a few months ago to take what was supposed to be a temporary job at the McCready Family Funeral Home and Bait Shop. And while her slick designer suits were still very much out of place in semirural Georgia, Frankie and the rest of the McCreadys were working like ants on a discarded Blow Pop to make her feel like part of the family.

"You comin' in?" Frankie asked. "Nope."

Frankie snorted. Her cousin took no crap from the local PTA-based social terrorists, but she was still pretty creeped out by the concept of embalming. Frankie tried not to judge. After all, she was creeped out by the concept of gluten-free cupcakes and juice cleanses.

"Sheriff Linden is here for you, Frankie," Margot said, training her eyes on a spot over Frankie's shoulder, away from the form of Benjoe Watts, lying under a pristine white sheet on table two. "They're bringing in Bobby Wayne Patterson."

"Oh, that's a shame." Frankie sighed, frowning deeply. "Yeah, my dad said that y'all—you all had been expecting this one for a while," Margot said, clearing her throat.

Frankie's momentary sadness over Bobby Wayne gave way to warm internal fuzziness over her cousin's casual use of *my dad*, something that wouldn't have happened just a few weeks before. After a lifetime of separation from the whole family, Margot wasn't quite ready to call Stan McCready "Daddy." But the two were able to stay in the same room and make pleasant conversation on a regular basis, which was a considerable improvement over when Margot had arrived.

Also, Margot had started to say "y'all," which made Frankie perversely proud.

"Could you tell *my* dad that Miss Eula's coming up on the elevator?" Frankie asked. "All prettied up and ready for her party."

"Will do," Margot said, the corners of her slick coral lips lifting.

"Your mom left your lunch in my office and said to remind you that you have to eat at some point. I believe the exact phrase she used was 'No excuses or I'll give her a whooping, just like when she was little.' "

"She's all talk. I never got whoopin's."

"I'd still eat the freaking sandwich, if I were you," Margot told her. "Your mother is a culinary genius, and bacon is her medium of artistic expression."

"Yeah, yeah," Frankie said, rolling the closed pink casket toward the elevator that led to the west chapel. She called after Margot, who was already halfway up the stairs to the funeral home proper. "Remind Daddy that Miss Eula ordered a full spray of white roses! She wanted them in place for her visitation. And she wanted to make sure Trudy Darnell saw them. She actually wrote it in her preplanned funeral paper- work: 'Make sure Trudy Darnell sees me covered in white roses.' They had a long-standin' feud over some pie-related incident at the 1964 county fair."

"The roses are already here. I'll place them myself," Margot promised from the stairwell. "Also, for the record, I did not expect the old church ladies to be *this* cutthroat. It's like *Game of Thrones* with less nudity and more denture cream."

"Just be grateful for the 'less nudity,' " Frankie yelled. "Trust me when I say that I am."

Frankie snickered and then heard Margot say, "She's ready to see you, Sheriff," before click-clacking her way up the stairs on her scary ice-pick heels. Frankie had no idea how Margot walked in those things, much less did stairs.

Frankie turned to see a tall man in a dark green Sackett County Sheriff 's Department uniform duck through the door. She kept her lip from curling in disdain, but it was a near thing. "Sheriff."

Blessed with a thick head of dark-blond hair and eyes the color of new moss, Eric Linden wasn't handsome in the classical sense. Frankie knew enough about bone structure to see that his sharp cheekbones and slightly crooked Roman nose didn't quite coordinate with his high forehead and square chin. His lips were oddly full and opened over white, but certainly not orthodontia-perfect, teeth. His top canines in particular were slightly off-kilter, which shouldn't have been charming but somehow was.

And damn, did that man know how to fill out a uniform. The fit of Eric's shirt alone was enough to make Frankie more than a little self-conscious. She liked to think that her sense of style made up for her own pale, under-toned physique. For instance, today's ensemble of a black tunic over tights printed with galaxies and comets lent her a certain air of quirky elegance. It would help her self-esteem considerably if she didn't turn to lady jelly in a lab coat every time she made eye contact with those big green eyes of his, while he seemed to remain unaffected. He was supposed to have been a fun highlight to an outstanding "self-care" weekend—a highlight she would never have to see again. But here she was, enduring regular awkward interactions with a guy who seemed to think she was some heartless sex marauder, all because she hadn't stuck around for postcoital pancakes a few weeks before.

"Ms. McCready," he drawled, his eyes catching on Mr. Watts. He seemed to blanch, and his speech faltered for a second. "I—Y —Your cousin was supposed to tell you Bobby Wayne Patterson is coming in. I think it's a possible homicide. Since you're the county coroner, I need you to give him the full workup before I can send him along to the state crime lab."

Jesus Herbert Christ. Not this again.

Eric Linden seemed to think that anybody who didn't die in intensive care surrounded by a circle of great-great-grandchildren was the victim of foul play. This was the second body he'd brought in as a "possible homicide" in the couple of weeks since he had taken over for the recently retired Sheriff Rainey. The first was Len Huffman, a poor tourist from Ohio who'd had no idea how to operate a fishing boat near a dam and ended up drowning. Sheriff

Linden had insisted the boater's pretty and much younger wife had something to do with his untimely demise and refused to release the body to the family until he had evidence. While Frankie could see the motive in a woman forced to spend her precious vacation driving to Georgia for fishing, ultimately overconfidence and poor boatsmanship were the only killers in this case. It took Frankie's autopsy report, a statement from the bass boat's manufacturer, and affidavits from the man's sons regarding his poor swimming skills to convince Sheriff Linden.

Her relationship with Eric had suffered several episodes of tragic dickheadery in the short time she'd known him. What had been a very pleasant encounter that they'd both enjoyed—several times—on one of Frankie's lost weekends in Atlanta was ruined when Eric was introduced to her as Lake Sackett's new sheriff. Eric did not appreciate Frankie's no-nonsense approach to anonymous short-term relationships and was not pleased to find he'd moved to her hometown. He'd proceeded to act like an asshat every time their jobs brought them together. He'd managed to make her feel unattractive, unprofessional, and unwanted without really trying. And when she'd thought they'd finally reached some sort of under-standing after resolving Len Huffman's case, he'd stomped all over it by accusing her of securing her evidence by inappropriately using her connections and natural charms.

Frankie considered herself a nice person, but she would dearly love to see Eric ugly-cry.

The buzzer by the back bay rang, letting Frankie know that a "delivery" was coming into her mortuary. She crossed the gray-tiled room and punched in the key code to electronically open the double doors. Naomi Daniels, the local day-shift paramedic, wheeled a gurney through the sunlit doorway. Poor Bobby Wayne was safely tucked inside a standard-issue black body bag. Frankie's heart ached for his long-suffering mama.

"Hey, Naomi," Frankie said, a note of finality in her voice, as if she'd been expecting this delivery.

"Hi, Frankie." Naomi's voice was resigned as she handed over the clipboard. Her messy brown hair hung limp around her cherubic face as she bent over the body. "Unresponsive at the scene. No breath, no pulse, cold to the touch. Pretty sure the cause of death is that big ol' missing spot in the back of his head, but you'd know better than me."

"Who found him?" Frankie asked, taking the state paperwork that assigned her official stewardship of the body.

"The Clay boys. Poor things skipped school to squirrel hunt and found a dead body for their trouble."

"Well, they'll never play hooky again," Frankie muttered. She checked over the paperwork one last time before signing and handing it back to Naomi. The paramedic used her considerable upper-body strength to transfer the body bag onto Frankie's central treatment table. Frankie noted that the sheriff hadn't even offered to help her.

"No, they will not," Naomi said, shaking her head. "Little Brody Clay threw up so much I thought I was going to have to drop him off at the ER before I brought Bobby Wayne in." Frankie grimaced. "Sheriff, this sort of thing can be pretty traumatic. You might make sure the boys get referred to the county's mental health services for follow-up counseling. You'll have to talk their daddy into it, because Allan Clay doesn't buy into that sort of thing."

"Already done," the sheriff said, his square jaw stiff. "I know my job."

Frankie pressed her poppy-bright mouth into a thin line, exhaled through her nose, and counted to eight. He didn't deserve ten.

Naomi saw the grim set of Frankie's normally cheerful mouth

and took a step back. "Okay, then. I'm going to head out. Sheriff, you have my statement. If you need anything else, let me know."

Sheriff Linden offered her a curt nod and Naomi carefully wheeled her gurney out into the sunlight. As she closed the double doors behind her, she mouthed the words *good luck* at Frankie.

Frankie took the necessary report forms out of the filing cabinet by her desk. The little Funko Pop! versions of the Avengers, plus half the Lannister family, standing sentinel over her desktop monitor didn't cheer her up like they normally did. She wanted Eric Linden and his big-city cop attitude out of her work-space, yesterday. He was a condescending ass in a town that had already met its condescending-ass quota. They didn't need to go importing them from Atlanta.

Frankie cleared her throat and turned carefully on thick-soled sneakers printed in cosmic blues, pinks, and purples. She thought they were a nice complement to the purple and blue streaks in her hair. "Can you explain to me why you think that Mr. Patterson's death is a homicide?"

The sheriff cleared his throat and several beads of sweat appeared on his brow. "If you would open the body bag, I'll show you."

Frankie shook her head. "After the deceased come through my doors, I don't like to let other people see them until I've prettied them up for their services. It's a little more dignified."

Eric frowned at her. "Do you understand how police investigations work? This isn't optional. I'm the sheriff. You're the coroner. I don't want to use the phrase 'chain of command,' because it's too damn early and I've spent my morning up to my ass cheeks in chiggers. So please, just open the damn bag."

"I might, if you would explain to me how you could possibly think this is a homicide investigation."

"The gunshot wound to the head doesn't seem suspicious to you?" he drawled.

"Not when you consider that Bobby Wayne Patterson drank *at least* a twelve-pack of Bud Light every day and he was an avid hunter who built his own deer stand about twenty years ago. Also while drunk. And he called the safety on firearms 'the sissy button.' So no, when I add all of those factors up . . . I'm not seein' homicide."

"Just because the man had a reputation as a drunk doesn't mean he couldn't have met with foul play!" the sheriff exclaimed. Frankie noticed that he'd gone oddly pale. "Every case deserves our full attention."

"I absolutely agree. But how many times have you pulled Bobby Wayne over for DUI in the weeks you've worked here?"

Sheriff Linden grimaced, which was answer enough for Frankie. He fumed, "So you're just going to sign off on it as an accident without even looking into it? Is that how you normally handle things around here, Ms. McCready?"

"No, I'm going to do my due diligence, just like I do with each and every body that comes through my doors. But I'm not going to waste the county's limited budget on expensive, unnecessary tests when we need to save it just in case there's an actual murder in our town . . . for the first time in more than twenty years."

Sheriff Linden glowered at her with those icy green eyes of his and she rolled her own in response. "Okay, do you have pictures of the scene?"

The sheriff took a mini tablet out of an oversize pocket in his cargo pants, tapped in an access code, and handed it to her without looking at the screen. She scrolled through the photos of the body, the deer stand, and the ground surrounding the scene, until she found one that featured the dry-rotted wooden steps Bobby Wayne had nailed into the broad oak tree when he was in high school. Frankie noted that the fifth step up was broken and dangling from the trunk by a loosened nail.

"That broken step's, what, eight feet off of the ground?" she said, manipulating the screen to zoom in on the step. Sheriff Linden frowned at the screen and nodded. Frankie snapped on a pair of sterile exam gloves.

"Excuse me, Bobby Wayne," she said in a polite but brisk tone. "I just need to take a quick look."

"You talk to the dead bodies?" Eric asked.

"I was raised well. Just because they're not breathin' doesn't mean I shouldn't be polite," she shot back as she opened the body bag and gently extended Bobby Wayne's hand. The sheriff took a rather large step back and she showed him the dark brown material packed under Bobby Wayne's ragged fingernails. "And this looks like tree bark, doesn't it? And those stains on his sleeves?" Frankie sniffed delicately at the green camo jacket. "Smell a lot like beer."

The sheriff nodded, his lips going the color of day-old oatmeal. "McCready, don't *sniff* the body. I gotta draw a line somewhere."

"From that height, given the scratches on the tree trunk and the bark under his nails, and what looks like a Bud Light can at the base of the tree, I think it's pretty safe to say that Bobby Wayne was trying to climb into his rickety old deer stand while holdin' a beer, because I'm pretty sure Bobby Wayne was born holdin' a beer. The step gave way under his foot, he dropped the beer, tried to keep hold of the trunk, but fell onto his back, with his rifle barrel right under the base of his skull, and the rifle went off. It's a terrible tragedy, but these things happen. Haven't you ever heard of the Darwin Awards?"

Sheriff Linden shook his head. "How would that even happen?"

Frankie took the sheriff's tablet and opened the photos from the crime scene. She noted the way he instinctually turned his eyes away from the images. She tapped the screen. "Bobby Wayne always used his granddaddy's rifle. He thought it was good luck."

"Okay."

"Well, modern firearms have that firing pin block thing that prevents a gun from firing accidentally if it's dropped."

"I'm familiar with the concept."

"Bobby Wayne's granddaddy's rifle didn't have that. So . . . not good luck after all." When he shot her a disappointed look, she added, "But just to make you feel better, I'll run tests on the back of Bobby Wayne's jacket to show the patterns of gunshot residue and determine how the rifle was situated against his back when it was fired. And I'll send the bullet to the state lab for comparison to his rifle."

"You can run GSR tests here?" Sheriff Linden asked, eyeing her workspace.

"As I've told you before, Sheriff, this is technically the county morgue. There's no major hospital for fifty miles. I've been the county coroner since my uncle, the last coroner, died. I know what I'm doin'."

"You ran unopposed," Sheriff Linden shot back, a tiny bit of color returning to his cheeks.

"No one else wanted the job," she told him. "Because people around here enjoyed dealin' with Sheriff Rainey about as much as I like dealing with you."

"Well, that's hurtful." He placed his hand over his heart. For the first time since he'd entered the basement, Sheriff Linden offered a hint of a smile and she saw a glimpse of that charming, adventurous soul she'd spent quality naked time with all those nights ago.

"I'm not tryin' to be hurtful. Just honest." Frankie carefully tucked Bobby Wayne's arm back in the bag and zipped it. The sheriff took a deep breath and his shoulders relaxed. Frankie rounded the table and he took several steps back toward Mr. Watts's table.

"I get that you're used to murders by the hour, but you're going to have to pump your brakes just a little bit. This is Lake Sackett.

Not every non-natural death is going to be suspicious. Sometimes alcohol and outdoor sports are going to combine in awful, permanent ways."

"Look, I'm an interim sheriff. I took the job knowing I would only have it until the special election in November. That doesn't make it any less demoralizing to campaign for the job I have. And difficult, since, as you like to point out at every possible opportunity, I'm an outsider. I have to make a good impression with voters or there's no hope of me getting elected." He pinned her with those frank, incredibly dilated green eyes. "Besides, I saw what happened to the last sheriff. I would like to retire without the words 'gross incompetence' written on my cake."

"Well, don't let your evidence room become a hoarder nightmare and you'll already be way ahead of Sheriff Rainey."

Eric wiped at his sweaty brow. "So, what, you're saying I should relax? Take up a hobby?"

Frankie opened a mini-fridge she kept near her desk and handed him a bottle of water. "No, I'm sayin' you're going to burn yourself out if you're not careful. And you're going to become the 'boy who cries murder,' which will make people laugh at you when you walk into the Rise and Shine. They'll pretend it's something else, but it will be you. Not to mention, it doesn't look great to the tourist trade if every hunting accident and drowning is investigated as the possible work of a serial killer."

The sheriff sagged against the autopsy table behind him. "You're right. But for the record, I want to do a good job, not just 'cause I want to be elected, but for my own reasons. I *have* to do well here."

"Um, I really appreciate this new level of emotional openness between us, but maybe you shouldn't touch Mr. Watts like that," Frankie said, timidly gesturing to the table he was leaning on.

The sheriff turned, saw the covered body on the table, and stumbled away, dragging the sheet with him in his haste. The barest hint of Benjoe Watts's gray hair became visible. And then Eric Linden did the last thing Frankie would have expected.

His eyes rolled up like window shades and he fainted dead away on the tile floor.

Chapter 2

ERIC WOKE UP with a cold cloth on his forehead and Frankie's hand waving a broken smelling salts capsule under his nose.

Inhaling sharply at the harsh ammonia scent, he blinked at her a few times and a dreamy smile parted his lips. And then his brows drew down hard over his eyes.

"I'm on an embalming table, aren't I?"

Frankie nodded, her purple-and blue-streaked ponytail bobbing over her ear in a jaunty fashion that seemed obscenely out of place. Eric yelped and launched himself off the slab. His boots skidded on the tile and he landed in a heap on the floor.

Despite her general lack of damns about Eric, she understood a good panic faint. She'd had them off and on for years—usually while she was waiting on test results from her physicals or felt some pain that didn't feel normal for a woman in her mid-twenties. On the rare occasion when she'd done it in front of her parents, she'd played it off as low blood sugar and long hours. Still, waking up on the floor, not knowing how you'd gotten there and how long you'd been there, was scary and humiliating. She was willing to cease hostilities until Eric was on his feet. A battle of wits was no fun with the unarmed.

"I wanted you to be more comfortable while I worked. Besides, I could hardly lift your heavy butt all the way over to the elevator," she huffed. "I only got you this far because the table lowers all the way to the floor."

"The table . . . where you embalm people."

"Oh, calm down, it's disinfected at least three times a day," she said, slapping his bottle of water into his hand. "So, you've got an aversion to dead bodies. A way-more-serious-than-the-average-person's aversion. I should have noticed before, at the Huffman drowning site, when you refused to make eye contact with, well, anybody. But I thought you were just being a jerk."

"It's a long story. I don't want to talk about it," he snapped. Frankie raised her hands in a defensive pose. "Fine. I did GSR tests on the back of Bobby Wayne's jacket while you were 'nappin'.' " She made sarcastic air-quote fingers. "In my professional opinion, the pattern looks pretty consistent with someone who was lying on top of a rifle when it fired, but I'm sure you'll want to send it along to the state lab to confirm." He cocked his head to the side and his eyes narrowed.

"You let me stay unconscious on an embalming table while you ran forensic tests?"

"It was only a few minutes. And I wanted to wake you up with good news," she said with a cheeky grin. "Well, that's not true, I wanted to wake you up with the news that I was right and you were wrong. But it's basically the same thing."

"What the—what?" he spluttered.

She placed a large evidence envelope in his hands. "Bobby Wayne's jacket. Scrapings from under his fingernails. I'll send you the blood alcohol content results, plus photos of the wound and the bullet as soon as I remove it."

"There is something very wrong with you."

"You're not the first one to say so," she said cheerfully, though his words stung a bit, even in his low honeyed-whiskey tones. "But gettin' back to the subject we were discussin' before you took your little floor nap, yes, I do think you need to relax a little bit and take up a hobby. Preferably one that gets you out of the house and into the community, so people see you as an actual person with feelings, instead of a cyborg sent from the future to accuse innocent people of murder."

"Let me guess, you're going to recommend I take up fishin'?"

"What's wrong with fishin'?"

"It's just a little self-interested to recommend I take up fishin' when your family runs the local bait shop."

"You aren't one of those outdoor superstore guys, are you?"

"No, I'm just not that into fishing," he said, shrugging. Frankie scoffed.

"I wouldn't tell anyone here that."

"I told you I'll get a handle on it. A little trust wouldn't hurt this uncomfortable workin' dynamic we have going."

"Okay, fine," she said. "I'll stop expressing concern for your wellbeing."

"Can you tell me where Margot's office is?" he asked. "I'm supposed to give her some reports about emergencies and incidents at the Founders' Festival. I tried telling her there were none, but she said she wants me to fill out a form and give some sort of sworn blood oath for a report to the county commissioners."

Frankie frowned at the tone of . . . intrigue in Eric's voice. She swallowed thickly. She'd given this guy some of the best . . . hours . . . of her life, and he wanted her to draw him a map to Margot's office? She'd never envied Margot her polished good looks, the always-smooth blond hair and the kind of skin that came only from good genes and fancy spas. But now, seeing her former hookup showing interest in her cousin, Frankie kind of wanted to shave Margot's head. She would feel bad afterward and apologize, but still, she wanted to do it.

This was a bad sign, in terms of her character. Nice Southern women didn't turn on family members when a handsome-but-judgmental law enforcement officer showed interest in them.

And what was Eric thinking, showing that much interest in her cousin? Surely he had to know that Margot and the local elementary school principal, Kyle Archer, were Facebook-official. Then again, being an outsider with no family in the area, he was cut off from most of the traditional channels for "local news"—the kitchen table, the beauty parlor, the church parking lot.

Oh, what did she even care? She didn't have any claim on Eric Linden. She didn't think she even *wanted* a claim. She just didn't want him looking like Christmas had come early when he thought about spending time in Margot's office. Because of reasons. That had nothing to do with Eric's face. His stupid, beautiful face.

"Just up the stairs. And she was only kidding about the blood oath," Frankie said, rolling her eyes. As soon as Eric relaxed just the tiniest bit, she added, "She'll accept tears."

Eric's mouth dropped open, making Frankie laugh as she turned to Mr. Watts. When she heard Eric move toward the stairs, she called over her shoulder, "Sheriff?"

His boots scraped against the floor as he stopped.

"The dead, they aren't scary. Even if they were scary in life, they're not any particular way in death. Not angry, not sad, not happy. They're nothin' at all. They're not there," she said.

"And yet you talk to them."

She turned and smiled at him. "Just because they're dead is no reason to be rude."

She told herself the little shudder in Eric's shoulders was due to the air-conditioning.

***

Ain't She a Peach is available for purchase in stores everywhere.

GIMME SOME SUGAR EXCERPT

Praise for the Southern Eclectic Series

"Packed with countless laughs and heartfelt moments....This romance is classic Harper, oozing snark and Southern charm in every scene." *(Publishers Weekly on Gimme Some Sugar)*

Selected for Target Recommends Book Club Pick in April

Chapter 1

NICE SOUTHERN GIRLS did not make money baking penis cakes.

Lucy Bowman Garten was going to hell on a road paved with devil's food and peach-toned buttercream.

Technically, she wasn't even supposed to be working in her bake shop, which would eventually be called Gimme Some Sugar, as it wasn't officially open. Hell, she'd only leased the defunct

Hardison's Meat Shop two months ago, before she'd even arrived back in town. And she'd had to do that under a limited liability company so her mother-in-law wouldn't find a way to interfere with the rental agreement. Evie Garten had a surprising number of friends around town, despite the fact that she was ten pounds of mean in a five-pound sack.

While the kitchen was cleaned and ready and could easily pass a health inspector's perusal—if the mealy-mouthed, liver-spotted bastard would ever show up for his damn appointments—the displays were still fitted for the enormous hunks of pork the former meat shop used to sell, and the "café area" looked like a hoarder intervention waiting to happen. Also, as a minor point, Lucy's business license was still mired in the initial hoops set up by Sackett County's small but byzantine government. So Lucy was doing this somewhat inadvisable job for a high school friend so far under the table she was practically subterranean. She wasn't even being paid—Maddie's fiancé was going to do some plumbing work for her in return for her obscene baking skills.

The next time she got a text message that started with *So, I'm hosting a bachelorette party* . . . she was going to respond with *Do I know you?*

Lucy finished the very last swirl on the royal icing *E* and stood back to survey her work—an eighteen-inch penis lying flat across a silver-foiled cake board, with eat me written across its testicles in hot pink.

She would not be taking pictures of this for her shop's website.

Lucy did not understand the compulsion to eat phallic baked goods for a girl's last hurrah before marriage. She re- membered how hopeful and excited she'd been before she'd married Wayne. She'd wanted to start her married life as soon as possible. She'd thought, *I can't wait to spend the rest of my days with the man I love.* She hadn't thought, *I better eat all of the buttercream-frosted appendage I can because I might not have the chance again.*

Then again, she'd been a hopeful, excited idiot before she married Wayne, so what the hell did she know?

She blew out a long sigh and said, "Well, it's grotesquely enormous and painstakingly detailed. And baking it has been the most action I've seen in years . . . so it's perfect."

Wiping her hands on her purple doughnut-themed apron, Lucy crossed to her carefully organized supplies and selected a large, unmarked sheet cake box—which, unfortunately for Lucy, had a little cellophane display window on top. She wasn't eager to show this cake off, but it was the only box large enough to accommodate it.

Once the cake was secured, she put a Braves cap over her coppery auburn curls and carried it out the front door, carefully propping it against the half-collapsed wooden flower box in front of the shop while she struggled to fit the key in the door's original and extremely tricky lock.

As usual, Main Street was bustling with midafternoon traffic: people driving home from work, ferrying their kids from school to baseball practice, the usual. She saw a couple of nearby shop owners out on the sidewalk, cleaning windows and hanging up flower baskets. February in Lake Sackett always felt like holding one's breath, the last few weeks of quiet before the tourists descended on the town's beautiful waterfront. At least, it had been that way when Lucy had been growing up—locals handed the town off to the tourists with smiles on their faces, happy to get their much-needed cash. However, it was always a relief when those same tourists cleared out in September.

After she and Wayne moved away for school, "mistakes were made" at the Sackett Dam and the Army Corps of Engineers released ten times the amount of water meant to be drained from Lake Sackett, right at the beginning of what became an ex- tended drought. Lake levels dropped to an all-time low. Tourists didn't want to risk their boats on a diminished, sad lake where they could potentially run aground in areas that used to be safe. That meant less money coming into the businesses, which meant less capital for those businesses to make improvements, which meant dilapidated motels and shops that fewer tourists were eager to spend their time at—and on and on the cycle went. Little extras like discounts and free samples were the first thing to go, followed by friendly smiles and easy conversations. Her dad said that tourists sensed this anxious energy and booked their weekends in areas that didn't seem quite so edgy.

The town's economy had stalled to the point where Wayne claimed that visiting their families was becoming "too depressing." Wayne didn't want to see their hometown all run-down and empty, like something out of a bad horror movie. He said he wanted to remember it as it was.

Well, he was never that eager to visit Lake Sackett in the first place, but nostalgic sentimentality had been a convenient excuse. If her dad wanted to spend Christmas with them, Wayne had said, he could come to Texas and visit. Lord knew his own parents had accepted enough airline tickets on Wayne's dime.

Lucy shook her head. Thinking about her daddy, or Wayne's mama, for that matter, was not going to improve her already tense mood. So Lucy would focus on the positive. Thanks to some very concentrated effort by the recently established Lake Sackett Tourism Board, tourism to the town's hotels, rentals, restaurants, and quaint little shops was slowly coming back to the numbers enjoyed before the water dump sent the town into a tailspin. Lucy was building a business in a town on the rise, no matter who thought she was a "damn fool" to do it.

"Would you just *lock*, you sonofabitch?" she hissed, jangling her keys as she struggled to get the lock to tumble. She leaned her ball-capped forehead against the glass of the door, glad that her four-year-old wasn't around to hear her using foul language. The little sponge would probably repeat it at some terribly awkward moment, like in front of the local Baptist minister.

"Hey, let me help you with that!"

She turned . . . and screamed internally to see Duffy McCready jogging down the sidewalk of Main Street.

Duffy had been her very best friend in elementary school. She'd neglected friendships with the girls in their grade so she could play trucks in the sandbox with Duffy. She shared the Goo Goo Clusters in her lunchbox with him and only him. And in high school, well, she'd harbored a secret crush on him that reduced her to some very embarrassing diary entries, not to mention late-night-call impulses that made adult Lucy very grateful Pete Bowman had never allowed his teenage daughter a cell phone. Duffy had been one of her favorite people on the planet for years and she was so glad to recon-nect with him after their years-long separation. But Holy Lord, right now, she wanted him to either go away or go blind.

Temporarily.

She wasn't evil or anything.

With the ladies-who-lunch crowd back in Texas, this was the sort of thing she would brazen her way through—smile, laugh it off, pretend it was a big joke. But this was Duffy McCready, her Lake Sackett Achilles' heel.

Duffy moved to take the keys from her while Lucy tried to angle the box out of his line of sight. This brought her closer to Duffy's tall frame as he hovered over her to work the lock. Between the warmth radiating off of his body and the smell of leather and cinnamon gum, Lucy had to brace herself against the brick to keep her knees from giving way.

Settle down, girls, she warned them. *That way lies madness and tears and a crazy ex-wife who tried to push you down the stairs in high school.*

Her knees argued that it had been a very long time since she'd been so close to a nice-smelling man. And Duffy was a reliable, emotionally stable sweetheart who wouldn't mind a sniff or two between friends. Her knees were a very bad influence.

Duffy grunted and managed to flip the key in the ancient lock. He turned to smile at her, his face only inches from hers. Her breath caught as she got her very first look at adult Duffy up close, and her knees were now giving her very bad ideas. Her childhood friend had turned into a hunk of something.

Long of limb, broad of shoulder, and possessed of *dear Lord, don't even get me started* blue eyes, what little baby fat Duffy'd had on his face had long since resolved into sharp cheekbones and a strong, square jaw. She stared at his mouth, somehow soft and inviting-looking even under that scruff of gingery beard. His brows drew together and his mouth opened as if he was going to say something. But his eyes cut toward the cake box, which had shifted during Lucy's knee failure.

Duffy frowned and tilted his head. "Is that a . . . ?" Lucy cringed, so very hard. Duffy had seen her penis.

She squeezed her eyes tight, even as she felt him move away from her. The blood rushed to her cheeks in a hot, humiliated wave. "Yes, yes, it is."

"Wha—Who—" Duffy's laugh burst out of him in a shocked bark. "*Why?*"

"I don't know!"

Duffy burst out laughing. Lucy's shoulders shook with her own giggles, despite the absolute mortification of Duffy knowing she'd spent the past few hours crafting edible genitalia from sugar and butter. "I honestly don't know. Maddie Paxton is having her bachelorette party and she insists she can't have a cake unless it's penis-shaped. I'm just glad I wasn't asked to order the penis gummy candy."

"Women are a mystery," Duffy said, shuddering as if he was

imagining those particular confections being consumed. "A beautiful, divine, horrifying mystery."

She sighed, moving toward her truck to put the cake in the passenger seat . . . far, far out of sight. "Yeah, I don't think this sort of thing counts toward the feminine mystique."

"If it makes you feel any better, it looks very realistic."

"No, that does *not* make me feel better." She shook her head and an enormous, blinding-white smile spread over his face, crinkling those big baby blues of his.

"So, welcome back to Lake Sackett," Duffy said, laughing, opening his arms in what could be construed as an invitation for a hug. She laughed and stepped toward him and he wrapped those long arms around her in an awkward embrace that didn't quite press their bodies together. A wave of disappointment swept through her, leaving her confused. Duffy was apparently one of those men—meaning pretty much all of them—who considered her a sexless nonentity now that she was a mother.

But that shouldn't affect her at all, right? Weak knees, lantern jaws, and full-body hugs had never been part of the equation for them in the first place, so why did she feel that keen sense of loss when Duffy kept his distance?

"So, what are you up to?" he said, frowning slightly as she shoved the truck door closed.

"I'm opening a bakery," she said, gesturing to the meat shop's windows.

"Really?" he said, the corners of his mouth lifting. "I thought you wanted to be a marketing guru. PR and crisis management, all that stuff? I always pictured you walking around in office buildings, barking orders while people handed you stuff to sign." Lucy laughed, thinking of her life back in Texas, which had mostly revolved around scheduling playdates for Sam and trying to find inventive new ways to hide Wayne's phone during dinner.

"Yeah, it was a real rat race."

"Well, I'm glad you got away from all that," he said. "So you're going to turn the meat shop into a bakery?"

"Sure. It's got the right wiring to support the new ovens, fridge, and cooler cases I've had installed, along with a new sink. And it's got loads of counter space for me to work with."

Lucy didn't mention the difficulty getting contractors who would work on the space on any sort of reasonable schedule, or how many she'd had walk off the job because they were distantly related to Evie or because Evie had sent Wayne's little brother, Davey, to harass them while they worked. She'd finally had to hire a crew out of Atlanta who didn't give a damn about local connections and made it clear they'd whoop Davey's ass if he kept coming around. Davey, who usually lost interest once someone his own size made it clear they would put up a fight, skulked away and the work was finally finished.

Instead, she said, "I've got all of the kitchen changes made, now I just have to finish prepping and painting the café area."

"You mean the place where people used to stand in line with deer carcasses waiting to have them processed?"

"It will be very bright paint," she told him. "People won't even recognize it."

"So are you gonna be doing wedding cakes and all that?"

"Sure, wedding cakes, birthday cakes, cupcakes, anything people will pay me to bake. It's something I started when my son, Sam, was a baby, making cakes for friends, just to relieve some stress, then doing birthday cakes for their kids as Sam got older. I got pretty good at it, took some classes and got some certifications, and now, here we are. I figured it would be a good way to make a living but have the flexibility to keep up with Sam."

"And you should be pretty popular. Ever since the Dunbars closed their bakery over Christmas, people have been getting all their bought cakes at the Food Carnival. From what I hear, they taste like freezer-burned feet."

"Which is great, because my slogan is going to be 'Doesn't taste like freezer-burned feet!' "

He barked out a laugh. "Well, you're the marketing guru," he said, nodding toward the storefront, where the former meat shop's faded weekly special signs and hanging meat hooks were still on display, like an art installation entitled *Failed Scary Commerce*. "Though the whole *Texas Chain Saw Massacre* theme, combined with the carb-based porno, might make me take that back."

Lucy spread her hands over her warm cheeks. "I will never do a bachelorette party favor for a friend. For anyone. Ever again."

"Good, I hear that's how bakers get reputations."

She laughed. She'd missed how easily Duffy could make her laugh. It was like his special talent in high school, taking everything in her life and making it seem like it wasn't so bad.

Because he's your friend, she told herself firmly. *Duffy is a friend, a good man who deserves a heck of a lot more than being dragged into your mess of a life right now or at any time.*

And suddenly Duffy wasn't laughing anymore. His ruddy cheeks went pale and he looked a bit sick. "Oh my Lord, I just realized, I haven't even said anything about Wayne. I just—I saw you and the penis cake and I just got so distracted."

"Oh, no," Lucy assured him. "It's okay."

"No, I was raised better than this," he said, stepping even farther away from her. "I was really sorry to hear about Wayne. That must have been awful for you. How are you holding up?"

She swallowed thickly. Right, awful. Because she'd only been a widow for six months. And she was supposedly in mourning.

Lucy had her share of regrets about Wayne. In high school, she'd thought he was one of the most interesting, ambitious people she'd ever met. He had a great sense of humor. He was charming and could be so thoughtful when it suited him. But eventually, the sense of humor became as sharp and biting as new vinegar. The charm was worn down by the grind of everyday life, and all the lead showed through the gold plating. She was left with a man who seemed like such a loving husband from the outside, a good ol' country boy who'd raised himself out of nothing to become a polished prince at Crenshaw and Associates Financial Management; but he couldn't see her as anything but a member of his "support team," a convenience, and occasionally, a source of embarrassment—certainly not as sophisticated as anyone they spent time with from his office.

Wayne had known she wasn't happy, toward the end; he just didn't understand why. He worked hard to provide for them. They lived in a beautiful home, took luxurious vacations, joined the best clubs. Sure, he had his dalliances with pretty much any female employee of Crenshaw and Associates, but that was par for the course for their circle. Hadn't the other company wives told her to expect as much? Hell, it wasn't exactly unheard of for men from Lake Sackett to stray, either. Besides, he didn't drink as much as his friends did, and he didn't spend *that* much money on his affairs. So why couldn't she at least be content with their life? And the worst part was that she couldn't make him understand, even when they'd gone two years without having sex because she wasn't about to expose herself to whatever he might have picked up from his "friends."

She didn't love him anymore. She wasn't sure she ever had, really, beyond the first wash of teenage hormones and blissfully stupid life-planning one did at eighteen. Wayne didn't see how sleeping with other women should affect his relationship with Lucy, an "evolved" opinion he'd neglected to share with her before they'd stood in front of a priest and promised to forsake all others. And while Wayne didn't see cheating as a reason to end the marriage, she wasn't about to let her actions teach Sam that those patterns were acceptable. She'd insisted on counseling, and Wayne had made a half-hearted effort. He hadn't stopped cheating, of course, but he had admitted that he should stop being so obvious about it. Then gravity had sort of ended the marriage for them, and sometimes she was at a loss as to how to feel about it.

"It's been difficult. But Sam and I are going to be okay. We're staying at my dad's place. Sam's raring to start kindergarten, but he'll settle for running the preschool like his own personal kingdom for now," she said with a snort.

Duffy's brows drew together again, noting her darker expression. "Yeah, Tootie said something about that. Is 'Mamaw Evie' still giving you a hard time about putting him in preschool instead of leaving him with her?"

Lucy rolled her dark brown eyes so hard she almost dislodged a contact lens. "No more than usual."

"It will get better," Duffy assured her. "Evie's just not used to anyone telling her no."

"Oh, she's used to it. She just refuses to hear it," she grumbled.

Duffy placed one of his enormous hands on her arm. "She's mourning. You all are. Wayne's death was a shock, and people lash out when they're grieving. They're scared, they're hurt. If anyone would know, I would."

Lucy nodded. Duffy had a unique understanding of grief. His family had owned the McCready Family Funeral Home and Bait Shop, the largest funeral home (and bait shop) in this end of Georgia, as far back as anyone could remember. While Duffy worked on the marina side of things, leading fishing tours and selling tackle, he'd seen enough funeral fistfights break out to recognize emotional wear and tear.

She'd hoped that moving with Sam back to Lake Sackett, living in her late father's home, would simplify their lives. In Dallas, she'd had "friends" that she lunched with and planned charity events with, but no one she could trust with even half of the personal details she'd mentioned in this single afternoon's conversation with Duffy. She'd hoped that things would get easier once she was in more familiar territory, with people she knew and cared about. Yes, most of her own family was gone, but she could swing a cat down Main Street and hit three people who had known her since birth. She wanted that for Sam, that permanence and familiarity, even if it did come at the cost of living near her in-laws, which was enough of a negative on her pro/con list that it had almost convinced her not to move back.

She pursed her lips and nodded. "I'm sure that's it."

"Well, if you need anything, just let me know."

Her traitorous knees could immediately name about ten things she needed, most of them requiring nudity and dim lighting. Very. Bad. Influence. Her brain scrambled for a much more appropriate and less naked answer.

"Um, actually, I need to get this cake over to Maddie. It's kind of warm out for February, and buttercream melts pretty easy. You can only imagine how much worse that thing looks when it's . . . melting."

Duffy shuddered at the image. "Yikes." "Maybe you could come by tomorrow?"

"Ah, can't, I've got a charter tomorrow. Bunch of guys from Clarksville, want to try their hand at crappie."

"Well, text me, and we'll work out a time."

Duffy scratched the back of his neck. "I don't have your number."

"Sorry," she said, her cheeks flushing pink.

Of course Duffy had no way to contact her, beyond the gossip grapevine. They'd emailed occasionally after she'd left, and stayed Facebook friends . . . until one day she'd checked her friends list and found that he wasn't on it anymore. She'd wanted to believe it was some sort of techno-error, that he couldn't possibly have unfriended her. But she'd never had the guts to contact him and ask if he'd meant to end their digital friendship, or even to try to refriend him. And now, realizing that he didn't even have her number? It made the distance between them stand in even sharper relief.

"Give me your phone," she said, holding out her hand. He slapped a very heavy chunk of plastic in her palm. "Sweet baby Jesus, can you call 1987 on this thing? Does it text or do I need to use Morse code?"

"Smartass," he grumbled, taking the phone back and opening his texting window. Or at least, he tried—it took him several seconds to think about it.

"I don't see a point in getting the fancy-schmancy models that can Google and scratch my back for me," he said. "It's not like I'm big on social media."

"Really?" she asked, her mouth going slightly dry. Was he really going to bring this up now? Just minutes after seeing her for the first time in years?

"Yeah, I quit Facebook years back," he said. "I just didn't see the point in it. Do I really need to know that the guy I used to sit next to in math class is 'drinking the weekend's first beer, hashtag-blessed?' And do I need to 'like' it?"

An old wound Lucy hadn't even realized was there closed just a little bit. He hadn't unfriended her; he'd walked away from the service entirely. Duffy hadn't intentionally cut her from his life. Life had just happened, as it had with so many of her old friends, and they'd lost touch. Sure, she'd thought her friendship with Duffy was different, that it would last until they were old and gray, living next door to each other and watching their great-grandkids wrestle in their backyards. If someone had told her as a teenager that they would be standing there on the sidewalk, virtual strangers, she would have laughed in their face. And maybe kicked them in the shin for good measure. But knowing that he hadn't deliberately pushed her away was welcome news.

"Probably not," she conceded. "But it's handy, when you move far from home. And when you're planning on opening a business."

"If this becomes the kind of place where people post pictures of their coffee instead of drinking it, I will boycott it," he warned her, though he was grinning. "Publicly. There may be dead fish involved."

"There's not much I can do about that," she told him. When Duffy's text function finally launched, she texted a message to her cell number. **This is Duffy.**

"You could bake ugly cupcakes that don't make for good pictures?" he suggested.

"That gets you on the Internet for other reasons," she said, pursing her lips. Duffy threw his head back and laughed.

"That's what I've been missing, that sense of humor," he told her.

"You're surrounded by women who have good senses of humor."

"Yeah, but they use them against me, which isn't as fun." She snorted. "I've missed you, Duffy."

A truck drove by and honked, a typical greeting in Lake Sackett, but she felt oddly awkward standing on the street, where anyone could see her, laughing and typing her number into his phone. It seemed like something a widow shouldn't be doing with an old high school friend just six months after her husband's funeral. Especially a widow who was hoping to open a business that depended on community goodwill in the off-season.

"I've missed you, too, Lucy. And the rest of my family will be descending on you soon enough. Be prepared for more gossip than your ears can stand."

She grinned. "I'm looking forward to it. I was so sorry to hear about your dad passing. I'm gonna miss having someone who's willing to eat my baking mistakes, no matter how misguided. Especially now that those mistakes will be on a commercial level."

Duffy smiled, the light in his eyes going just a bit sad. "Thank you. And he would have loved to see you open this place, no matter how many mistakes you bake. He always liked you, said you were a darling."

"Well, he was right, because I am a darling," Lucy said primly.

"With a penis cake in her truck," Duffy noted. "Come on, we'd just forgotten about the penis cake." Duffy shook his head. "Had we?"

"Oh, I'm already pretending it never happened," she told him. "Solid plan."

Chapter 2

DUFFY DROVE THROUGH town at a snail's pace. He was clearly getting too old for after-charter drinks with clients. He knew a greasy breakfast from the Rise and Shine would help his sorry condition, but he wasn't sure he had the energy to get out of his truck to buy it. So he crept along Main Street and prayed for Aunt Leslie's chewy coffee to work its dark magic.

He'd meant to get up much earlier to run to the post office and pick up the shipment of lures, but he'd overslept and ended up leaving his mother to open the bait shop on her own. Donna was not going to be a happy camper when he returned. Maybe he should stop and get a greasy breakfast for her, just to avoid the inevitable ass chewing.

If Lucy's bakery were already open, that would have solved his problem. Donna was a sucker for a cinnamon roll, with the rare exception of Ike's over at the Rise and Shine. She said they tasted like "frozen, prepackaged crap," which seemed impossible given that Ike prided himself on making everything from scratch. Donna swore Bud Dunbar made the only decent cinnamon rolls in town, but Dunbar's Bakery was the last of Lake Sackett's businesses to fall victim to the water dump. Well, the bakery had also fallen victim to the fact that Bud's son, Junior, was an idiot and Bud had serious doubts about letting him run a business that involved sharp objects and hot appliances. But the water dump hadn't helped.

Cousin Margot's Founders' Festival had reversed Lake Sackett's plummet into the outhouse. His uncle Stan's girl had spent years in the big city planning parties for fancy people, and she'd channeled all of that know-how into planning the Founders' Festival the previous fall, an event so aggressively quaint that it showed up on travel blogs and magazines all over the country as a "spot to watch." And then they'd had an especially rainy winter, which was slowly building the lake back to normal levels.

Despite running late, Duffy paused and pulled to the side of the street as a funeral procession rolled into view, a nicety that his grandpa E.J.J. had drilled into his head from childhood. As his uncle Stan drove past in the hearse, he pointed at Duffy and then pointed at his watch. Duffy nodded his head and gestured back for Stan to speed it up because it was Stan's slow-ass driving dragging the funeral procession in the first place.

The key to making McCready's work was keeping the marina side fun for the boaters while remaining respectful to the people who were grieving for a lost loved one. And the poor Burtons were grieving the death of their matriarch, Mama Winnie, to a decade-long battle with breast cancer. Winnie was one of those rare women who had spent her entire life getting her way, but being so loving and supportive of her family that they never minded her total control. Grandma Tootie had aspired to be just like her, but the McCreadys were a little tougher to wrangle than the Burtons.

At one point, he'd been distantly related to the Burtons through his marriage to Lana. Her mother, Wanda, was the daughter of a distant Burton cousin. But the Burtons had always been quick to assure Duffy that they had little to do with his wife or that branch of the family, even before he married Lana . . . which should have been a red flag, he supposed.

Duffy and Lana had been "nod in the hallway" friends for years, but never thought about dating until her friend Carletta Leehigh set them up for homecoming junior year. They just sort of fell into being a couple. Lana's high school friends had teased her for years about being the only one in their group without a steady boyfriend or a pre-engagement ring. And Lana was deathly afraid of being left behind.

Like a lot of couples in Lake Sackett, they'd gotten married right out of high school. She'd come to him while they were lining up for graduation in their royal blue caps and gowns, her eyes wide in panic because her period was late. She must have gotten knocked up on prom night, she'd told him, when they'd joined the rest of their class partying on Make-Out Island. On prom night, Duffy had been six beers in when Lana sidled up to him, and he hadn't quite built up the hops tolerance he had now. Earlier that night, he'd heard that Lucy was going to follow her sweetheart, Wayne, to Texas A&M that fall instead of going to Georgia State and staying close to home. His best friend in the world was leaving him for longhorns and a shithead. Consolation sex with his not-quite-girlfriend had sounded like the best idea Duffy's beer-soaked brain had ever heard.

So when Lana had come to him with tears in her eyes, Duffy had done the "right thing"—immediately after the graduation cere-mony, he'd dropped to one knee and proposed with his class ring. After his mother, Donna, stopped screaming at him, they arranged for the quickest quickie June wedding ever performed in Lake Sackett.

Tootie said that when everything involved in the ceremony is a rental, it should be considered an omen for a short-lived marriage. Why she felt the need to cross-stitch that on a sampler and give it to them as a wedding present was another matter entirely. And then, about three weeks after their honeymoon in exotic Knoxville, Lana told him that her period had shown up after all, that sometimes she was irregular and had these little "scares." Donna had an outbreak of the "I told you so's," insisting Duffy should have demanded a pregnancy test and an ultrasound before the wedding. Duffy started having nightmares about bear traps and having to gnaw off his own foot to escape. Between her plans to move to Texas and Duffy's new status as a married man,

Lucy kept her distance and faded from his life.

And he was stuck in Lake Sackett, in more ways than one. Duffy turned the truck onto the McCready's lot, wondering whether he should head back to town and grab that greasy breakfast after all, because he was not prepared to face a busy day tuning up boat engines. He pressed his hands over his eyes to try to relieve some of his headache. He hadn't been this hungover since the morning after he'd heard Lucy had gotten married. He and Carl had gone through four jars of Dawson family brew, which didn't sound like much, but Carl's family moonshine recipe could easily power a space shuttle launch.

His marriage had dragged on longer than it should have through mulishness (Duffy's) and infidelity (Lana's) because, well, Duffy had the unenviable combination of the McCready stubborn streak and the refusal to admit his mother was right. But Lana had gotten it into her head that sleeping with one of Duffy's well-off friends was going to lead to greener pastures, and had filed divorce papers. Duffy had recognized a reprieve when he saw it and signed them immediately.

He knew he wasn't in love with Lana anymore. He wasn't sure if he ever had been, truly, or if he had just been so blinded by loneliness and disappointment that his teenage brain had got- ten its wires crossed. He did know for damn sure that he didn't want to be married to her anymore. But unfortunately, he was just attached enough to let her slip back into his life every now and again when her ego got bruised.

Every few months, Lana came to him crying, hoping for some comfort over her latest heartbreak—some dipshit ATV salesman who didn't keep his promise to take her to Daytona for the weekend or, worse, that time a dipshit Jet Ski salesman did take her to Daytona for the weekend and left her without a way to get home. And the sight of a woman he'd once thought he loved, miserable and broken . . . it was like he had no control over his pants.

In the morning, Lana would skip off with boosted self-confidence, leaving Duffy soaked in Designer Imposters perfume and resignation that the whole cycle would start over again in a few months. He knew it was unhealthy. He knew he should keep her at a distance. He just didn't want to be one of the extensive line of people who'd added to her hurt over the years. She got so caught up in attention from men, in the whirlwind of a new relationship, but she never looked before she leaped. She was sensitive. She was insecure.

She was waiting for him in the parking lot of McCready's.

Duffy opened the truck door and spotted her climbing out of her El Camino, which was parked outside the back staff entrance for the funeral home.

"Oh, shit."

E.J.J. had made it very clear that unless Lana was burying somebody, she was not welcome on the McCready's property. There had been several "confrontations" between Lana and Duffy's mama. One of them involved a boat anchor. What was she doing here, instead of following the funeral procession?

Lana leaned against her El Camino, waggling her fingers at him. He crossed to her, scanning the parking lot for Donna. If he could get Lana back in her car without incident, maybe he could get through his morning without bloodshed. He glanced toward the bait shop, where he could see his mama rummaging around in the tackle racks, facing the lot. Maybe not.

"Hey, Lana, what are you doing here?" he asked.

As she moved closer, kitten pout firmly in place, Duffy was enveloped in the familiar scent of imitation Obsession. Lana wore her usual combination of skintight jeans and a low-cut tank top in a loud tropical print. Her only concession to the late-winter weather was a jean jacket. Her short dark-blond hair was swept back from her face, which had changed over the years, mostly in the frown lines etching deep brackets around her bright red cupid's bow of a mouth.

"I brought something for you," she purred, pulling a blue plastic glasses case from her shoulder bag. "I guess I must have knocked it into my purse while I was leaving your place."

"This isn't mine," he said, lifting a gingery eyebrow as she handed him the case. "I don't wear glasses."

"Are you sure? I could swear it came from your place," she chirped, though her green, narrow-set eyes weren't quite meeting his. "Thanks for keeping me company the other night. I was just so upset about Randy. You're such a good friend to me, Duffy. Just like you always promised. I know I'll never be alone as long as you're around to make things better."

Duffy swallowed heavily. It always made him squirm inside, hearing her describe him as a "friend" so pointedly, like she was trying to friend-zone him, when she was the one who came looking for him every time she had an itch. Why did he keep doing this? Was it guilt? For leaving when he had the first chance? For not fulfilling his marriage vows of forever and end- less patience?

His sister, Marianne, had always said he had a savior complex, which could stem from having so many relatives living within throwing distance, not to mention growing up with an active alco- holic and a very ill child in the extended family. Someone always needed a hand, needed a favor. Marianne also offered "being an incurable dumbass" as a potential explanation. Lana trailed her fingers across his chest, a gesture that would have sent shivers down his spine just a few months ago. Now it made him step back, putting space between them. "They cut my hours at the store again and I've moved in with my mama. So you might be careful about calling. You know she doesn't like you since you divorced me."

"You filed the papers," he said in the flattest tone he could muster. Because she always got so upset when she thought he was mad at her, and that derailed the conversation like a couch on the tracks.

"Yeah, but she says you were a real asshole to sign them," she said, smiling sweetly. "I don't know where she gets these funny ideas. I don't say anything but nice things about you."

"Mm-hmm. I thought the cops got called the last time you moved in with your mama. Something about you setting all her shoes on fire with a can of Sterno?"

Lana's lips curled into a sneer and he knew that he'd pressed the wrong button. Lana did not like it when people reminded her of her interactions with the legal system. She snipped, "Well, I didn't have a choice. It's not like I could move back in with you with how your family feels about me."

"No, you cannot," he told her.

"I wasn't asking," she huffed, poking her bottom lip out in a pout.

He gritted his teeth. Right, like she "wasn't asking" two years before when she'd been dumped by the local weatherman and showed up on his porch with a Hefty bag full of her clothes. When Duffy refused to let her crash on his couch for "a while," Lana had told a very nice nurse he was dating at the time that he had crabs.

"Because we are not married anymore. Because *you* filed divorce papers," he said, with a little more heat in his tone than he usually used. The crabs rumor had taken months to die down.

"Well, I didn't realize it would be a federal case, wanting to spend time with a *friend*. If you don't want to see me, I'll just go."

He didn't want to disagree with her, because getting her out of the parking lot as soon as possible would prevent her from interacting with his family. But at the same time, it might be better to placate her a little bit because once he'd bolstered her up, he usually wouldn't see her for weeks. Not for the first time, Duffy realized how absolutely fucked-up it was to have to negotiate with his ex-wife like she was some sort of terrorist holding peace and quiet as her hostage.

"McDuff Marion McCready!"

Shit-fire, his mother had used his full name. This was not going to end well.

He turned to see Donna McCready standing at the steps leading to the dock, her hands propped on her hips. Her angular face, never what one would call "pleasant" these days, was thunderous.

"Son, you're already winning 'Jackass of the Week' for being late to work and leaving me to open up the shop alone," she said. "Don't compound the idiocy."

"Mother McCready, why are you always so grumpy in the mornings?" Lana asked, her tone all peaches and cream and arsenic. "You know they're making prunes in all sorts of new flavors now."

Duffy sighed in defeat. From the beginning, Lana had tried too hard to force a close relationship with his mama, who was like a cat when it came to, well, anybody. Donna only wanted to spend time with people who weren't super keen about spending time with her. And after it became clear that Donna wouldn't be penning Lana's name in the family Bible, Lana seemed to delight in poking at Donna's antisocial underbelly.

Donna growled lightly. "Don't call me 'Mother McCready.' Any family connection between us was severed by the divine wisdom of the state of Georgia!"

"Okay, let's just stop the insanity right here before I have to call Eric and he sees how bug-ass crazy our family is and runs away from the only remotely healthy relationship Frankie has ever had," Duffy barked, hurting his own head with his volume. "Lana, thank you for bringing me the glasses case. Now, Mom and I have a lot of stocking to do and we need to get to it."

"Oh, I can help!" Lana said brightly.

Donna's growl was no longer light. "March your little skinny chicken legs over to your car before I have you towed."

"Mama, calm down. You're gonna have a stroke. Get back to the shop. I'll be there in a minute. Lana, you need to leave. You're just stirring the pot right now and that's not all right," Duffy said, opening Lana's car door.

"Oh, fine." Lana sighed, rolling her eyes but smirking heavily. She straightened her shoulders and winked at him. "I'll see you later, Duffy. Mother McCready."

Donna took a threatening step toward Lana. Duffy stepped back and stopped her. "Mama, I do not have enough cash on hand to bail you out. I'll have to raid Uncle Bob's swear jar. It ain't classy to have to count out your bail money in stacks of quarters."

Lana gunned her engine and waggled her pink-frosted finger-tips as she sped out of the parking lot, barely missing Duffy and Donna with the spray of gravel she threw. Donna glared at him, her whiskey-colored eyes sharp as razors over her aviators. "What sorry excuse do you have to say for yourself?"

"I know I'm late," he said. "I took those clients out for beers at the Dirty Deer, since the charter was kind of a bust, and who knew a bunch of Vols fans could drink so damn hard?"

"Oh, no, you're not late," his mother scoffed. "You're just in time to do all the restocking your damn self. I'm gonna go have a coffee with Leslie in the Snack Shack."

"I deserve that," he conceded.

"And the bait crickets got out again," she called over her shoulder as she walked down the dock.

"Wha— How?! I locked the barrel!"

"Well, I unlocked it and tipped it over!" she yelled back. "Yeah, I deserve that, too," he muttered.

***

THE CRICKETS DID not go down easy. Duffy spent a good portion of his day chasing the critters around the bait shop and dumping them back into the bait cage. About a third of them escaped, which was going to cost them, so his mama had to have been pretty pissed off to do that on purpose.

Pulling into his driveway at the end of the day, Duffy stepped out of his truck and surveyed the little collection of cabins on the lakeshore that his cousin Margot called a "compound." Considering the fact that the whole family worked together all day and then lived in houses within shouting distance, a body would think they'd hate the sight of each other.

But somehow, they made it work. With the exception of Frankie, McCreadys minded their own business.

The McCready family descended from a pair of brothers, John and Earl Jr. Earl built a little bait shop on what became the shore of Lake Sackett, offering tackle and lunches to fishermen and tourists. His brother, John, a carpenter by trade, was called on to give up cabinets for coffins when the Spanish flu epidemic took out a good portion of the town's population. When John needed more workspace, Earl offered him the use of the back of his shop and a family legacy was born.

Some McCreadys—his cousin Frankie, Grandpa E.J.J., Uncle Bob, and now Cousin Margot—buried Lake Sackett residents with all the expected pomp and frills, while others—Aunt Leslie, his mother, and himself—devoted their time to stuffing customers full of delicious deep-fried delicacies and guiding them on fishing tours through some of the best crappie beds in the county. In the best cases, one half of the family was able to help the bereaved with funeral planning and then the other half could distract the bereaved from their grief by feeding them and taking them out for some postburial cheer-up fishing. Grandpa

E.J.J. loved cross-promotion.

Duffy knew his family wasn't quite normal. Most people had nightmares about mortuaries. They didn't spend Christmas in one. But he was proud that the McCready Family Funeral Home and Bait Shop was a Lake Sackett institution. Or the McCreadys belonged *in* an institution. It was a thin line.

Rolling his sore shoulders, Duffy shuffled toward his cabin, exhausted, looking forward to a cold beer and a warmed-up portion of Aunt Leslie's special macaroni and cheese. She used four kinds of cheese and none of them was Velveeta, which she called her "secret noningredient." She did use bacon, because this was Georgia and no respectable side dish should remain unbaconed. Tootie and Leslie were nice enough to deliver Tupperware dishes to him every Sunday to keep him from relying on TV dinners and carryout. His mother did not participate in this food prep relay because "he's an adult, not a dumbass teenager." Also, Donna's cooking was basically poison.

Shampooing his difficult-to-manage curls gave Duffy something to do while considering his strange encounter with his ex that morning. Something about Lana's behavior was sticking in his craw. His ex avoided Donna whenever possible. Why would she come to McCready's, where she was sure to see Donna, Frankie, or Leslie, none of whom tolerated her? Was it because she was moving in with her mom? Was she trying to wangle an invitation to stay with him? She had to know that wasn't possible. He was willing to commit to a little comfort on a long dark night, but surely she had to know they were never getting married again.

Oh, fuck a duck, what if she didn't realize they were never getting married again?

After showering and microwaving his mac 'n' cheese, Duffy settled onto the front porch swing with a beer and his laptop, an early model held together with duct tape and positive thinking. He usually checked sports stats or news while he was eating, but tonight he fired up his seldom-used email, attached a picture of the ugliest cupcake he could find on Google, and wrote, *A humble suggestion from a friend.*

He signed off with just *Duffy* and hit send before he could over-analyze it. And then he logged onto Facebook. Well, technically, he tried to sign into Facebook, entered an old password, and had to reset it because it had been years since his last login. He rarely updated his timeline. He didn't see the point in posting pictures of his food or deep philosophical thoughts about which pants he was going to wear that day.

Margot had informed him that his social media footprint was "shamefully small" during her revamp of McCready's online profile. But she noted that his timeline was free of political rants and inappropriate memes, which she appreciated. Tootie's account had been a mess of both, because Tootie was a bit more tech savvy and a lot less circumspect than the average senior citizen. Duffy's updates informed him that he had more than forty new friend requests pending, most of them from old school classmates or distant relatives on his mom's side. But other than that, his account was pretty stagnant. His real friends knew that if they wanted to contact him, they had to do it through his phone or talk to his face, like he was a person.

He scrolled by Tootie's feed because that way lay madness and dog memes. Frankie had posted a picture of her pale, smiling face snuggled up to Eric's photogenic mug. She looked so . . . weirdly and completely happy. He'd never seen her grin like that. He'd seen her smile with puckish delight, with gleeful anticipation of vengeance. And then there were those rare, scary moments when Frankie smiled because she was mentally calculating how long it would take to disintegrate your body in the crematory. But he'd never seen her beaming like her whole world was right.

Duffy was glad Frankie was settling down after so many years of "casual" dating. She had waited long enough to find someone who seemed to enjoy her crazy, even if Eric didn't seem to fully understand it. Duffy was happy for her, just like he was happy for Margot and the L.L.Bean-catalogue-perfect life she was starting with Kyle and his girls. He didn't even want to think about what happened in his sister's marriage to the guy he'd sworn blood- oath loyalty to in the sixth grade (the sister-kissing traitor). But Marianne was content, too, and that was all that counted.

A beagle mix, just out of his puppy stage and most likely one of Grandma Tootie's pack members, toddled onto Duffy's porch and sat at his feet, waggling his tail so hard that the whole back half of his body shook. "Hey, there, pup, what are you doing?"

The dog whimpered and zeroed in on Duffy's mac 'n' cheese dish with huge, glossy brown eyes.

"Oh, hell no," Duffy told him. "The minute I do that, Tootie comes over here yelling at me because I gave you something you're allergic to and I spend the rest of my night on puppy puke patrol."

The dog's butt stopped wiggling and he simply stared up at Duffy, as if he could make the mac 'n' cheese move into his belly through sheer force of will. Duffy moved the dish out of reach and pulled the dog onto the seat with him, scratching behind his ears. The dog seemed willing to accept this offering instead of cheesy, carby goodness, and leaned into the scratch.

Taking a deep breath, he typed in Lucy's name with the hand not occupied with scratching. She immediately popped up as a friend of Marianne's and Tootie's. The sight of her face seemed to make his chest tighten up. She'd been a looker ever since their elementary school days, swanning right through that awkward phase unfazed with her deep brown eyes and high cheekbones— not to mention the obstinate set to her soft pink lips that she'd inherited from her late mama.

Lucy had her arms wrapped around a boy of about four, who had Lucy's coloring but Wayne's stocky build. She gazed at her son with the sort of motherly love they wrote about in storybooks.

She'd looked happy with her husband. They'd had a nice life. And he felt like an asshole for being salty over it.

She didn't need him coming at her with his unresolved feelings. She was mourning a man she loved. She needed time and space. She needed a friend. And he wasn't sure he could be her friend right now. He wanted so much more from Lucy.

He remembered the moment he fell in love with her. They'd been in seventh grade. Lucy had hit her growth spurt well before Duffy had, and stood three inches taller than his springy ginger curls. Wayne Garten and some other older boys had been poking fun at him in the cafeteria, calling Duffy a freak because his daddy cut up dead bodies all day.

Lucy had yelled, "Shut your mouth before the toilet fumes make us pass out!" And then she had walked right up to Wayne and punched him in his stupid face. Blood had spurted in a beautiful, gruesome arc from Wayne's nose as he toppled to the floor, arms windmilling comically. She planted one pink Con- verse on Wayne's chest and asked him if he had anything else to say to her friend Duffy. Wayne insisted that he did not.

Jimmy Greenway, the principal at the time, informed Lucy that she'd earned herself a three-page essay on alternatives to fighting. She crowed that it was worth it and she would make it four pages. Duffy knew then that no girl would ever be as awesome as Lucy Bowman, and none of them should even try.

"It's not pathetic if I close the browser now, right?" Duffy asked the dog. The dog dropped his chin on Duffy's leg and avoided eye contact. "Oh, what do you know?"

Duffy glanced up at the purr of an engine rolling toward him. Carl, the aforementioned sister-kissing traitor, was steering his massive red tow truck over the gravel drive. He rolled to a smooth stop directly in front of Duffy.

"What are you doing out here?" Duffy asked.

"I got beer that needs drinkin'," Carl said, hopping out of the truck with two six-packs of their favorite brew.

"I can help you with that," Duffy said, throwing his feet up on the porch railing.

"Marianne said you'd had a rough day," Carl said, handing him a cold can. "Frankie told her something about a plague of crickets and your mama being all pissed off?"

"I don't want to talk about it," he said.

"She also said Lana dropped by and threw her particular brand of joy around."

"It was not a red-letter day," Duffy said, cracking open his beer. "A man can't even walk across the parking lot of his work- place without getting caught in the cross fire of his mother and his ex-wife cat-fighting it out . . . and then getting ratted out by his cousin . . . who tells his sister."

"Has it occurred to you that the women in your life exercise a little too much control over you?" Carl asked.

"I try not to think about that too much," Duffy said, shaking his head.

"Yeah, one issue at a time. Every one of those women is terrify-ing," Carl said as he slumped onto the swing next to Duffy. He scratched behind the beagle's ears, prompting the dog to crawl into Carl's lap and attempt to lick his beer can. "I mean, I love your sister more than my own breath. But one time I ate the last peanut butter cup in the house, and she replaced the batteries in the remotes with duds she'd been saving in a drawer."

"Which remote?"

Carl took a long draw of beer and shook his head. "All of them, Duff. All of them."

Duffy nodded. "She learned that one from Frankie. I feel like I should make some sort of warning sheet for Eric. 'If you do "this stupid thing," Frankie will respond with "this particular act of pointed smartass vengeance" when you least expect it.'"

"Nah, if he's hitching into this family, he's gotta run the gauntlet. There are no shortcuts," Carl said, frowning. "So, it must have been weird seeing Lana again. After all, you told me that you haven't hung out with her in weeks. A new record, you said. Finally over her, I think you said."

Duffy tilted his beer back and drained the rest of it in one gulp. "I knew it." Carl sighed and picked up a fresh beer.

Duffy shrugged innocently. "Knew what?"

"Dammit, Duffy! You know I don't like talking about feelings," Carl told him.

"I am really not looking forward to whatever comes after this." "I love you like only a brother can," Carl said. "But Lana is poison. She always has been. You put up with stuff from her that you'd never allow from anybody else."

"That . . . is a fair assessment."

"Don't you want someone to share your life with? Somebody you can spend more than a few hours at a time with? Kids?"

"Are we really having this conversation?" Duffy scoffed. "This is not porch talk! This is what Marianne and Frankie talk about when they have girls' nights at Margot's. Are you gonna paint my toenails for me next?"

"I wouldn't touch your nasty-ass feet with a ten-foot pole.

Answer the damn question," Carl countered.

Duffy picked at the ring of his beer can. The bitch of it was that Duff *was* lonely. With everybody in the family pairing off but him, he was starting to feel left behind. The only other singles in the family were Stan, an avowed bachelor after the disappointment of his first marriage, and Donna, who was basically a puffer fish when threatened with human interaction. So sometimes, with Lana, he felt a little bit less alone.

"Yes, I would like kids of my own one day," Duffy said. "As much as I love hanging out with the boys . . . yeah, I would like a couple of girls, I think."

"Asshole."

"Tell Aiden to stop putting his homemade superglue on people's chairs and I'll change my mind."

"That boy's either gonna be an astronaut or a supervillain," Carl said with a sigh. "But you're never gonna have one like him if you keep this crap up with Lana. Girls like Lucy Bowman—who I happen to know is back in town, thanks to my lovely wife—do not put up with playing second fiddle to crazy ex-wives and their drama. Hell, look what happened when you tried to take that cute girl from the Bass Pro Shop out to the movies."

Duffy shuddered. AnnaBeth, the fishing lure consultant, had not been amused when Lana sent an usher into the theater, searching for Duffy by flashlight, because his "wife" was having a medical emergency at the concession stand. Duffy ended up spending most of the night cleaning popcorn out of his hair, as AnnaBeth had dumped the bucket over his head. Sadly, this was not the first of Duffy's dates that had ended this way.

"You don't love Lana," Carl noted. "You just feel bad for her."

"Yep." Duffy sighed.

"Well, last time I checked, TiVo-ing a bunch of *Oprah* don't make you a life coach," Carl muttered.

"Marianne wasn't supposed to tell you about the *Oprah* thing. I feel betrayed," Duffy said.

"McDuff, one of the great things about you is the fact you're one of the nicest guys in the world. I mean, everybody in town knows that if they need something, they can call you, day or night, and you'll be right there for 'em. But maybe it's time for you to put some of that nice guy aside and think about yourself first."

"What in the hell does that mean?"

"Stop answering Lana's calls. Stop humoring her when she shows up wanting attention like a stray cat. And when she invades your dates, pretending you're still married, tell her to take her ass home."

"Fine," Duffy told him. "I will."

"And stop being such a gutless wonder and ask Lucy out on a damn date."

"I'm not a gutless wonder. I'm full of guts. And those guts know that if I tried to date Lucy and messed things up with her, that would be the end of our friendship. And I'm not willing to risk that. And hell, that's assuming she wanted to date me in the first place. I caught her loading an eighteen-inch penis cake into her van and I can't imagine I can offer her anything much in comparison."

Carl choked, spraying his beer down the front of his shirt. "What?"

"Long story."

***

Gimme Some Sugar is available for purchase in stores everywhere.

ALSO BY MOLLY HARPER

Discover More by Molly Harper

all lists are in reading order

The Southern Eclectic Series (contemporary women's fiction / romantic comedy)

Save a Truck, Ride a Redneck (prequel novella)

Sweet Tea and Sympathy

Peachy Flippin' Keen (novella)

Ain't She a Peach?

A Few Pecans Short of a Pie

Gimme Some Sugar

The Mystic Bayou Series (paranormal romance)

This series publishes in audio first; the ebook and print editions come out six months after

How to Date Your Dragon

Love and Other Wild Things

Even Tree Nymphs Get the Blues (out in June, 2019)

The "Sorcery and Society" Series (young adult fantasy)

Changeling

Fledgling (out in August, 2019)

The "Nice Girls" Series (paranormal romance)

Nice Girls Don't Have Fangs

Nice Girls Don't Date Dead Men

Nice Girls Don't Live Forever

Nice Girls Don't Bite Their Neighbors

Half-Moon Hollow Series (paranormal romance)

The Care and Feeding of Stray Vampires

Driving Mr. Dead

Undead Sublet (A story in The Undead in My Bed anthology)

A Witch's Handbook of Kisses and Curses

I'm Dreaming of an Undead Christmas

The Dangers of Dating a Rebound Vampire

The Single Undead Moms Club

Fangs for the Memories

Where the Wild Things Bite

Big Vamp on Campus

Accidental Sire

Peace, Blood, and Understanding (out 10/7/2019)

The "Naked Werewolf" Series (paranormal romance)

How to Flirt with a Naked Werewolf

The Art of Seducing a Naked Werewolf

How to Run with a Naked Werewolf

The "Bluegrass" Series (contemporary romance)

My Bluegrass Baby

Rhythm and Bluegrass

Snow Falling on Bluegrass

Standalone Titles

And One Last Thing

Better Homes and Hauntings

ABOUT THE AUTHOR

Molly Harper worked for six years as a reporter and humor columnist for The Paducah Sun. Her reporting duties included covering courts, school board meetings, quilt shows, and once, the arrest of a Florida man who faked his suicide by shark attack and spent the next few months tossing pies at a local pizzeria.

Molly has published over thirty books. She writes women's fiction, paranormal romance, romantic comedies, and young adult fantasy. She lives in Michigan with her husband and children.

Please visit her website for updates, news, and freebies! https://www.mollyharper.com/

Twitter: @mollyharperauth

Facebook: https://www.facebook.com/Molly-Harper-Author-138734162865557/

CPSIA information can be obtained
at www.ICGtesting.com
Printed in the USA
LVHW041426010920
664636LV00003B/203

9 781641 970877